A FORBIDDEN LIAISON WITH MISS GRANT

Marguerite Kaye

MILLS & BOON

First Published in Great Britain 2020
by Mills & Boon, an imprint of HarperCollins*Publishers*
1 London Bridge Street, London, SE1 9GF

© 2020 Marguerite Kaye

ISBN: 978-0-263-27716-6

MIX
Paper from
responsible sources
FSC® C007454

This book is produced from independently certified FSC™ paper
to ensure responsible forest management.
For more information visit www.harpercollins.co.uk/green.

Printed and bound in Spain
by CPI, Barcelona

Prologue

~~~~~~⚬⚬~~~~~~

The Clachan Estate, Scottish Highlands
—June 1816

Constance Grant stood on the brow of the hill, gazing dejectedly down at the charred remains of what had once been the village of Clachan Bridge. Though a month had passed since the razing and burning, the acrid stench of smoke still filled her mouth and her nose, scorched into her memory for evermore.

Last October, when the Sheriff Officer first tried to serve the writs, the villagers had defiantly torn them up. He returned in November, this time escorted by several constables and with the laird's own factor in tow. His name was Robert Lockhart, the minister's son who had once been one of their own, until the laird elevated him. The man once admired by all and dear to the heart of one foolishly blinded by love was the harbinger of their downfall now. Reluctant he might have been, but he had ensured the writs were officially and legally served.

Still, despite the fate which had already befallen the other villages on the Clachan Estate and the surrounding estates, the people of Clachan Bridge were not minded to capitulate and had hoped and prayed for a reprieve. For natural justice to prevail. Or for Lockhart to derail his employer's plans. He'd already secured a stay of execution for them. They had been allowed to wait out the harsh winter before the evictions were enforced. Some took hope from this, planting their kailyards as usual, ploughing their runrigs in readiness for the new year's crop. But when Lockhart came again in May with his posse of men, incomers recruited from the Lowlands armed with picks and axes, the villagers were forced to accept that he was no longer on their side. They were about to lose their homes, their land, and their livelihoods.

This destruction and mass eviction was in the name of what they called improvement, these days. Stark disbelief turned quickly to fury and fear, and then wild panic that day, as

Marguerite Kaye writes hot historical romances from her home in cold and usually rainy Scotland. Featuring Regency Rakes, Highlanders and Sheikhs, she has published over fifty books and novellas. When she's not writing she enjoys walking, cycling—but only on the level—gardening—but only what she can eat—and cooking. She also likes to knit and occasionally drink martinis, though not at the same time. Find out more on her website: margueritekaye.com.

women tried to save their bairns and salvage their prized possessions, while the menfolk desperately tried to prevent the factor's men from pulling down their homes.

Fifteen minutes' notice to leave, they were given. Fifteen wretched minutes, to drag all they owned from the cottages. Heavy wooden kists stuffed full of shawls, precious plates, family heirlooms, were hauled into the kail-yards. Dressers too heavy to move were stripped of bowls, of pots, spirtles and spoons. Kettles and griddles were unhooked from the fires they'd hung over for decades. Panic gave way to a grim determination as the minutes ticked past. Bairns tottered back and forth carrying what they could—a stool, a jug, a fireside rug, a stone warming pan. Women grabbed their spinning wheels, men their working tools.

Walking among them, Constance's father had railed at Lockhart, one of his formal pupils and who, as a grown up, he had welcomed into his home when he had come courting his only daughter. The factor made no attempt to defend himself. His eyes sought hers over her father's shoulder with a final plea for understanding. Or was it forgiveness? Constance turned away. Sick at heart, she didn't doubt Lockhart was torn, but he had made his choice, and she would not pity him for it, nor ever absolve him.

The villagers called frantic instructions to each other. Panicked chickens ran in circles, clucking and squawking. Dogs barked. Cattle lowed in terror. But when Lockhart checked the silver watch the laird had given him on his promotion to factor, announced in a shaking voice that the fifteen minutes had elapsed everyone, from the smallest babe in arms to the oldest grandmother carried out on her bedding, fell silent.

The factor hesitated, temporarily unwilling, or unable, to order the commencement of the destruction. It was his henchmen who acted, tearing down the back wall of each cottage, felling the crux that supported the roof, ruthlessly kicking the doors from their hinges. When the fires were lit, the wailing started. And the crying. And the screaming. The roofs, thatched with bracken and heather, dry as tinder from the previous week's spring sunshine, were engulfed by the flames in a matter of seconds. The heat was so fierce it forced everyone back. There was no need for Lockhart's men to form a barricade here, not since the tragic events at the burning last year on a neighbouring estate. No one dared risk defying the men by remaining in their home. They knew better now. It was not murder apparently, not according to the law, to allow a man to burn to death in his own cottage while he was being evicted.

So they'd watched, growing silent once more, save for the sobbing children and the howling dogs and the minister, Lockhart's own father, praying uselessly and far too late for his flock to be spared. The flames intensified, the smoke became a thick black pall, the stench of it filling their mouths and their noses, making their eyes sting and stream.

Lockhart stood slightly apart, grim-faced, studiously avoiding her gaze now. The villagers were too stunned to plead with him, far less berate him. Constance stood silently among them, convinced she was witnessing a vision of hell. She'd had no notion that worse was to come, until she heard the strange rattling in her father's throat that was no sob, as her heartbroken father sank slowly to the ground. Mhairi, the village fey wife ran to his aid, but not even she could revive him.

A month had passed since that awful day. The memories made Constance's eyes burn, but she didn't cry. She had no tears left.

Turning her back on the ruins of the village, she made her way up the crooked path to the schoolhouse. She'd been born here. Her mother had died here. Her father had lain here in his coffin before his last journey to the little churchyard a mile distant over the moor. He was buried in the family grave, with his wife and their two wee ones, the brothers born too soon that Constance had never known. They were all together now, reunited in death. She fervently hoped they were at peace.

As for the villagers, some had accepted the secured assisted passages to Canada paid for by the laird. Some were trying to eke a living from the hitherto unpopulated hinterland on the coast. Others were dispersed to the four winds, seeking charity with their kin or scraping a new living in the cities. A diminishing few slept every night in the schoolhouse, creeping down from their hiding places under cover of darkness for the shelter and food she provided. Did her presence protect them? How would they survive when she left as she must, for there was nothing and no one to keep her here.

The fledgling shoots from the seeds which had been sown in the spring had withered and died in the kailyards, just like the hope which had been extinguished once and for all. The village would be turned over to the four-legged incomers, the sheep. She hoped that the people, generations of whom had been taught by her father and lately by herself, would endure. They were all hardy souls, but the loss of their land had broken their hearts and their spirits.

Constance too was broken, consumed by grief and by guilt. Could she have done more to prevent it, argued more persuasively, pleaded more passionately? She would never know now. Her wooden chest was packed with the few things which would accompany her. At least she was assured of sanctuary at the end of the journey south. She was luckier than most.

As for this home, the only one she had ever known, what use was a schoolroom with no children to teach? It was a substantial building with a slate roof, glass in the windows, a hearth in every room. Doubtless the laird would find a use for it. A new home for the factor who'd served him so well, perhaps. Would Lockhart be able to live with the ghosts that would surely haunt him here? Constance cursed the man. Good luck with that.

The carrier was due any moment now.

She'd said her goodbyes to her parents at the graveside earlier. Picking up her basket, Constance turned the key in the lock of the front door for the last time and left it there. Then she went back down the path to sit on her plain wooden trunk, and await the cart.

Chapter One

A little bird informs me that Scotland can expect an exotic and rare visitor this summer. A plump royal peacock is about to alight on our shores, albeit briefly, before returning to the Capital, his natural habitat, a migration mirrored by the seasonal habits of the so-called Scottish aristocracy, who will be lining up to greet him. They, who flaunt their Highland heritage, in truth view their vast estates as a cash cow to fund their London society lifestyle, their hard-working tenants merely a means to an extremely comfortable and privileged end. Our regal visitor will find himself very much at home in such company. After all, birds of a feather flock together.

Since it's been over two hundred

years since we were last blessed by the presence of a monarch, one would be forgiven for thinking fair Caledonia very much the poor relation in our so-called union of equals. The burning question for us mere citizens is, whether we should roll out the red carpet and display our famed hospitality to guests, or roll out the rotten fruit and display our famed hostility to those who would oppress us? Given that the King is a renowned trencherman, though prone to excess and gout, Flora prescribes fruit. Lots of it. Administered with gusto and precision. His Majesty deserves no less.

If some of our Caledonian elite end up slightly spattered in the process, that might well be considered poetic justice. It must not be forgotten that those same people studiously avoid getting blood on their hands, preferring to let their factor do their dirty work when it comes to driving hard-working families from the lands they have worked for generations.

Flora MacDonald, *New Jacobite Journal*

*Newhaven, near Edinburgh
—Monday, 8th July 1822*

Though the fishing village of Newhaven was located no more than two or three miles from the centre of Edinburgh, it felt like another world. For a start, the air was much sweeter, with not a trace of the pall of smoke which hung over the city, even on the brightest of summer's days such as this. Constance wended her way down the cobbled main street past the rows of distinctive cottages where a steep forestair led to the front door on the second floor of each, the ground floor being given over to drying fishing nets.

It was quiet, with none of the clatter of traffic she'd become inured, rather than accustomed to, in the New Town. She hadn't set out with the intention of coming here. She'd left the house in Coates Crescent with no clear purpose at all, save to walk and to think. She had walked all right, though she couldn't even recall how her meanderings had brought her down to the Firth of Forth, but as to thinking, she'd made not a whit of progress. The opposite, in fact, for as she reached the harbour, a melancholy stole over her that was quite at odds with the blazing sunshine.

The tide was out, leaving the fishing boats stranded at drunken angles on the gritty silt. The fresh tang of salt mingled with the smell of sun-baked seaweed, overlaid with the distinctive, sweetly rotten odour of the catch that had been sold in the market over on the other side of the harbour, where empty fish boxes were stacked on the jetty. Newhaven was nothing like the landlocked Highland village she'd left six years before. Yet something about the air of quiet contentment, of peace and calm, reminded her of Clachan Bridge, engulfing her in a wave of longing to be back there in happier times.

Usually she tried not to dwell on the past, but the memories, long supressed, crowded into her mind today, the ghosts of those she'd lost clamouring to be heard. What had the bairns she'd taught made of themselves? Had any of them survived long enough to prosper? Was there any trace left to remind the shepherds who now roamed the land of the thriving village that had once stood there? And what of the loyal factor the absent laird had employed to enforce his orders? Had he found an alternative use for the schoolhouse, or let it fall to ruin, a poignant memorial to all the ghosts who must surely haunt the place? Perhaps he'd moved into it himself. That would be taking irony to the limits, right enough. She didn't care. She wouldn't waste her time worrying about any of those unfeeling orchestrators of misery. *Marbhphaisg orra!* A curse on them!

Her oath lacked bitterness. The laird would have found another factor, had Lockhart refused to do his bidding. That he had not refused, despite her pleas, had taught her a valuable lesson. Her wishes would always come a poor second to his. She had not been heartbroken when she left Clachan Bridge, but she'd been heartsore. Back in those early months after the Clearing, when Pearl had taken her in, she'd barely had the will to leave her bed of the morning. Days passed without her even being aware of them. Without purpose or desire she had drifted through her first Edinburgh summer, barely noticing the months edging from autumn into winter, and then back into spring. It was easy to miss the changing seasons in the grey city, easy to surrender to a perpetual, self-indulgent listlessness.

Until Pearl, dear Pearl, had introduced her to the man who had forced her to take a long hard look at herself, and to ask, was this all there was to look forward to, maudlin acceptance? Was she going to let the likes of the laird and his factor continue to destroy lives unopposed? Stop mourning and start protesting, Paul had said. Help open people's eyes. Use your experiences to show them the appalling suffering that continues in the Highlands to this very day. Let's force people to stop hiding their heads in the sand, to sit up and listen. Let's make an outcry that can't be ignored.

Smiling at the memory, Constance's mood lifted a fraction. Pearl had given her a haven and Paul had breathed life back into her, giving her a purpose. For the last four years, she'd worked tirelessly alongside him, determined to convert hearts and minds to their cause, desperate to speak out on behalf of those diminishing numbers left in the Highlands who had no voice of their own to air their grievances. She'd been convinced that her voice would help turn the tide of public opinion, for if only people knew what was happening, they must surely call for it to end.

But the Clearances had not ended. Far from it. Progress in the name of sheep farming was spreading inexorably through the Highlands and as a result, Paul was beginning to lose heart. Though his passion for their cause burned as brightly as ever, they had been shouting into a void for too long, he had insisted yesterday. Perhaps it was time to admit defeat. Constance had protested passionately, begging him not to give up, but something of his resigned acceptance had wormed its way into her mind overnight. *Was* she wasting her time? Had this crusade lost its purpose, leaving her in limbo, unable to give up on it, yet failing to make any headway? Six years she'd lived in Edinburgh, lost for most of the first two, pouring her heart and soul into her work for the last four, and all to no avail.

She had sacrificed so much. Had it all been in vain? Six years was a big chunk of a life to be rootless and homeless, expending her time on a cause few cared about. What the so-called elite promoted as the tide of progress was proving impossible to turn. The old ways were being destroyed. Soon there would be no indigenous people left in the Highlands. The sheep would reign imperiously, unopposed.

And she would be forty next week. Forty, and what did she have to show for it? The only kin she had ever known were buried at Clachan Bridge. What hopes she'd had for a family of her own had died there too, crushed at the hands of a man who had put his ambition before her. The nature of the work she did now forced her to keep her own counsel. Save for Pearl and Paul, she had no friends, and no confidant.

Oh, for heaven's sake, what was wrong with her? The day stretched out before her, and here she was indulging in a fit of the blues, rather than enjoying it. Her life might be uneventful, but it was still a life, and a damned sight more comfortable a life, she was willing to bet, than most of the others who'd left Clachan Bridge enjoyed. A life that was for living, not frittering away.

As she began to walk along the sea wall, past the shuttered fish market and on to the entrance to the harbour, Constance made a determined effort to shake off her sombre mood, but for the first time in her life, she had the horrible feeling that time was inexorably ticking away.

Age was just a number, she reminded herself firmly. She would wake on the morning of her birthday no different from the woman who had gone to bed the night before. Which was, it dawned on her, precisely the point! She didn't want to dwindle slowly into middle age. She wanted to recapture the sparkle she'd once had, to wake up wondering what the day had in store for her, to look forward to it, rather than simply endure it. She wanted to make each day stand out, not blur one into the other in sepia tones. She wanted colour.

Finally, Constance's mood rallied. She had sacrificed too much to give up now. If the King came to Edinburgh, as seemed now to be extremely likely, then the eyes of the world would be on the city. It would be the perfect opportunity to make a song and dance that surely could not be ignored. Scotland's aristocracy would flock to the city proudly sporting their clan colours, while the true Highlanders were being banished from their lands. No one could fail to see the hypocrisy of it. This visit could well be the catalyst for true change. One last chance to make people listen, to put an end to injustice. Now was not the time to be defeatist. If she must turn forty—*forty!*—then she would make it a turning point, a day to launch herself full-tilt at the future, rather than hide her head under her pillow and wish it over. She would persuade Paul not to give up. She would throw herself into making the most of the golden opportunity the royal visit presented.

Smiling, her mood finally fit for the day,

Constance decided to give herself a respite for the rest of it, from worrying about the future. She had reached the furthermost point of the harbour wall, where the incoming tide was already lapping at the entrance to the harbour. Constance closed her eyes and tilted her face up, giving herself over to the simple pleasure of the sun on her face.

Grayson Maddox surveyed the area of Leith docks known locally as The Shore, located within the protective wall that curved around the entrance to the harbour. Assuming that King George did come to Edinburgh, this was where he would probably land. The visit had yet to be officially confirmed, but Grayson knew, from his own sources, that His Majesty's yacht was being made ready at Greenwich. Until the *Royal George* set sail, nothing was certain, he'd reminded Shona and Neil, but they'd been beside themselves with excitement. A visit to the capital city in the height of summer, to vie with thousands of others for a fleeting glimpse of a monarch Grayson had no time for was not his idea of fun, but his children saw the matter very differently, and it was a rare thing these days, for him to be able to please their increasingly sophisticated palates. He'd been sceptical, truth be told, when they begged him to make the trip to Edinburgh in order to secure accommodation in advance, but the thought of a few days purely to himself had been vastly appealing. So he'd journeyed east, arriving yesterday, astounded to find that his children had been in the right of it, for the city was already swollen with visitors, the atmosphere of excited anticipation almost tangible.

Despite the fact that he'd decided to take a break from work and had no intentions of heading down to Leith when he set out for a walk this morning, Grayson had inevitably been drawn to the waterfront where, despite the workaday bustle, a soothing calm prevailed. He tried to picture the place filled with cheering crowds ready to welcome the King. He imagined a band playing a rousing march stationed by the Martello Tower which marked the entrance to the pier. The drawbridge would have to be raised so that the barge which would ferry the monarch from his yacht could enter the inner harbour. Grayson's shoulders shook with laughter as he imagined the King, portly and red of face, dressed in one of his selection of garish ceremonial uniforms—an admiral, perhaps—

clambering up from the barge, sweating and wheezing. They'd probably need a block and tackle from one of the nearby wharfs to hoist him on to the jetty, like a fishing boat landing a monster cod.

Smiling to himself, he felt the tension he hadn't even been aware of begin to ease from his shoulders. Much as he loved his children they were, contrary to his expectations, becoming more rather than less of a worry as they got older. And his precious shipyard too—it wasn't a concern as such, for it was doing extremely well, but the fact remained that his business absorbed every moment that his offspring did not. He couldn't recall the last time he'd had even half a day to himself.

What to do with the time? The question flummoxed him. He should probably return to the city and start on the task which had brought him here, seeking out a suitable hotel, but that held little appeal. So what then, did he want? Not a question anyone, himself included, had been interested in for a very long time. For heaven's sake, he was more than a father and a shipbuilder, wasn't he? The honest answer was, not any more. He had been a husband once, but tragedy, then the day-to-day business of simply getting by, and of seeing that those nearest and dearest to him did more than that, had taken its toll. He'd never seen it as a sacrifice. He wasn't exactly a slave to his weans and his workers, for he'd chosen to take on a duty of care for both, and fought bloody hard in the case of Shona and Neil to shoulder the burden of their upbringing himself. Not that they were a burden, but...

But it was good, it was damned good to be here by himself for a bit, Grayson acknowledged ruefully. He was past the age of kicking over the traces, but that was what he'd like to do. Forget the world. Do something daft. Something that would shock the living daylights out of those who knew him. Something that would divert him from the path other people expected him to tread, if only for a wee while.

What though? Puzzling over this, he made his way across the bridge, meandering through the docks and quays that linked Leith and Newhaven, his practised eye unable to resist assessing the boats berthed there. Heading for the vantage point at the end of the harbour wall, his eyes drawn to the view it commanded out over the Firth of Forth to the flat coastland of Fife which seemed no more than a stone's throw away, he didn't see the woman standing in the shadow until it was too late to retreat gracefully.

She was tall but slight, dressed plainly in a grey gown, a dark blue shawl and a straw poke bonnet. She could be any age between thirty and his own early forties. Shona would doubtless say her garb was outmoded, but he thought she had an elegance in the way she carried herself and an air of confident aloofness that intrigued him. 'I beg your pardon, madam, I didn't mean to intrude.'

'It is a public jetty, sir, I cannot lay claim to it.'

She looked up and met his eyes, and Grayson felt a jolt of something like recognition. Yet they had never met, he was sure of it. Her voice was low, with the distinctive soft lilt of the Highlands. Her skin was clear, pale with a dusting of freckles across her nose and her brow. She had ordinary brown hair, unremarkable features save for her eyes, which were almond-shaped and green. He would have remembered her if he'd met her before and besides, it wasn't familiarity he was feeling but something far more visceral.

Her smile faltered. 'Do I know you?'

He dragged his eyes from her face, shaking his head. She'd be utterly appalled if she knew the effect she was having on him. He was appalled himself. Mostly. 'The light today is so bright,' Grayson said, 'I am convinced I can see all the way to Stirling.'

'Dunfermline anyway, I will grant you,' she answered.

'I've never been here before.' He stood beside her, his eyes on the Fife coastline, acutely aware of her at his side. Desire was a rare and rarely persistent visitor in his life, easily quashed or sated if the circumstances allowed. This was something very different. 'I didn't intend to end up in Leith, when I set out,' Grayson said, risking a glance in her direction.

'I did not have Newhaven in mind either.'

She met his eyes only briefly, but he felt it again. A physical jolt of awareness. Like drawn to like. Did she feel it too? 'I only arrived in Edinburgh yesterday,' he said. 'I'm from Glasgow.'

He was granted another smile, and this time she didn't look away. 'I gathered as much from your accent. What brings you to Edinburgh, Mr…?'

'Maddox. Grayson Maddox.' He held out his hand, and she took it. Unlike him, she was wearing gloves, but his fingers tingled at the contact all the same. 'How do you do, Mrs...?'

'Grant. Constance Grant. And it's Miss.'

Miss! Daft of him to be so ridiculously pleased by the fact she wasn't married, and preposterous to imagine it mattered one way or the other. But it did matter, because if she was married then what he was feeling, looking into her eyes and holding her hand, was inappropriate. But if she wasn't married, the fact that Miss Constance Grant looked as if she was feeling it too was...

Ah, but that was wishful thinking on his part. And he was still holding her hand. 'I'm in Edinburgh to make arrangements for the King's visit,' Grayson said, letting her go. 'I mean, I'm not personally interested if I'm honest, but Shona and Neil are, and they've been on at me to make sure we secure somewhere decent to stay, and though I thought there was no rush, it turns out they were right and I was wrong, and—and so that's why I'm here. In Edinburgh, I mean. I didn't plan to come to Leith, but the docks—I build ships, you see. Maddox Shipyards on the Clyde, though why you should—and why I am—' He broke off, realising he was babbling. 'You did ask.'

'I did. Shona and Neil, they are your children, I take it?'

'Aye.' He was surely mistaken in taking that look for disappointment. 'Their mother, my wife, she died some time ago.'

'I'm so sorry.'

'Indeed, and so am I. I never planned on being a widower, or having to raise two motherless children. But we can't always have what we want, can we? It was eight years ago, and now I've been single almost as long as I was married. Pardon me, Miss Grant, I haven't the faintest idea why I'm telling you all this.'

He had certainly shattered the mood, for she was looking at him quite differently now. Perhaps it was as well. 'I'll leave you to enjoy the view,' he said, regretfully.

'No. Don't go.' She put her hand on his arm to stay him, surprising them both. 'I myself moved to Edinburgh six years ago. Until then, I was a teacher in a school in the Highlands. I had planned to marry, to settle there, but the laird cleared the lands for sheep. You can't teach in an empty school, and as it turned out, I couldn't marry either because—it doesn't matter why.' Surprised at herself, she withdrew her hand, looking down at the water, which was rolling in through the harbour opening. 'What I'm trying to say, Mr Maddox, is that I understand what you mean when you say we can't always have what we want.'

'That is obvious, though I have to say not many people would have been so frank.'

'Nor would I be, normally. I'm not in the habit of talking to strangers, you know. Or to talk in such a personal vein at all, God's honest truth. You've caught me in a very strange mood.'

'How so?'

'Oh, I don't know. I have a birthday next week, one of those ones that are momentous, though they shouldn't be, and I find myself wanting to rail against it by doing something a bit daft, you know, throw over the traces?'

Grayson laughed. 'Would you believe me if I told you that I'd been thinking the very same thing a wee minute ago?'

'You have a significant birthday looming too?'

'No, though I suppose I was thinking how fast the years had been flying past and how precious little of the time I'd had to myself. Mind you, now I *have* the time to myself,' he added with a wry smile, 'I'm struggling to decide what I want to do with it. Maybe the fates decided what I needed was you.'

She gave a little huff of laughter. 'And in turn, they decided that what I needed at this moment was to meet you?'

Grayson smiled. 'Maybe they did.'

'You don't look to me like a man who believes in letting the fates dictate his life.'

'Oh, I'm not. I'm a man at an unexpected loose end, wanting something novel from the day.' It was back again. A connection. Not recognition exactly, not so simple as desire, though that was part of it. And she felt it too, he was sure of it. He decided to stop wondering where it might lead and simply enjoy it. 'So here you are, at a loose end too, wishing for a change. It must be the fates who decided to match us up, don't you think, for what else are we to make of the fact that I didn't intend to walk to Leith and you didn't intend to walk to Newhaven—assuming you did walk?'

'I did.' She smiled. Bloody hell, but she had a lovely smile. 'I walked all the way from the New Town.'

'In this heat! You must be thirsty, I reckon. Maybe even hungry?'

'Do you know, Mr Maddox, I think you may be right. About the fates intervening, I mean, though I am hungry.'

'So if I asked you, Miss Grant, to take a

bite to eat with me and honour me with a little more of your company, you wouldn't take it amiss?'

'I would not. Though if you can find somewhere in Newhaven that serves anything other than navy rum to fishermen, I shall be seriously impressed.'

Chapter Two

'Wait here, I'll go and see what they can rustle up for us.'

Grayson Maddox disappeared into the tavern, and Constance took a seat on the bench outside. She'd thought at first she was imagining it, the hint of interest in his eyes, but she was sure now that she was not. She reckoned he must be in his early forties, not too much older than herself. He was tall, a good head above her, and leanly built, though not scrawny. Rangy, that was the word. He had the look of a man who spent his life outdoors. Maddox Shipyards, he'd said, though she didn't think he actually built the ships. His clothes were not those of a labourer. The coat and waistcoat were plain, but the cloth was fine wool, and his boots were soft leather, the sort that only a man who did not have to mind

about wearing them out or getting them dirty
and scratched would buy. His linen too was
pristine, and his watch fob was gold.

A well-to-do man, though not born to
money, not with that accent. He wore neither
hat nor gloves. Not a man who aspired to be
labelled a gentleman, then. She liked that. She
liked the way he looked too. A strong-featured
face, the deep-set grey-blue eyes crinkled at
the corners, framed by dark lashes. His hair
was black, streaked with grey at the temples,
cut far too short to be fashionable. A practical style, like the practical tailoring of his
clothes. What on earth did a man like him see
in a woman like her? If any other stranger had
tried to strike up a conversation with her on
the harbour wall on any other day, she'd have
spurned him. Maybe the fates had indeed in-
tervened to bring two kindred spirits together,
in which case it would be unwise of her not
to follow their lead.

'Bread, cheese and coffee.' Mr Maddox returned, bearing a tray which he set down on
the bench between them before taking a seat.

His accent had a rough edge to it that he
made no attempt to disguise. Not harsh, but
soft, a low growl that Constance found dis-

tractingly arousing. 'What happened to the tot of rum?' she asked.

He thumped his forehead. 'What an eejit I am, I totally forgot to order some.'

She chuckled, taking one of the tin mugs from the tray. 'I can live without it.'

Picking up his own mug, Grayson Maddox touched it to hers. 'Here's to chance encounters. Can I help you to some of this fine repast?'

'Please.'

She watched as he cut the cheese with a fine silver knife that he produced from his pocket, making delicate slivers of it, arranging it neatly on the pewter plate with some bread, producing an apple from his pocket, peeling it and making a little fan of the segments. He worked quickly and efficiently, a task he'd obviously carried out many times before. For his wife? She banished the thought. His hands were tanned, the nails neatly trimmed and very clean, though the backs of them were covered in scars and the skin on the right one was puckered.

'Never get into an argument with a steam engine,' he said, noticing her interest as he handed her the plate, 'not even a model one.'

He made no effort to finesse his own meal,

cutting a slab of cheese and dumping it on to an equally thick slab of bread, though he ate with slow pleasure. The bench they sat on faced on to the Newhaven harbour. The tide was making headway, waves rocking the grounded fishing boats, making the seaweed-encrusted ropes that tethered them to the harbour creak and strain. Above them, the sky was light blue with barely a cloud in sight, the sun for once determinedly shining.

'Another couple of days of this and we'll be able to claim we've had a great summer,' Mr Maddox said when they had finished, stacking the empty plates on the tray and setting it on to the ground under the bench. 'Though it's probably raining over on the west coast, for it almost always is. There's times I wonder that we're not born with fins instead of limbs.'

'Is that why you build boats for a living?'

'I build ships, Miss Grant. Those wee things moored in the harbour, those are boats.'

'I do beg your pardon. What pray, is the difference?'

'There is a saying. A ship can carry a boat, but a boat can't carry a ship. Oh, and as far as I am concerned, any vessel powered by steam is a ship.'

'Are the ones that you build steam powered?'

'Most of them, though we've one yard still dedicated to building clippers, since it's currently the most profitable line of business, until someone comes up with a way to power a steam ship clear across the oceans.'

'You don't dream of being that person, Mr Maddox?'

He angled himself towards her, stretching an arm along the back of the bench. 'Grayson. If you don't mind.'

Grrrrayson.

'Grayson,' Constance repeated. Her voice sounded strangled to her own ears, but it made heat flare in his eyes. 'Then you must call me Constance.'

'I will, gladly.'

Good heavens, that smile! Surely hers was not so—so wicked? She leaned back just a tiny bit, so that her shoulders rested against his arm. 'Do you have plans to build an ocean-going ship?'

'If someone comes up with a practical design for one. I'm no engineer, I'm a business man, and happy to leave others to do the inventing. I specialise in putting inventions to practical use.'

Prrrractical use.

There it was again. Rough and yet smooth,

like a—dear Lord, Constance, stop behaving like a schoolgirl. 'As a confirmed landlubber I am woefully ignorant when it comes to boats. What is the advantage of steam over sail— besides speed, that is?'

'The biggest advantage is that you don't need to rely on the vagaries of the weather. Even on a flat calm day like today—not that we have many of them, mind—my ships can go about their business while sailboats are becalmed. They are great wee workhorses, my steam ships, and sturdy too. What's more, we're experimenting with iron hulls at the moment, which will mean they will be even more robust. You'd be surprised, even out on the Clyde estuary, just how rough the weather can get. But my steamers can work year-round, taking cargo and passengers doon the watter.'

Her shawl had fallen down the back of the bench. His fingers had found the nape of her neck. A butterfly touch, it could almost be mistaken for a breeze. Though her body knew different. She shifted on the bench so that her knee brushed his thigh through her skirts. *'Doon the watter?'*

'That's the journey from Glasgow by paddle steamer to the towns and the islands at the far reaches of the Clyde.'

'I see.' How had they managed to become seated so close together? His head was bent towards her, as if he was confiding his deepest secrets or whispering sweet nothings, instead of talking about shipping lanes. While they spoke, their bodies were conducting another, altogether different conversation. There was a light in his eyes that she could not mistake. She was pretty sure it was reflected in her own eyes. She had forgotten what this felt like. She didn't remember it being anything like this, truth be told. In any case, this had nothing to do with love and everything to do with lust. The word, with all its dark and sinful connotations sent a delicious frisson down her spine. She was almost forty, and she was in lust!

Constance moved a little bit closer. 'I've never been on a paddle steamer,' she said, daring to put her hand on his knee. 'I'd love to sail on one. What's it like?'

The sharp intake of his breath made her think, for a split second, that she'd made a huge mistake. Then his hand covered hers. 'I'm afraid it's not as romantic as it sounds. It can be a bit noisy. In the engine room you can't hear yourself think, but some steamers have passenger decks and cabins that are much quieter.' He turned her hand over and began to draw circles with his thumb on her palm. 'Basically, the more you pay for your ticket, the more civilised your journey will be.'

She was having difficulty breathing. She couldn't believe this was happening. That she was actually encouraging it to happen. Don't think, Constance! The fates wanted this. Ridiculous excuse, but she didn't care. 'And is it dangerous?' she asked. 'That scar on your hand...' The hand that was working magic on hers. 'And that was only a model, you say?'

'A fully working model built to scale. I shouldn't have tampered with it. Serves me right for getting burned. Constance...'

'Grayson?'

'Talking of getting burned. Are we both in danger of doing just that?'

'I don't know. I hope so. I don't mean *burned,* but—' She broke off, unable to voice what she actually meant, not because she was mealy-mouthed but for fear of being wrong. 'What exactly do you mean?'

'I mean that I would like to make love to you, but I'm worried we might regret it,' he said softly. 'And if I've got it completely wrong then forgive me, but I thought...'

'You haven't got it wrong. And I wouldn't regret it.'

His eyes widened. 'You mean you want to…'

'Make love.' Her heart thumped. Her body thrummed. 'Yes,' Constance said. 'Though I can't believe I've just said that.'

'I am very glad you did.'

Verrry.

He smiled at her in a way that made her belly flip. 'I reckon this tavern likely has rooms to rent. Shall I go and find out?'

The bedchamber was situated at the rear of the tavern, the single window looking out into a yard where washing was strung out on a line, empty save for a dog listlessly scratching itself. Constance pulled the shutters closed. The room was sparsely furnished. A washstand. A chair. A chest of drawers. A bed. The boards were bare but neatly swept. She couldn't believe she was here. With a man she barely knew.

Grayson closed the door. 'I told the landlady that my wife had had too much sun.'

'Did she believe you?'

'I don't look the disreputable type any more than you do. She didn't question it.' He leaned against the door, surveying her in the light of the sun, which was filtering through the gap in the shutters. 'I've never done anything like this in my life.'

'Nor have I.'

'But you have—you are not…'

'This is not my first time, if that's what you're asking.'

He didn't move. 'And are you truly sure, Constance, that you won't regret this?'

'I have no idea. I hope not. I am pretty certain that I would regret walking away now.'

He smiled at that, turning the key in the lock and joining her by the shuttered window. 'Me too. If you change your mind at any point, you'll tell me?'

'I will. But I won't.'

'I mean it.'

'I know.' How could she possibly know? She'd barely met him. Yet she trusted him, implicitly. He stooped to kiss her lightly on the lips, and for the first time, nerves fluttered in her tummy. 'It's been a while, Grayson.'

He laughed softly, untying the ribbons of her bonnet. 'Then you're in good company.'

He kissed her again, and this time she kissed him back. He tasted of coffee, and then of himself. His arms slid around her waist, but it was she who closed the gap between them, wrapping her arms around his neck and deepening the kiss. Her senses reeled as his tongue touched hers and his hands tightened around her. The wool of his coat, a lemony tang of soap, sweat, and him, she could smell him—or was it them? She was already hot, tense, deeply aroused. She could feel it was the same for him. He was hard. Oh, dear Lord, he was so hard.

She ran her fingers through the cropped, bristly hair at the nape of his neck, pulling him closer, kissing him more deeply. She could feel his breath, shallow and fast, and his hands on her bottom pulling her up against him, then wrestling with the fastenings of her gown, tugging impatiently with the buttons and the ties. She slid her hands under his coat, feeling the heat of his skin through his shirt and waistcoat. He let her go to shrug himself out of it, and she reached up to untie her gown.

Kissing again. How could she have forgotten how delightful it was to kiss? Had it ever been this delightful? She couldn't remember. She didn't want to compare. Her gown fell to her feet and she stepped out of it. His waistcoat fell beside it on to the floor. More kisses. He was kissing her neck, her throat, down to the tops of her breasts, and her nipples were aching for his touch.

His waistcoat was added to the heap of garments on the floor, and she tugged his shirt free from his breeches, relishing the way her touch made him shudder, the way his chest expanded as he exhaled sharply, the way the muscles of his back rippled.

Her corset laced at the front. He untied the knot, loosening it, no longer fumbling but utterly intent, sliding it down over her hips, leaving her in only her chemise, drawers and stockings. Her undergarments were perfectly clean, but plain, practical and past their best, not designed to be seen by anyone other than her. Like her almost-forty-year-old body. What on earth was she doing here? But the question had barely formed when he pushed her chemise aside and took her nipple in his mouth.

Oh, dear heavens, don't stop, she begged silently. *Keep doing this! And that! And that too!*

His mouth and his hands set up paths of fluttering sensations all over her body, all of them leading to the tightening, clenching knot of desire between her legs. She could hear herself panting, whimpering, as he sucked her, stroked her, kissed her, pausing only to yank his shirt over his head. His skin was pale but his physique was exactly as she had guessed, with the hard muscles of a man who used them. She clutched at him, her hands roaming frantically over the rough hair of his chest, the hard nubs of his nipples, the dip of his belly.

He lifted his head from her breasts, but her moan of protest was smothered as their mouths met again in a deeper kiss and he rucked up her petticoats, unerringly finding the gap in her drawers to slide his fingers inside her. He slipped in so easily, and she tensed around him. She was so ready for him that her climax began to build as soon as he started to stroke her. Expertly, she noticed, he knew exactly what he was doing. Then she forgot as sensations gripped her, his touch tipping her over the edge too quickly to resist, making her legs buckle, forcing her to grip his shoulders, burying her face in his shoulder to muffle her cries, arching against him.

He was so hard. And she *needed* him inside her. Kissing him wildly, careless, heedless of anything save her urgent need, she fell on to the bed, watching him unashamedly as he cast off the last of his clothes, her body responding to the sight of him, aroused, blatantly male.

He swore softly under his breath as he stepped between her legs, pulling her towards him, and they kissed again and she wrapped her legs around him, falling back on the bed as he entered her. Later, she would wonder at the lack of strangeness, at the way her body welcomed him, at the way they found a rhythm so quickly, urgent, without finesse but in perfect unison. But that was later. When he entered her, she was beyond thinking, beyond anything save the wild, desperate need to take him with her over the edge, to lose herself in this moment with this complete stranger and to forget who she was, who she had been, what she might become.

She had no reserve in making clear what she wanted, and he wanted it too, tilting her towards him to drive deeper, harder, until she climaxed again and he pulled himself free of her, coming with a guttural cry, falling on to his back by her side when it was over, his chest heaving, his eyes tight shut.

His heart was thudding. His whole body was thrumming with pleasure. He was weightless, empty, sated. It had been so long since he'd felt like this. No, that was wrong. He'd never felt like this. Making love to his wife had been a much gentler, very different experience. A tender, loving act. This was— different. Had it really happened? Grayson opened his eyes, half expecting to wake up alone in the aftermath of a dream, only to encounter a pair of almond-shaped green eyes staring at him. Though she looked hurriedly away, rolling over on to her side, turning her back on him.

'Constance?'

She grabbed the sheet from the dishevelled bed, wrapping it around herself, squirming out of reach. 'I must look a sight.'

Embarrassment, not regret. He was about to tell her that she looked delightful, with her hair half out of its pins and her cheeks flushed and her breasts only barely covered, but thought better of it just in time. 'You're not the only one.' Grayson grabbed his breeches from the floor and pulled them on. He barely recalled taking any of his clothes off. All he'd wanted was to feel her skin against his, to have her body pressed against his, to be inside her, to lose himself in her. He'd certainly done that!

Stooping down to pick up his shirt, slanting a glance at the unfamiliar back which was still turned to him, he was swamped by the urge to do it all again. Bloody hell, that was taking making up for lost time to new heights! Pulling his shirt quickly over his head he wondered, just for a moment, how Miss Constance Grant would react if he propositioned her. Again. *Had* he propositioned her the first time? No, it had been a mutual decision, that he was sure of. Entirely mutual, from beginning to end.

Her chemise and corsets were in a heap on the floor tangled up with his waistcoat and stockings. Who'd have imagined such prosaic garments clothed such a passionate creature. It had been a while, she'd said. Who, he wondered, and when? She wasn't married. Did they have different customs when it came to that sort of thing in the Highlands? He had absolutely no idea. He had just had a passionate—extremely passionate—encounter with a woman who was more or less a complete stranger, and what's more he would happily have another.

Which is when it hit him what was missing. Guilt. Donning his waistcoat, he examined his conscience but no, there was not a trace of it, nor regret either. Now that really was something new. Glancing over at Constance, he saw that she'd huddled deeper under the sheet. Picking up her clothes, he shook them out. 'It's as well the landlady keeps a clean house, or the pair of us would be head to toe in oose.'

'Put my clothes down, for goodness sake. Leave them there on the bed. I'll get dressed when you're gone.'

'I'm not leaving without you.'

'I'm most certainly not getting dressed in front of you.'

'Aye, that might be a bad idea right enough.'

'Oh! Well, thank you for being so understanding.'

'I'm not being understanding.' Grayson sat down beside her. 'There's nothing I would like more than to see you naked again.'

She whirled around. 'You don't mean—you cannot possibly mean…'

'But I do.' She looked so desirable, and he could just see the tip of one nipple peeking out of the sheet, and her lips were swollen with their kissing. 'I should be embarrassed. I'm forty-two, not twenty-two, but you, Miss Constance Grant, have given me a considerable appetite for what I've been missing.'

'Really?'

He risked a kiss. 'Truly.'

'I'm still not getting dressed in front of you.'

'If you kiss me again, it's my clothes that will be coming off, not yours going on.'

'Grayson! We can't possibly…'

'Ah, but you want to, do you?'

She was blushing, but her smile—lord, but her smile was wicked. 'I think I too have found an appetite for what I've been missing. I think…'

The tap on the door made them both jump. 'Mr Maddox, I was wondering if your wife was recovered enough to take some tea,' a voice said primly.

Stifling a laugh, for Constance had thrown herself under the bedclothes and pulled them over her head, Grayson went to the door, glad he had at least his shirt and waistcoat on. 'Thank you, that would be very welcome,' he told the tavern's landlady. He winked over his shoulder at Constance. 'She's fair tuckered out, for some reason. A cup of tea will be just the job to get her back on her feet.'

Chapter Three

'This has turned into the most unexpected day imaginable,' Constance said as they headed back up the hill towards the city.

Grayson glanced down at her, smiling wryly. 'That's a bit of an understatement.'

'If anyone knew what I'd done, they'd be shocked to the core.'

'But they won't, unless you tell them.'

'No,' Constance said uncertainly, for she felt as if her actions were written plainly over her face.

They walked apart, but she was acutely conscious of him striding along beside her, of the easy way his arms swung, of the way he matched his pace to hers. Just over an hour ago she had been naked in his arms. She had of her own accord allowed a complete stranger to lock himself in a room in a tavern with her, and she had not for a single moment questioned the wisdom of doing so. And now here they were, fully clothed, looking as if they were simply strolling along among the evening crowds instead of indulging in a promenade of shame, following a decadent afternoon.

Was she ashamed, though? Not a whit of it, astonishingly. Part of her was still floating on a cloud of sated desire, longing to be alone so that she could replay every delicious moment, recall every touch, and savour it all over again. No, she was not one whit ashamed, but she felt as if she was dreaming. When they said their farewells and went their separate ways as if nothing at all had happened, perhaps then reality would bite.

'Where are you putting up? Not that I need to know,' Constance added hastily. 'I'm not intending to come calling or anything. I was simply…'

'Oman's Tavern Hotel on West Register Street. Do you know it?'

'I know of it. I'm at the other end of the New Town.'

'I'll walk you back.'

'There's no need, Mr Maddox.'

He quirked an eyebrow. 'Mr Maddox?'

'Grayson.' She could feel herself blushing like a foolish girl, which was how she'd behaved. No! No foolish girl would have thrown herself at a man with such very adult intentions. She'd known exactly what she was doing and she had relished every moment of it. Until it was over that is, and there was no passion to make her forget her imperfections, the fact that her body was almost forty years old and the clothes which lay crumpled on the rented bedroom floor looked as if they were of a similar vintage. It didn't help at all that Grayson showed no trace of embarrassment then or now. She eyed him from under the shadow of her bonnet in mild astonishment. He looked so collected, so self-contained.

'I reckon I'm feeling the same as you, you know,' he said, sensing her attention. 'I can't quite believe it. That wasn't just out of character, it was pretty much unique in my experience. But I don't regret it, unless you do.'

'I don't. We are both adults with no ties,' Constance said firmly. 'We knew exactly what we were doing, and have harmed no one else in the process.'

'Bravo!'

'Though if anyone ever did find out! Oh,

my goodness, Grayson, your children— Ah, but, no, they are far too young, and besides...'

'They're not bairns, Constance. Shona is sixteen and Neil is fourteen.'

'Dear God.' She stared at him, appalled. 'Not bairns at all. If they knew...'

Grayson swore. 'Now, that really doesn't bear thinking about. Fortunately they are in Glasgow, and since we didn't meet anyone I know in Newhaven...'

'But what about here in Edinburgh?'

He frowned, pondering the question for a few moments before shaking his head. 'It's highly unlikely that I'll meet anyone who knows me, so there's no need to walk a yard apart from me, nor to look about you like we're about to be ambushed by some minister of the kirk telling us we've sinned, and promising us hell and damnation.'

'Believe me, I've long since stopped letting any minister dictate how I lead my life.'

'Then who is it you're worried might see us together? Have I been thoughtless? You live here and I don't, there's bound to be friends, neighbours...'

Constance closed the gap between them again. 'My circle of friends is very small. Anyway, even if I am spotted with you, it's hardly likely that anyone would rush to the conclusion that we'd spent the afternoon—well, why would they, given our age and circumstances. It's hardly a habit for either of us.'

'The way I'm feeling right now, it's a habit I'd happily acquire.'

'You don't mean that!'

'Would I take the chance again, if you offered it? I would. Would you? Ah no, don't answer that, I shouldn't have asked...'

'Yes, I would,' she answered promptly. 'Though of course I may only be saying so because I know that this was a quite unique afternoon that will never happen again.'

'That is me put firmly in my place. Seriously though, you know that I will keep this to myself, don't you? I'm not going to insult you by saying that I don't think any less of you, for I don't know what to think about any of this at all, but I—dammit, what I'm trying to say is that I don't see why two adults who are footloose and fancy free shouldn't indulge in...'

'...a delightful afternoon, without it damaging their reputation in any way.'

'Aye. That,' Grayson answered with a crooked smile. 'To be honest, until you mentioned Shona and Neil, I hadn't thought about that aspect of it at all.'

'Do they think their papa a monk, then?'

'They think me a father, which precludes me from being a man and they'd be shocked to the core if they discovered otherwise. The very thought of what would happen if—it really doesn't bear thinking about.'

Doesnae bearrrr thinking aboot.

'There then, it's as well you met me in Edinburgh and not Glasgow,' Constance said, 'and that we've absolutely no common acquaintances. In fact, my social circle is pretty much restricted to my friend Mrs Winston, who is currently out of town visiting relatives,' Constance said. Which was true enough. Technically, Paul was not an acquaintance but her employer.

'I thought you said you were a teacher.'

'I used to be, in the school my father founded.'

'That must have made it particularly painful to have to leave.'

'Yes.' But that was six years ago and there were plenty of other schools, she could see him thinking, looking at her with a mixture of sympathy and curiosity. She was oddly tempted to explain, and had to remind herself that despite what they had shared, he was still a complete stranger, and the secret was not only hers to share. 'Mrs Winston, my friend, is also my godmother, and was my mother's oldest friend,' she said instead. 'When I came to Edinburgh, she very kindly took me in and gave me a roof over my head. Her mind is sharp, she's excellent company, but she is getting on a bit, and is rather frail, so I run errands for her and so forth. It suits us both, my staying there.'

It was weak, and it made her sound shallow, but after all, she would never see Grayson again. The thought dented her mood. It was a rare thing for her to take to someone instantly the way she had with him. He made her laugh. She liked him, and she knew he felt the same about her. But they were already over half-way up Leith Walk now, and what in other circumstances could have been a promising beginning was about to be an abrupt farewell.

How would they say their goodbyes? As if they were perfect strangers, with a nod and a polite handshake? Well that would be appropriate since they *were* perfect strangers! She would have liked the chance to know him better.

'A penny for them? You were miles away,'

Grayson said, interrupting her thoughts and smiling quizzically.

'I was wondering—I was just wondering how you came to be a shipbuilder?'

'Unlike you, I didn't join the family business, though my father *was* a shipping clerk.'

'I'm not exactly sure what a shipping clerk is,' Constance replied. Nor was she particularly interested, but if it kept the conversation in safer waters—*ha!*—then she was happy to be enlightened. 'Do tell.'

'Because you'll not sleep tonight unless I do?' Grayson retorted, quite undeceived. 'Well then, on your head be it. A shipping clerk keeps an eagle eye on everything that enters or leaves the warehouses and the ships. Purchase orders, bills of lading, invoices, that kind of thing. Documentation was my father's province. He was very good at it and highly trusted, with ten clerks working for him. But as far as the ships themselves were concerned—no. My father hated to cross a bridge, never mind sail.'

'Whereas you?'

'That's why the west coast weather suits me. Did you not notice my webbed feet? Aside from a head for numbers, my father and I were chalk and cheese. I was expected to follow in his footsteps, but I'm not suited to sitting at a desk all day.'

'No, you certainly don't have the look of a man with a sedentary occupation. I mean—' Constance broke off, appalled, as an image of exactly how he looked naked and aroused popped into her head. 'I mean, you have not run to fat as some men do in their middle years.'

'My middle years! And here was me thinking, after this afternoon, that I'm not past my prayers after all.'

'Were you thinking that? Before? That you were past your prayers, I mean?'

'I will be forty-three next birthday. In my dotage, as far as my children are concerned.'

'I will be forty next week. A confirmed old maid.'

'Aye, that's exactly what I thought when I saw you, and this afternoon has proved it.'

She laughed sheepishly. 'I shall wake up tomorrow morning and this will all seem even more unreal than it does just now.'

'If it was a dream, it was a delightful one.'

'Yes.' She met his gaze, caught her breath at the warmth in his smile, then looked away hurriedly. 'It was.' They had reached the top of Elm Row at the busy junction of Picardy

Place which led into the heart of the New Town. 'There is talk of building some sort of gate here, if the press is to be believed, to allow the King to be presented with the keys to the city.'

'And bonfires on Calton Hill too,' Grayson said, gazing up at the folly, intended to be an imitation of the Acropolis, that had begun construction at the summit. 'There will be a fine view of proceedings from up there.'

'Do you really think that the King will draw the kind of crowds the press are predicting? I think they are being far too optimistic.'

'Now there we must disagree. Aside from the fact that a trip to Scotland will keep him from meddling in the conference at Verona at the same time as making him feel useful, I reckon the great and the good and the native hordes too, will be delighted to make him welcome. Everybody loves the excuse to put on their finest and make merry. When, after all, was the last time a king set foot in Scotland?'

'Depending on your allegiance, it was 1746 when Bonnie Prince Charlie was hounded out. But if you mean a *crowned* monarch, then it was, I think 1633 when Charles was crowned here. That would be the first Charles for the English, though he was our sixth. The one who was beheaded. I wonder if that is a portent of things to come?'

Grayson laughed. 'You are talking treason.'

'Oh, no! I am simply speculating.'

'As opposed to your expressing a desire to make it so?'

'You may interpret it that way, I most certainly would not.'

Once again, he laughed. 'It's a fine line none the less, and though I'm inclined to agree with your sentiments, I think we'll be in the minority. Fat George's visit to Ireland last year was deemed a great success. Despite what you and I may think, he is reckoned to be charming and people like a spectacle, don't they?'

'Including your son and daughter?'

'I'm afraid so.'

She stopped, for they had reached the imposing façade of the Register House. 'Oman's Tavern is just in there, isn't it?'

'Yes, but I'll see you safely home first. The other end of the New Town, did you say? Come, let me walk with you, I'm not ready to part from you just yet.'

She had no more desire to end their encounter than he did. Physically sated she might be, but she was very far from bored with his company, quite the contrary, so she nodded her assent. 'Along Princes Street to the end, then. Coates Crescent is just beyond that on the way to Haymarket.'

It was after six, and the traffic was beginning to thin. They walked together in a silence that became more strained with every step. On their left, the castle loomed high up on its volcanic plug, the echo of a battalion marching on the Esplanade spilling down into the marshland left by the draining of the Nor' Loch. 'There is to be a parade from the castle all the way down to Holyrood Palace,' Constance said. 'A ceremonial handing over of Scotland's crown jewels, what is left of them.'

'Another of Sir Walter Scott's notions, doubtless,' Grayson said sardonically. 'The man will have the world believing we wear nothing but tartan, and go about our daily business armed with claymores and dirks.'

'You are not one of Mr Scott's admirers, then?'

'No, but Neil, my son loves his novels.'

His children, she was realising, were a touchy subject, and so Constance ventured nothing more than a polite, 'Really?'

'Really. Neil,' Grayson continued to her

surprise, 'would love to inhabit the romantic Highlands that Mr Scott conjures up. He has no head for commerce and no interest in engines. He's very much his mother's son in looks and temperament.'

'And your daughter?'

'Shona. Ah, poor Shona, is far too much like me for her own liking and others too. Their grandparents—their mother's family— they never approved of my marriage. It has led to complications which I'd rather not go into, if you don't mind.'

'Of course not. They are none of my concern.'

'It's not that. It's only that I'm enjoying being myself with you, just the two of us, for the moment. Tell me, what do you do to occupy yourself all day?'

His smile reached his eyes again. They were horribly near Coates and their parting of ways, though of one accord their pace had slowed. At least she hoped it was of one accord. 'I deal with Pearl—that is, Mrs Winston's correspondence. I read the newspaper to her, and sometimes novels—she too is very fond of Sir Walter Scott. She cannot walk so far these days, but I accompany her when she takes the air in the park, and I keep her company when she has no other alternative. Oh, yes, and I walk her dog.'

'Aren't you bored?'

'Oh, no, for I have my own...'

'Your own what?'

'My own reading. From the lending library. I am not an admirer of Sir Walter, and Mrs Winston does not mind my borrowing my own reading matter with her subscription.' It was lame, but it was all she could think of. Grayson would think her idle, but that couldn't be helped.

'Reading, talking, dog-walking. It's a long way away from teaching bairns. You must miss teaching, surely?'

Every day. Disconcerted, for she had not permitted herself to admit it until now, Constance shrugged. 'I have plenty to occupy me. And here is Coates Crescent,' she declared, both relieved and depressed by the sight of the familiar terrain, coming to a halt in front of the gardens that fronted the row of houses. 'This is where we must part.' Taking a deep breath, she held out her hand. 'Goodbye, Grayson.'

He took it, covering it with both of his own. 'Must it be goodbye?'

'What else can it be?'

'I've no idea. Nothing, not in the sense of— of anything.' He grimaced. 'I simply meant that I've enjoyed my time with you. I don't only mean—though that was—well, we both are agreed about that. But the rest—I don't know. Sorry, I'm not usually a man with a problem saying what he means. When I met you this morning, I felt I knew you. I've never felt such an instant connection before, and I'd like to spend a bit more time with you. A bit more talking, just me and you and letting the world go hang. Ach, never mind, ignore me, I'm havering.'

'No, I have the feeling we are kindred spirits,' Constance said, as he turned to go. 'The oddest thing, isn't it? I like you, knew I could trust you, right from the start.' She curled her fingers into his. 'You might be interested to know that I walk with Angus every morning.'

'Lucky Angus, who's he?'

'He's Mrs Winston's Scotch terrier, and if he were human, I'd call him thrawn.'

'And where and when do you and this stubborn creature take your walk?'

'In the mornings between nine and ten, in the afternoons between five and six. Angus can't walk very far, he's old as well as thrawn, so I take him to the parkland at West Coates. It is just over there.'

'So if I just happened to be passing I might bump into you?'

'Another happy accident?'

'Sometimes fate needs a helping hand.' He smiled down at her, and his smile made her belly tighten. Then he lifted her hand to his mouth, pressing a kiss to her knuckles, and his smile changed, and for a moment she felt as if she couldn't breathe. Then he let her go.

'Until tomorrow,' he said, turning away to head back towards Princes Street, raising his hand in farewell, but not looking back.

Chapter Four

~~~~~~~~~~~~~~~~~~~~~~~~~~

Tuesday, 9th July 1822

Coates Crescent, with its small formal residents' gardens, bordered the main thoroughfare of Maitland Street, which led to Princes Street in one direction and the Haymarket in the other. It was already busy when Constance set out with a reluctant Angus on his leash the next morning, the road crowded with handcarts, drays, and coaches flooding into the city. Her nose twitched, for though the New Town had none of the open drains that polluted the Old Town, the air was still smoke-tinged, even on this balmy summer's morning, and the constant traffic of cattle and horses was adding its own distinctive aroma to the mix.

Having spent a good part of the night telling herself that it would be best if Grayson didn't show up, her heart leapt when she saw him. She was early, but there he was, sitting on the grass, his back against a tree, writing in a notebook. His coat was olive-green today, worn with buff-coloured trousers strapped under his shoes in the new fashion. It suited him. He would, she thought, look very becoming in a plaid with those legs. Not that she should be looking at his legs, for it made her recall in vivid detail how they'd felt naked, sprawled on top of her in the aftermath of their lovemaking yesterday. Was it only yesterday? She still couldn't quite believe they'd been so bold. She could feel herself blushing, and had a strong urge to flee.

But before she could make up her mind, Grayson did it for her, getting to his feet with enviable ease to greet her. If she'd been sitting leaning against that tree, she'd probably have had to roll over on to all fours to get up. 'Good morning. Fancy meeting you here! I take it this is Angus?'

The terrier was sniffing at his legs, yapping as usual, and for once a welcome distraction. Constance tugged on the lead and the dog bared his teeth at her before returning to his sniffing. 'I'm afraid he doesn't take to strangers but don't worry, he doesn't bite.'

Grayson knelt down, taking the dog's muzzle firmly in both hands. 'No, but I do. Enough of that, do you hear?' he said gruffly.

To her astonishment, Angus's straggly tail started to wag. 'My goodness, you are honoured.'

'He just needs to know who's boss.'

'Be careful though, because...'

'Bloody hell!' As Angus lunged to lick his face, Grayson recoiled in horror. 'His breath's minging!'

'I know.' She tried in vain to smother her laughter as she hauled Angus back. 'It's his teeth—or lack of them.'

'Hence the reason you were so sure he wouldn't bite me!'

Watching him brush the grass from his trousers, Constance's doubts returned. 'I shouldn't have come. I mean, I shouldn't have hinted so heavily that you'd be able to find me here.'

'You'd rather that I left?'

That wasn't hurt in his eyes, she told herself, it was more likely relief. 'You're probably only here because you felt obliged.'

'I was the one who engineered another meeting. I thought—if I was mistaken...'

'No! I want—I don't know. It's difficult, I've never been in this situation before.'

He laughed softly. 'I'm as confused as you. I thought I'd made it clear that all this is completely new to me too.'

'You did.' She didn't have to explain herself, but she wanted to. She didn't owe him anything, he was a complete stranger. But he wasn't. 'Yesterday was perfect. A moment out of time for both of us. I simply wonder if it would be better to leave it at that?'

He thought for a moment, a slight frown pulling his brows together. 'Of course, if that is what you wish, but—Constance, for me yesterday was not only about what happened, delightful though it was. I took a real shine to you. You make me smile, and that's a rarer thing than it should be. I feel as if we're in tune, somehow. I know that probably sounds daft, but...'

'No, it's not daft, it's what I was thinking too,' she confessed.

'That's a relief. Look, I'm only going to be in Edinburgh for a few days. What I'm trying to say is, I'd like to spend as much time with you as you can spare.'

Which was exactly what she wanted too. Yet still she felt obliged to put up some sort of resistance. 'I do have some free time, with Pearl being away, but we might find we have nothing in common.'

'In which case we'll say goodbye, and no harm done, but if we said goodbye right now...'

'We'd both regret it,' Constance said impulsively, casting caution to the winds for the second time in as many days.

'Aye.' She wasn't imagining it. He almost visibly relaxed. 'My thoughts exactly. Shall we stop fretting about what we're doing, and just enjoy each other's company then?' Grayson eyed Angus, snuffling about in the grass. 'How about we leave him to do his business, and take a stroll around the gardens?'

'Oh, no, poor wee thing, we can't abandon him, he might run off—well, trot off, he's not really up to running. Pearl would be devastated if she came home to find I'd lost him. She and Angus are perfectly matched.'

Grayson took the leash from her, tugging Angus into action. 'You mean Mrs Winston has no teeth either?'

She laughed, only now admitting to herself how much she craved this little bit of extra time. 'Oh, no, she has a full set, unlike Angus here, though they are not her own. Unfortunately they don't fit well either. She finds them a hindrance rather than a help when chewing, so she takes them out and hides them under her napkin. She forgot, one night after dinner, to retrieve them, and there was a new footman clearing the table, and the teeth ended up in the laundry with the napkin. Fortunately, I managed to get to them before the laundry maid was confronted with them smiling up at her.'

'What big teeth you have, Grandmama,' Grayson said, grinning. 'It's from the tale of Red Riding Hood, a wee lassie who meets a grisly fate at the hands of a wolf who has eaten her grannie.'

'It never fails to amaze me how much children prefer dark tales to happy ones. Ghosts and ghouls were what my pupils loved best. Changelings being snatched by the fairies. Kelpies, and sea monsters, they couldn't get enough of them.'

'It was the same with Shona when she was wee, though her mother considered her too young to read lurid tales such as Red Riding Hood, promising her that she would have the book when she was old enough. It was only after—after. I found Shona crying over the book, and had not the heart to take it from her. I told her it would give her nightmares but she clung to it for grim death.'

'Sometimes,' Constance said gently, 'it's good for children to escape into a fairy-tale world, no matter how gruesome.'

'Aye, that's one of the many things I learned.'

'I can't imagine how difficult it must have been for you,' Constance said, 'having to cope with two motherless wee ones while mourning your wife.'

'They kept me sane, not the other way round.'

She could not recall that he'd mentioned his wife by name. Her parents didn't approve of the marriage, he'd said yesterday. A grandmother would have been an immense help to a widower with two bairns, but it didn't sound as if much assistance had been forthcoming. How many men would have devoted themselves to raising two children as he had, and not a hint that he'd resented it either—quite the contrary. Here was proof that it was possible for a man to put his personal responsibilities first, rather than his career. The contrast with Lockhart was impossible not to draw. 'So some stories have a happy ending,' she said brightly, noting Grayson's bleak expression, 'unlike poor Red Riding Hood! Eaten by the wolf, same as her grannie.'

'Well, it was a happy ending for the wolf.'

Constance couldn't help laughing. 'That's one way of looking at it. I think we had better slow down a bit if you don't mind. Angus's legs are much shorter than yours.'

'That looks like a nice patch of grass under the tree over there, and it's in the shade. Will we sit down and let the dog have a well-earned breather? You see Angus is well ahead of the game, making himself comfy.' He'd let go of the lead and the dog, having circled his chosen spot, fell panting to the ground while Grayson took his coat off. 'There, you can sit on that.'

'Thank you.' Constance managed to do so with a modicum of grace, praying that she'd manage to get up again with the same ease, and knowing for a fact that she wouldn't.

Grayson sat down beside her, stretching out one long leg, curling the other under, angling himself to face her. 'Mrs Winston was your mother's friend, you said? Is she a Highlander too, then?'

'Not at all. She's originally from the Borders, which is where she is now, and only moved to Edinburgh when she married.'

'Then how...'

'My parents are also from the Borders. Even after they'd lived in Clachan Bridge for years, they were still referred to as the Sassenach Settlers. My father was an orphan who did well for himself, becoming a teacher. My mother's family were well to do, and didn't approve of their daughter falling in love with him. They had ambitions beyond a mere teacher for their daughter, and so they used their influence to have my father dismissed, thinking that would precipitate the end of the romance.'

'I am assuming, given your presence here, that it did not?'

'They eloped, and through a more sympathetic but distant connection of my mother's, moved to Clachan Bridge village, and set up the school there.'

'And what of your mother's family?'

'I have no idea. I've never met any of them. I've managed without them my whole life and they have never shown the slightest bit of interest in me. When Màthair died, Athair, my father, wrote to them. At the time he told me he expected no reply, and none came.'

'That's hellish.'

'You can't miss what you've never had,' Constance said. 'I consider myself a Highlander, and was raised to speak Gaelic and to teach it too, though we always spoke English at home. For my parents, Clachan Bridge was a haven. They were very happy, we all were, while the old laird was alive, but he died ten years ago, the same year as we lost Màthair, and that's when everything changed.'

'I'm sorry.' Grayson caught her hand. 'I didn't mean to upset you. Don't say any more, it's obviously a painful subject for you.'

'But I want to explain.' She had removed her gloves and bonnet when they sat down. His skin was cool against hers. 'The folk who inherited Clachan, which is the name of the estate, had no interest in it you see, and the house, all the lands were sold.'

'To an improver, I presume?'

'An improver!' Constance swore under her breath in the Gaelic. 'If you class burning down villages and chasing families from their homes as improvement then yes, that is what he was. Ours was just one of the many villages he set his factor to *improve*. The last one to be cleared, as it happens. There's no village now, it was razed to the ground. There are no crofts, and no one left to farm them, even if there were.'

'Dear God. You don't mean they actually set alight to people's homes?'

'To prevent them from returning,' she said bitterly. 'To ensure they relocated to whatever godforsaken patch of land they could call home, or took a ship to some far-flung wilderness overseas, as is increasingly the preferred option.'

'Constance, wait. You can't force people to emigrate.'

'Put the rent up every quarter until they are deep in debt and starving. Then the law is on your side when you evict them for nonpayment. Burn down their cottage, give their crofts over to sheep, make sure their minister is right by your side, telling his flock that it is God's will to obey their laird. Then offer them an assisted passage to Canada. No,' Constance concluded, her chest heaving, 'of course you can't force people to emigrate.'

'I had no idea.'

'You have that in common with most of Scotland.'

'You saw this? You actually witnessed this take place, in your own village?'

He looked so shocked that her flare of anger

died. 'Athair—my father, he—his heart failed him while we watched. The schoolhouse was the one building left standing. It was a shelter for some of the villagers, in the weeks after, but I doubt Lockhart would have permitted them to remain there after I left.'

'Lockhart, he was the laird, I take it?'

'No, his factor, who did the dirty work while the laird was safely far away in his big fancy London house. Lockhart was our minister's son.'

'The minister who stood by while his flock were evicted?'

'I'm not making it up, I assure you.'

'No.' Grayson ran his hand through his hair, shaking his head. 'I can see you're telling the truth, but it beggars belief.'

'Ah, but it gets worse, for Lockhart was the man I once planned to marry.'

Grayson's jaw dropped. 'Your future husband burnt down your village?'

'I had broken the engagement the year before, when it became clear to me that he would put his ambition before all I thought we both held dear but yes, he did, acting on the laird's orders.'

'I don't know what to say. I simply can't imagine what you must have gone through.'

Constance shook her head, unable to speak for a moment for her throat was clogged with tears. 'What I suffered was *nothing* compared to some,' she said passionately. 'There was one old woman. Her family carried her out on her bed, for she was too frail to walk. And there was another family, who...' Her voice broke. 'I'm so sorry, I didn't mean to blurt all that out. I don't know why I did. I never talk of it.'

Grayson swore under his breath. 'I'm not surprised. Here.'

She took the handkerchief, mopping her cheeks and blowing her nose. It was fine cambric, but there was no monogram, in keeping with the rest of his raiment, good quality but plain. 'Thank you, don't worry, I'll have it laundered before I give it back to you,' she said, tucking it into the pocket of her gown.

'Don't worry about a daft handkerchief,' Grayson said, still trying to come to terms with what she had told him. 'After an experience like that, it's testament to your strength of will that you're even here to tell the tale.'

'It's a tale that no one wants to listen to.

What happened to my village is happening on almost every estate in the Highlands, but no one seems to care.'

Every estate? The Glenbranter lands belonging to his in-laws and how they were run were none of his concern, that was what he'd always told himself, and what he'd had drummed into his head too. No matter what he thought of the Murrays, and he could make a list as long as his arm of their failings, they were not brutes. Shona and Neil said little of their regular visits north, but he couldn't believe they would have failed to notice such barbarous measures, had they been taken. They'd have told him, wouldn't they? Uncomfortably, Grayson was forced to admit that he had no idea if they would confide in him, and he certainly didn't want to get into a discussion on the subject with Constance.

What he really wanted, looking at her tear-stained face and brave smile, was to pull her into his arms. 'I can't believe I've known you less than twenty-four hours. Maybe we have met after all, in another life.'

'That sounds like something Mhairi, our village fey wife would say. You don't really believe it, do you?'

'Not really, though I can't shake off the conviction that something brought us together.'

'Well then, let's call it fate for want of a better explanation.'

He frowned at the mutt contentedly sleeping a few feet away. Angus was making snuffling noises, one of his rear paws twitching. 'I'm not used to having time to myself, with no business issues to occupy me and my weans being looked after by someone else. I've no time to feel lonely, but I've not much time for making friends either. Self-sufficient, is how I'd describe myself, and happily so, but it feels good to talk to someone who wants nothing from me, save to know me a bit better, and to share something of herself too.' He shifted on the ground, moving closer to Constance. 'Does that make sense?'

'Perfect sense.' She smiled at him. 'We really are kindred spirits.'

'So you won't be surprised then, that what you told me of your parents' marriage struck a chord. My late wife was from a very well-connected family. They thought a rough Glaswegian shipbuilder who, at the time, had not yet made his fortune, was not nearly good enough for her. They opposed the match, and so we married without their consent. Her parents disowned her at first, but she was the light of their lives and unlike your mother, they welcomed her back into the family fold after a few months of exile. Their forgiveness never did extend to me, though.'

'That's what you meant yesterday, when you mentioned complications.'

'You wouldn't believe the half of it. While my wife was alive, it didn't matter so much, she'd take the children to visit, leaving me to concentrate on business for a few weeks at a time. But when she died, they wanted to take Neil and Shona away from me.'

'No! Oh, Grayson, how awful. And self-ish, too. Your children are all you have left of your wife.'

She was so obviously indignant, it made him feel considerably better. 'They thought they could offer them things I can't, open doors for them socially. They still think that way, and constantly point this out to Neil and Shona whenever they see them. I sometimes wish…' He sometimes wished that the Murrays and their blandishments would disappear in a puff of smoke and spare him sleepless nights! If it would have been wrong of them, all these years ago to take his weans from

him, it would be tantamount to a crime now.
'Ach, never mind them,' he continued, as
much to himself as Constance, 'I wouldn't
stop Shona and Neil seeing them, even if I
hadn't promised Eliza.' It provoked an odd
kind of relief to speak her name. 'My wife,
I mean.'

'Even I can see you're a devoted father, and
I barely know you. I'm sure your children
know how much you love them.'

'Loving them is the easy bit. Making them
happy, that is more of a challenge with every
passing year. You could say they are my life's
work.'

'A task you're happy to undertake.'

And one he was determined to keep to
himself. 'I wouldn't have it any other way,
though as I said, it leaves me little time for
myself.'

'You've never thought of marrying again?'

'Never. Neil and Shona are well past the
age of needing a replacement for their mother,
and as far as I'm concerned, it wouldn't be
worth rocking the boat. We're happy just the
way we are. What about you though, have you
no thoughts of ever marrying?'

'Lockhart—Robert, his name was Robert—
we were what you'd call childhood sweet-

hearts and if it had been up to me, we'd have married and settled down long before he became the laird's factor. But he was ambitious. He followed his father into the church, spent several years away from Clachan Bridge training for the ministry, though it didn't work out for him. I waited, I was happy enough teaching. He came back, and took up the post working for the laird as I told you.'

Constance bit her lip, staring down at her hands. 'I thought I knew him so well, but when it became clear I could not persuade him to put the people he had grown up with, never mind the woman he said he loved, before his own ambition, I had no option but to end our arrangement. Since then—no, I've no desire to marry, not now. I'm too set in my ways to give any man control over how I live my life, and I've long given up on the idea of having children of my own. If I ever return to teaching, there will be children enough for me to care for.'

'Do you have plans to do that?'

'Not yet. I have other undertakings I must complete first. Not least of which,' she added before he could ask what these might be, 'is surviving the ordeal of my fortieth birthday. I never used to think I looked like my mother, but as I get older, when I catch a glimpse of my reflection in a shop window or a glass, there she is, staring right back at me. She told me once that when she looked in the mirror she was always surprised to find *her* mother staring back at her. Which must have disconcerted my father. He referred to his mother-in-law as Morag the Monster—you know, the mythical beast who is supposed to live in the depths of Loch Morar?'

Grayson accepted the very deliberate change of subject equitably, being no more eager to let the mundane business of everyday life intrude on their time than she. 'I can't say I've come across Morag before, but she sounds like a very friendly kind of monster.'

Constance chuckled. 'Not if my father is to be believed.'

'Well I can assure you that there is nothing of the monster at all about you.'

'Why thank you kindly, sir.'

'Not the most effusive of compliments, I'll grant you.'

'Oh, at my age, one gratefully accepts any praise.'

'At your age!' Grayson lifted her hand to his mouth, pressing his lips to her knuckles. 'Aye, you've one foot in the grave right enough.'

'Well maybe a toe.'

She looked charmingly flustered by his touch. A simple kiss, and not even on the mouth, had him feeling a bit flustered himself. 'Bollocks,' he said, just for the sake of shocking her into one of her sinful smiles.

He was amply rewarded. 'Your language is most uncivilised.'

'That's your fault. You make me feel very uncivilised.'

'Verrrry.' She leaned across him to flutter her fingers over his jaw, to curl them into his hair.

'Constance?'

'What?'

'I think it's only fair to warn you that I'm going to have to kiss you if you come any closer.'

'Surely not in front of Angus,' she said her lips a whisper away from his.

'We'll have to do our level best not to wake him.'

Their mouths met, their lips only just touching for the longest, tantalising moment before they opened, and the kiss began. Such a kiss. Slow. Lingering. Lips and tongues.

Her eyes drifted closed. It was the kind of kiss that made the world disappear, to leave only the two of them, melting into each other. The kind of kiss that could go on and on and on until...

Until the reek of a small, impatient terrier's breath got between them and made them pull apart with mutual cries of disgust that quickly became laughter.

Looking anxiously around her and relieved to see that they were still alone, Constance grabbed her bonnet, stuffing her hair, which had come out of its pins, underneath it. 'I can't believe we did that. In a public park, for goodness sake.'

'In front of Angus, too. Look at him, he's shocked to the core.' The dog was distractedly scratching his ear.

'I don't know what came over me.'

'The need to slake a thirst after a drought,' Grayson quipped as he stood, holding out his hand to help her up.

'Do you think so?'

He kept hold of her hand. 'No, I don't. That was a vulgar joke, which I apologise for. I don't know what it is, and I've no mind to put a name to it either. It was delightful, that's all that matters.'

'I had better get back, for I'm sure it's much later than I think and there's a man coming to the house to measure up for some new curtains and I have a host of other domestic tasks that I won't bore you with. What will you do for the rest of the day?'

'Count the hours until I see you again. What about tomorrow?'

'I'm afraid I can't. As I said, I have a list the length of my arm to complete, but I should be free all the next day. I could help you to look for a hotel, if you like.'

'I would appreciate that, though there's no rush. I was thinking I might stay on a few days. I reckon I've earned a wee holiday. The yard is in good hands, and Neil and Shona have one of their mother's cousins staying with them.' Grayson grimaced. 'Like the rest of that family, she's more than happy not to have dealings with me. So I'm in no rush to get back to Glasgow just yet. What if I was here to help see you through this birthday you're dreading?'

'You might be well and truly fed up with me by then.'

'I'll take my chances.'

'You'll be able to become bosom friends with Angus.'

'Temptress!'

Constance laughed. 'Now that's a description that's not ever been applied to me before. Till Thursday then.'

Chapter Five

Though the self-proclaimed Jacobite King languishes still in the English capital, my little bird with his ear to the ground tells me that Lord Montagu has offered the home of his ward, the young Duke of Buccleuch, as a temporary residence suitable for a monarch. So confident is Lord Montagu that his generous offer will be accepted, that he has already decanted from Dalkeith House to take up residence in the Barrie Hotel. A self-imposed Clearance, if you like. A tribute to the actions of his fellow landowners or a mocking parody? You decide.

Meanwhile, that expert in creating Highland myths, no less a personage than Sir Walter Scott, himself a rela-

tive of Lord Montagu, has taken it upon himself to supervise the preparations for the visit which must surely be imminent. Look out your tartan, abandon your credulity, and prepare to take part in a pageant designed to advance the fiction that our nation is both united and a fair and just society. In order to achieve this a thick plaid veil will be conveniently drawn over the vile Clearing of the Highlanders from their lands. Why not send them overseas to test their mettle, and rid Scotland of those too lazy or ignorant to improve themselves? some say. They just happen to be the very people who would profit most from their absence. They believe the noble Highlanders who have fought their causes, ploughed their lands and lined their pockets for centuries, now consider them less valuable than the sheep who replace them. And while they are believed, while the myths they propagate go unquestioned, the Clearing will continue unabated, right under the King's florid regal nose.

Flora MacDonald, *New Jacobite Journal*

Thursday, 11th July 1822

Grayson had arranged to meet Constance on the Esplanade in front of the castle, and was rather taken aback to discover the space crowded with what he at first thought must be troops from the barracks, drilling. But there seemed to be at least three separate groups, and none of them wore the official Government Tartan. Bagpipes were wailing discordantly as each cadre was drilled to a different beat. Some of the men wore plaids, some were armed to the teeth, but others appeared to be dressed for a day ploughing the fields. One man, garbed in the full regalia of a warrior complete with eagle feathers crowning the bonnet perched over his flaming red locks, carrying a sword and shield, was bellowing orders at his better-dressed band of Highlanders from atop a large carthorse.

'I'm sorry I'm late.'

'Constance!' Grayson whirled round. 'Where did you spring from?'

'I had business in the West Port, down near the Grassmarket.' Her brow was furrowed, her smile seemed forced.

'Not altogether pleasant business, by the looks of you.'

'It can be difficult, when you feel passionately about something, to accept that others might feel quite differently. Or even worse, be completely indifferent.' She blinked rapidly, obviously on the verge of tears, before catching herself, forcing a smile. 'I'm not one to give up without a fight though. Never mind that, have I kept you waiting long?'

Clearly she did not wish to be questioned. Curious as he was, he followed her lead. 'No, and anyway, there's been plenty to keep me entertained. I like your gown, the blue suits you.'

'Oh. Thank you. It's new. Not my usual style, more fussy, but...'

'I like the ruffles, and the braiding on the neckline. It's very stylish, all the more because you're wearing it. You know, when you blush so charmingly like that, I want to kiss you.'

She relaxed, her smile softening. 'If you want to shock the living daylights out of the world and his wife, then please do so.'

'I can never resist a challenge.'

'Grayson! Act your age.'

'When I'm with you, all thoughts of lambswool vests and felt slippers go right out of my mind.'

Constance giggled. 'I confess, that though I saw the perfect walking stick when I was shopping yesterday, and it was a bargain too, I decided to postpone purchasing it until after you've returned to Glasgow.'

A bellow from the red-haired man in the feathered bonnet made them both look over. One poor unfortunate seemed not to know his left from his right and was consequently causing chaos and pile-ups.

'That strutting peacock is the legend that is MacDonnell of Glengarry,' Constance said. 'He was apparently the role model for Walter Scott's Fergus McIvor from *Waverley,* and he seems determined to live up to it. Would you look at him, prancing about on that horse like he owns the place.'

'Aye, he's a right arrogant wee shite, isn't he—if you'll pardon my language.'

'Feel free to call him whatever you want.' Her lip curled. 'He's one of those men who never walks five yards without his trail of grovelling courtiers to demonstrate his importance. That outfit he's wearing is of his own invention. He calls it the Garb of the Old Gaul, though when he imagines any Old Gaul wore it or for what purpose, I've no idea. He has another costume he wears when he plays the soldier, as opposed to the Lochaber chief, with a red coat and a plume of black ostrich feathers.'

'I can see that you're much taken with him. Aside from looking like a tartan peacock, what's he done to rile you?'

'He's the epitome of a type that's become all too prevalent in the Highlands, that's all. He prides himself on being called the laird, yet he's dispatched all the real Highlanders who were his tenants off to the wilds of Canada so that he and his cronies can hunt stags, and play at jousting with claymores.'

'Jousting with claymores! No, surely that's an invention of Walter Scott's?'

'It's not, I assure you. Glengarry makes sure his exploits and those of his wee Highland society are reported in the press. The dinners he gives for other so-called Highland gentlemen and their wives, are eaten to the tune of the pipes.'

'That would certainly put an end to any conversation, to say nothing of ruining your digestion.'

'I couldn't agree more, but there's worse, when the meal is over.'

'Dirk dancing on the table?' Grayson hazarded, laughing. 'No wait, he expects his guests to sing for their supper.'

'No, for then they might upstage him. You'll never guess. He has his own bard. A blind man, who recites obsequious poetry in praise of his laird.'

'Good grief. Are you teasing?'

'I wish I was.' Constance turned her back on the marching groups. 'He'd be a more honest chieftain if he was parading his sheep about.'

As yet another about-turn resulted in raised voices and pushing and shoving, Grayson snorted. 'Sheep would be more intelligent and easier to marshal. Come away from this risible spectacle and take a look at something worth admiring. The view out over the New Town, it's splendid,' he said, ushering her over to the low ramparts. 'Hard to believe that was once a loch down there, isn't it? You can see quite clearly from here, how well planned the New Town is, all those straight streets and neat blocks. There are parts of Glasgow being constructed in a similar way.'

But Constance's attention had returned to Glengarry. 'Doesn't it make you sick to your back teeth, this pageant Edinburgh is putting on to celebrate the Highlander, when there's likely to be no Highlanders left if what they call progress is allowed to continue?'

'It's shocking, and your own experience of it is tragic, but I don't see how it can be stopped. That cockerel crowing over there, he's a joke figure who's come to believe the myth Walter Scott has created for him, but he's not breaking the law, unless there's a law against being a bigger horse's arse than that belonging to your steed.'

'You have a way with words that I cannot compete with.'

Turning her back on the parade, she smiled up at him, and Grayson's heart lifted as they stood side by side, looking out over the New Town. She was such a slight wee thing, yet there was iron at the core of her that awed him. She, who had suffered and endured so much, saved her pity for those who had suffered more. She was bitter, not at the hand fate had drawn for her, but at the perpetrators. He'd never met a woman like her. He felt no urge to protect her, to shield her, to cushion her path. She wasn't in the least bit like Eliza. But if he was younger, if he didn't have Shona and Neil to care for, if he was setting out again to establish his shipyard, he'd be fortunate to have a woman like Constance at his side, to counsel him and to bolster him. For there had been times in the past when he'd doubted himself, wondered if he'd been over-ambitious or insufficiently so, if his judgement was flawed.

Eliza had given up so much to marry him, he did everything he could to make the life she'd chosen comfortable and free of worries. He'd loved her with all his heart. He'd known Constance for three days. What he felt wasn't love but an affinity, the like of which he'd never felt before, and he knew she felt it too. It was a terrible shame they only had a short time to enjoy it.

'It's an amazing view, isn't it?' She smiled up at him. 'All those neat rows of houses, such a contrast to the sprawl of the Old Town. The streets down there will be awash with lairds and clan chiefs, lord, ladies, marquesses and countesses and all their entourages, all of them clad in tartan, if Walter Scott has his way. Though contrary to what he believes, Highlanders don't go about their daily business wearing fancy plaids and matching stockings, never mind sporrans.'

'If only my business was weaving and not shipbuilding, I'd make a fortune.'

'If you're planning on attending the gentleman's levee at Holyrood or escorting your daughter to the ladies' drawing room, you'd better think about how you're going to deck yourself and your children out, you know.'

'I'm not thinking we'll be invited to attend any such events. They'll be for the great and the good, not humble men like me, who build ships.'

'But your daughter, will she have expectations? She's sixteen, old enough to make her curtsy in front of the King, and to have her cheek kissed.'

'I'm not going to allow anyone to slobber on my daughter's cheek, not even the King.'

'It's considered an honour.' Constance's mouth was prim, but her eyes were alight with laughter. 'I believe that Harriet Siddons, the actress, may be hired to teach the young ladies the correct way to receive the royal embrace.'

'My daughter isn't going to receive any embrace, royal or otherwise, until she's a good deal older.'

'Are you planning on locking her up in a keep, and throwing away the key until she's— what, twenty?'

'Oh, no, thirty at least.' He held his hands up to forestall her protest. 'No, don't say it, I know perfectly well that's ridiculous, but I'll be damned if Shona's first kiss is going to be from a fat king several times her age squeezed into a kilt.'

'Oh, my goodness! I hadn't even considered— can you imagine the King in a kilt?'

He shuddered theatrically. 'Like a sausage bursting from its skin. Surely he wouldn't be so misguided. He'll make himself a laughing stock.'

'Then I most sincerely hope he is so misguided, though sadly, I'm beginning to think you were right when you said that the people of Edinburgh would welcome him with open arms.'

'It's not so much the King, as an excuse for a celebration or twenty. You can't blame people for wanting a bit of fun.'

'Will you consider it fun, I wonder, escorting your daughter to a ball?' Constance laughed, seeing his expression of horror. 'Fortunately for you, invitations will be at a premium.'

But Grayson cursed under his breath. 'I don't know why it didn't occur to me before now. Shona and Neil's grandparents,' he said impatiently, for Constance was looking blank, 'they are bound to be here for the festivities.'

They wouldn't have a problem getting themselves invited to any levee or drawing room, and they'd make damned sure their grandchildren knew it. Dear God, they might even offer them the chance to take part, let them catch a glimpse of what life could be like if they—what was the phrase—*embraced their heritage.* And abandon their father in the process. 'I'll just have to make a point of studiously avoiding them,' he said, as much for his own benefit as Constance's. 'The city will be packed to the gunnels, it shouldn't be too difficult.'

The plaintive skirl of the bagpipes became one cacophony of sound as the pipers from all three faux regiments joined up. 'Is your wee Highland heart stirred by this?'

Constance wrinkled her nose. 'I have always loathed the sound. And to think this is just the beginning of the gathering of the clans, as Sir Walter will doubtless call it. Where on earth will they all stay?'

'Not in any comfort, that's for sure. There will be tents pitched down there before long, where the Nor' Loch once was, I'll wager. Your Mrs Winston could likely make herself a small fortune renting rooms out for the duration. Perhaps you could ask her to put us up?' The skirl of the pipes was so loud that he had to pull her close, and to speak into her ear to be heard. Which was no hardship. 'You and I, under the same roof? Now there's a thought that's both terrifying and oddly tempting.'

'Tempting! You'd wake Angus, if you went creeping about the house in the night, and then Angus would wake everyone else.'

The pipes dwindled to a discordant drone. 'Angus and I are best friends, don't expect him to guard your virtue.'

'This conversation is taking an indecent turn. Don't look at me like that!' Constance was blushing again. 'Time is getting on. If we're to take a look at some hotels, we should make a start.'

'If Oman's on Charlotte Square has some decent rooms we won't need to look any further.' He took her hand, kissing her palm through her glove. 'Shall we?'

Castle Hill was steep, narrow and crowded. The sun had given up on the city this afternoon, and the sky was grey, lowering, the tenement buildings looming so high that they all but blocked the light. At the Lawnmarket the road widened, but the noise increased tenfold as various roads converged. Carts and carriages clattered on the cobblestones on the way up from the High Street laden with goods from the docks, meeting occupied sedan chairs and horses and ponies and donkeys from the bridge that crossed over into the New Town, and from the Grassmarket below. Walking was a task that required a great deal of attention if a person was to keep one eye on the traffic and another on the cobbles, which were treacherous with mud and thankfully unidentifiable filth.

'At least in Glasgow, there is room to walk, and the tenements are not so near nor so tall,' Grayson muttered. 'Did you say there's going to be some sort of procession here?'

'Parading the ceremonial chest holding the Scottish crown all the way from the castle down these streets to Holyrood Palace,' Constance replied. 'Then it's planned that the King will take the same route, from the palace back up the Royal Mile to the castle to the cheers of the watching masses.'

'How will anyone see anything, for heaven's sake?' He pulled them both into the shelter of a narrow wynd to allow a boy with a barrow to pass. 'There's hardly an inch of space as it is.'

'They are planning to put up viewing platforms by the roadside.'

'Death traps, those will be, especially if

some enterprising person sells the space twice over. I certainly won't be one of the customers.'

'When the King lands, he will be driven in state from Leith and given the keys of the city near Picardy Place—you remember, where the road widens out at the top of Leith Walk? If you are quick, you may be able to rent a window seat in one of the tenements there for your children.'

'Thank you, I'll look into it. I take it you'll not be competing with me for a place to watch the spectacle?' Grayson slanted her a smile. 'One thing's for sure, there's no need for you to book a lesson from an actress in kissing.'

'One kisses the King's cheek, not his lips!'

'You're more than welcome to practise on me.'

'I won't be attending a lady's drawing room,' she said, her mouth prim in her effort not to smile. 'Nor will I be paying three shillings a yard for plaid to make a sash for my ballgown. That's what they are charging you know, in the Scottish Tartan, Shawl and Silk Warehouse over there.' She indicated a large shop front on the North Bridge that they were crossing. 'A shilling a yard is what it usually sells for, and when Mr Scott's dress code is published, and his notion of the Garb of Old Gaul described, I reckon they'll put the price up to at least five.'

'A dress code! Are you joking?'

'Indeed, I am not. There is a dress code for everyday wear, and a specific one for each of the set-piece entertainments too. You will be expected to wear a plaid or some form of tartan in the King's presence, you know.'

'Then it's as well I'm not planning on being in his presence, for I refuse to wear a skirt.'

'That's very unpatriotic! It's also a crying shame for unlike some, it is my humble opinion that you have the legs for it. Mind you, since my experience is somewhat limited, that's not exactly an informed opinion.'

'It's the only one I'm interested in,' Grayson retorted. 'If we go this way, we'll avoid Princes Street, it might be a bit less crowded. Watch now, while we cross the road.'

'I'm capable of crossing the street unaided, you know. I've been managing for some six years.'

'Accept my apologies.'

But he held tightly to her all the same until they had crossed and were heading up St David's Street to St Andrew's Square, where the bustle did indeed lessen somewhat. They slowed their steps and walked in a companionable silence along George Street until they reached Charlotte Square. The palace fronts of the houses were designed by Robert Adam, and though work had begun in the previous century, the square had not long been completed.

Oman's newest and most prestigious hotel was located at Number Six Charlotte Square, and occupied the central pavilion on the north side, with an impressive frontage in the Palladian style, complete with large fanlight above the front door, and Corinthian pillars. The reception hall smelled of fresh flowers and beeswax, and the large drawing room, dining room and library which made up the rooms on the ground floor were opulently decorated in, to Constance's mind, a rather oppressive style.

'Good afternoon. I am Nigel Urquhart, I have the honour of being in charge of this fine establishment.' The man who greeted them, dressed in black trousers and coat, with a gold waistcoat, had a stately gait and an owlish appearance. He had a beak-like nose and a supercilious expression. 'I'm afraid that all the superior suites have already been reserved for the royal visit,' he informed them after

Grayson had introduced himself and stated his business. 'Our clientele includes some of the most eminent members of the Scottish peerage, and all will be arriving here in August to pay homage. Their Graces, the Duke and Duchess of Argyll will be residing here for His Majesty's visit, as will the Marquis and Marchioness of Lothian, and—'

'And myself, accompanied by my two children, if you have rooms I consider fit for us,' Grayson interrupted. 'Do you have any, or am I wasting my time? This might jog your memory.'

It was a banknote he slipped the man, Constance noticed, not a coin, and it bought them a considerably warmer smile and a set of keys. 'I've just remembered that we had a cancellation only this morning. The Caledonian Suite is available, though I'm afraid it must be reserved for the whole month of August, since we are not yet privy to His Majesty's plans. There are two bedrooms and a sitting room where you would be able to dine in private if you so desire. However, most of our guests choose to eat in the main dining salon. As I'm sure you are aware, Oman's reputation for fine food is second to none in the capital.'

'Then I suggest we put that proud boast to

the test for ourselves with an early dinner, once we've had a look at the rooms, assuming you've a table?'

'But of course, Mr Maddox. I am sure you and your wife won't be disappointed. The dining room is on the left. There is a salon just through there, facing out on to the gardens, where our guests can relax after dinner, and there are—excuse me—retiring rooms just here, if you or your wife wish to refresh yourself. No? Well, allow me to show you the Caledonian Suite. It's on the second floor, if you'll follow me.'

'After you, my dear Mrs Maddox.'

Grayson smiled mischievously at her. Constance allowed him to usher her towards the impressive oak staircase, casting him a quizzical look over her shoulder but saying nothing, conscious of Mr Urquhart watching them. The panelling of the first-floor landing was adorned with a number of landscapes which were presumably meant to depict the Highlands, if the abundance of purple hills and stags at bay were anything to go by. On the second floor, gilded wall sconces took the place of portraits. A corridor led off in each direction, a long runner of red carpet covering the polished floorboards.

Mr Urquhart ushered them to the right, stopping at the first door, which he opened with a flourish before standing to one side to allow them to enter. 'The Caledonian Suite.'

If Grayson was impressed he kept it well hidden, but Constance struggled not to gasp in astonishment. Closing her ears to Mr Urquhart's eulogies, she wandered around the sitting room, trailing her hands over the rich gold and cream brocade of the two sofas which sat facing each other in front of a white marble hearth. The gold velvet curtains which hung in heavy folds over the three sets of windows had a thick, soft nap. The cornice was patterned in latticework, painted stark white, while the walls were duck-egg blue adorned with more purple heather landscapes, the only jarring note in the otherwise extremely tasteful room. There were fresh flowers in the grate and on the occasional tables. A huge mirror hung over the fireplace, with gilded wall sconces on either side. A large chandelier hung from the ceiling. Her feet sank into the rich, soft rugs.

The smallest of the bedchambers was obviously designed for a servant, containing only a small bed, a nightstand and cupboard, and a chair, though the boards were polished and a rug was positioned by the bed. The second bedchamber was substantially bigger, painted all in white with a Chinese paper on the walls above the waist-height panelling, and a huge bed draped with too many pillows to count. The final bedchamber, obviously Mr Urquhart's pièce de résistance, was a study in pink. The huge bed had a cerise damask canopy with gold tassels, the headboard gilded with gold leaf. The bedcover was rose-pink, woven from silk and velvet, the walls were flocked in magenta. The *chaise longue* which sat at the foot of the bed, the chairs which faced each other across the fireplace, and even the chair which sat at the escritoire, were all covered in pink.

As the clock on the mantel began to chime, Mr Urquhart frowned, checking the time with his watch. 'If you will excuse me, Mr and Mrs Maddox, I'm afraid I have a pressing matter of business to attend to. Please take your time and have a good look around. I will be available downstairs later if you have any questions. Mr Maddox, if you will grant me a word.'

'What did he want?' Constance jumped guiltily off the pink bed as Grayson returned.

'To confirm that I could afford the price, and to inform me that he'd want a portion of it paid in advance since I'm not yet a regular customer.'

'Is it expensive?'

'No, it is exorbitant, though I'm not such a bumpkin as to have agreed to what he quoted me, which amounted to extortion. You learn quickly in business that everything is negotiable.'

'I had no idea that hotels could be so luxurious.'

'It's not remotely to my taste, but Shona and Neil will like it, and that's what matters.'

'You'll have a fight on your hands over which one of them has to sleep in the servant's room.'

'No, I won't, for that will be mine.'

'But...'

'Come on, can you see me in this room, lounging around in a silk dressing gown?'

A burst of laughter escaped her. 'No, perhaps not!'

'Don't tell me you like all this ostentation?'

'I prefer the other room, the white one with the Chinese wallpaper.'

'It is very nice, I'll grant you,' Grayson said, following her into the room, 'but it will have to be Neil's or else, as you say, I'd have a fight on my hands.'

'You must be very well off, to be able to afford all this, even if you did barter the price down. You could have fitted our entire school-house into two of these rooms, and a village cottage into one.'

'I was not born into money, Constance. I was raised up in a tenement close in Glasgow. Two rooms, one for living and one for my parents to sleep in. My bed was in a recess in the kitchen.'

'I don't mean anything by the comparison,' she said shutting the lid again, 'save that this is luxury beyond anything I've experienced.'

She sat down at a walnut escritoire. Carefully opening the lid, she tried to imagine writing on the pristine green leather blotter. She'd be too worried about leaving ink spots on the white upholstery.

'I don't have any objection to those who have earned it enjoying their wealth. Despite what some might think, I'm not a revolutionary.'

'Who thinks that you are?'

Paul's words of caution this morning, her failure to reignite in him the passion which still burned so fiercely in her own heart, made her long for a more sympathetic ear. For a moment, she considered confiding in Grayson, but only for a moment. She had lived and breathed her crusade for so long. Grayson was a much-needed respite from the battle she was coming terrifyingly close to losing.

'I simply believe it's wrong to profit from the suffering of others,' she hedged.

He was turning a porcelain figurine around in his hand, frowning down at it. 'Are you thinking that I'm the type to exploit my workers, so that I can afford to house my children in the lap of luxury?'

'No! Good grief no, that's so preposterous it never crossed my mind. Though I must admit, I had not thought you so wealthy.'

Grayson set down the figurine. 'If that means you're about to shun me on a matter of principle, I promise I'll give it all away, the moment I get home.'

'Your children would have something to say about that.'

'True, very true. I'm afraid that Neil and Shona are a wee bit too used to living in what you call the lap of luxury and I would be very reluctant to do anything that might estrange them. Would it be all right with you if I let them stay on at Queen's Gate, as long as I camped out in a tent in the back garden?'

'Queen's Gate sounds very grand.'

'Oh, it is, and every time I step through the front door, I feel like I'm an interloper, though it's nearly ten years since we moved in. I'd have been happy to stay where we were, but my late wife had put up with living in a cottage for long enough. Not that it was a cottage mind, it was a perfectly good house, but she was used to better.'

'And you worked hard to make sure she had it.'

He wandered over to stare out of the window, his hands dug deep into his coat pockets. 'Don't get me wrong, Eliza never demanded, or expected, or complained. She never once said that she'd married beneath her, though it was clear from the start that's what her parents thought. And she *was* ashamed of our circumstances, I know she was, though she never said. She wouldn't invite any of her friends to visit, though there was room enough and I told her often enough that they'd be welcome. It was too far for them to travel, she always said. I wondered sometimes if it was me she was ashamed of.'

He pressed his forehead to the glass. Indignant as she was, Constance kept her thoughts to herself. Grayson was such an honourable man, and for such an immensely successful one, surprisingly self-deprecating. It wasn't fair of her to condemn a dead woman, and his Eliza must have had some guts, to go against her family's wishes and marry him in the first place.

'I had a perfectly happy marriage. If Eliza had not died, we'd be happily married still. When I lost her, I thought my world had ended, but when you've two young ones to look after, you can't afford to indulge in self-pity. It took some adjusting, I won't deny it, but I'm content enough now. I'm busy, Shona and Neil are happy. Like I said before, I don't want to risk rocking the boat. We miss Eliza, but there's no big gaping hole for her to fill. If she was miraculously restored to us, I wonder if she'd even fit in now.'

Grayson turned back to face her. 'That sounds harsh, but it's the truth. What is it about you? I've never told a living soul any of this before. I wasn't even aware I was thinking some of it. I'm just going to take another look at that wee room, make sure my feet won't hang out of the end of the bed. Why don't you wait for me in the sitting room?'

Constance did as he bid, for it was obvious he wanted a moment alone. There was a seat built into one of the windows of the sitting room, strewn with tasselled cushions. If this was her room, she would sit here in the morning with a book and a pot of tea. If she could afford to live in this place, she could afford a portable writing desk, so that she could work here too.

Sitting down, hugging one of the cushions to her, she tried to imagine such a life, but it was pointless. She couldn't see beyond the life she was living now. If Paul had his way it would end, and soon. She had a matter of weeks to succeed in doing what she'd signally failed to do over the last four years. Her work was her heart and soul, her life's blood. She ate, slept and dreamt her work. It was all she had, and all she was. Failure was simply not an option.

Frowning, she set the cushion down and went over to look at herself in the mirror. The weight of her self-imposed mission, the pain and the passion she had expended over the years, was almost too much to bear. She rarely thought of her sacrifices, rarely considered them sacrifices at all, but meeting Grayson had brought home to her how isolated she'd been.

'A penny for them?'

His face appeared over her shoulder in the mirror. He stood behind her, close enough to send her heart racing, but not touching. Even though they had been as intimate as it was possible for any man and woman to be, he never assumed any rights over her. Robert's proprietorial touch had been something that irked her, she remembered now. After they had bedded for the first time, his manner changed, as if he had gained something that she had lost.

She turned away from her reflection. 'Do you ever look back at yourself and wonder if it was really you, who did those things, who felt those things?'

'Do you mean, would I change the past if I could?'

'No, but I mean, if you were back in the past now, would you behave differently, make different decisions?'

'Hindsight is a marvellous thing.'

'I don't mean hindsight, I mean—actually, I'm not sure what I mean. What you said about my making you think things, say things you've never said, it's the same for me. You've stirred up all sorts of feelings I didn't know I had. I've only known you three days, and already I know—' She broke off, embarrassed.

'I'll miss you too, if that's what you were going to say.'

He had such a look in his eyes, of longing and desire that so perfectly reflected her own feelings. She *knew* what he was thinking, and when she stepped closer, reaching for him, his arms went around her, and she knew she'd been right. 'Grayson,' she said softly, simply for the pleasure of saying his name.

'Constance.' His hand on her waist pulled her closer. His other hand found hers. When he lifted it to his mouth, pressing a kiss to her knuckles, he seemed pained. Slowly, his head dipped towards hers, giving her every chance to step back, to end the moment, but even if she'd wanted to, it would have been impossible. His breath was hot on her cheek. There was a tiny frown drawing his brows together.

'Oh, Constance,' he whispered, and she heard in his voice what she felt too, all the sweetness they were doomed to miss out on, knowing the clock was already measuring out the hours before they parted, knowing that it was inevitable.

Their lips met because they were meant to meet, because they were made to lock together. This kiss was not like before. Their lips clung, and their hands remained twined, pressed between them, against their hearts. His free hand tangled in her hair, cradling her head. She flattened her palm on the roughness of his cheek. Time stopped as they kissed, and there was nothing in the world that mattered in that moment save the meeting of their mouths, the press of their bodies, the languid sweep of his tongue, the taste of him and the scent of him, the dizzying, sensual delight of him.

They broke apart slowly and reluctantly, gazing at each other, dazed. The world had shifted, they both acknowledged that in the look they shared, in the way their fingers still clung. And then the clock on the mantel chimed out a tune, and they blinked, released each other, stepped back. From what? Constance wasn't sure, but it was best not to speculate, she was certain of that.

Chapter Six

❧❧❧❧❧

The dining room of Oman's Hotel was situated at the front, on the ground floor. One large central table was set though as yet unoccupied, but several of the smaller round tables were busy with a mix of single gentlemen, two elderly couples and a group of four matronly women in the far corner beside a covered grand piano. The walls were painted moss green, decorated with pilasters of brown marble topped with gilded, moulded acanthus leaves, and the ceiling was ornately moulded. An austere head waiter with waxed moustaches and a pronounced French accent showed them to a table in one of the window embrasures, his minion snapping the starched napkins out with a flourish. Silver cutlery gleamed. Light sparkled off the crystal glasses.

Grayson watched Constance drinking it all in, trying not to look nervous as she was handed the large leather-bound menu. Taking the wine list from the hovering sommelier, he listened with half an ear to the man eulogising about the hotel cellar while perusing the list for himself, before selecting a decent claret that, he noticed wryly, surprised and impressed the wine waiter.

'You are obviously accustomed to such places,' Constance said, as the sommelier departed. 'I've never eaten in a restaurant before.'

'I am forced to endure business dinners about once a month. Don't let them intimidate you, it's their job to make a song and dance. It allows them to justify their prices.'

'But there's so much choice, and a good few things I've never heard of.' She wrinkled her nose. 'Hodge-podge? "A traditional Scottish stew made from neck of lamb, served in an ale and barley broth with seasonal vegetables", according to what is written here.'

'Another of Walter Scott's traditions in the making, I reckon,' Grayson said. 'It's listed under Traditional Highland Dishes, along with haggis and sheep's head, which is something I remember my mother making, and I hope never to have to eat again. The stink of it hung in the air for days afterwards.'

'And you obliged to sleep in the kitchen recess too. In fact it is traditional to cook a sheep's head broth in the Highlands, though thankfully my mother never did so. There was one wee wifey in the village, Mrs Angus McLeod, who was famed for it, and also for her black puddings, which I must admit I am rather fond of. I don't see those featured here.'

'Blood mixed with oatmeal is probably a stretch too far for the Oman Hotel's diners who include, let us not forget, the Duke and Duchess of Argyll,' Grayson said, in the obsequious tones of Mr Urquhart.

'You'll be dining among exalted company when you're here. Mind now, to take cream with your porridge instead of salt, lest you betray your humble origins.'

'It just won't taste the same, made fresh and served with cream. My mammy used to make it but once a week, to save the coals, and let it set cold in an old drawer.' Grayson grinned. 'We were poor but we were happy. We'd have a slab of it every morning, fried on the griddle.'

'You should recommend they do the same here, during the King's visit, for the sake of authenticity,' Constance said, her eyes alight with laughter. 'The food of Old Gaul, served to their patrons dining in the garb of Old Gaul. Instead of braised cod cheeks, which they have here, they could offer crappit heid.'

'That sounds so disgusting I'm scared to ask what it is.'

'Cod's head,' Constance informed him, 'stuffed with oats and a bit of suet.'

'You're having me on.'

She chuckled. 'I've never tasted it myself, but old Mrs McLeod served it up with boiled turnip tops. I don't see any of those on this menu either. Really, it is somewhat lacking in authenticity.'

'If there is a specific dish that Madam would particularly like, I am sure the chef would be able to prepare it for you,' the waiter, who had appeared from nowhere, opined. 'Although we do have an extensive menu, it is our aim at Oman's to please...'

'No. Of course. There is more than sufficient choice here.' Constance's cheeks were scarlet, her eyes helplessly roaming the menu again.

Grayson cursed the cat-footed functionary under his breath. 'Shall I choose for both of us?' Receiving her grateful nod, he did so.

Their wine appeared then, and by the time he had finished tasting, and singing the sommelier's praises to the high heavens for his own choice, Constance had recovered her composure.

'Delicious,' she said, taking a tentative sip from her own glass, 'though I'm not the connoisseur you clearly are.'

'I've simply more experience than you.'

'Are there hotels as elegant as this in Glasgow?'

'There are, though their clientele tends to be merchants rather than marquesses.'

'Do you live near your shipyard?'

'Lord, no. My yard's in Govan, on the south side of the River Clyde, and my big fancy house is across the river, in the west end of the city. I take it you've never been to Glasgow?'

'I was born in Clachan Bridge, and had barely travelled beyond the boundaries of the estate until I came to Edinburgh,' Constance replied. 'Is not one city very much like another?'

'You couldn't get more of a contrast than Edinburgh and Glasgow. We don't have a castle or a palace, though we've a fine cathedral, a first-rate university, and a great deal more green space—that's what it means, Glasgow, dear green place.' Grayson took another sip of wine. 'My city's a bit rougher around the edges than Edinburgh. We're more down to earth. It's a workhorse kind of city, full of merchants and shipbuilders, not lawyers and doctors. Trade, that's what Glasgow is all about.'

'And that is why the King is coming to Edinburgh,' Constance said sardonically.

'Aye, you're in the right of it. He'd look down his nose at us, and we'd have no compunction in telling him where to go if he expected us to go bowing and scraping.'

The first course arrived, and with it the head waiter, overseeing the delivery, removing the silver covers from the serving dishes with a theatrical flourish. Stewed carp, lobster vol-au-vent pastries, and pigeon pâté with toast. Grayson made the appropriate noises, aware of Constance, no longer embarrassed or overawed but amused.

'It is like a piece of theatre,' she said, leaning over the fish to inhale the aroma. 'My goodness, that smells delicious. And those little pastries there look so delicate. My mouth is watering. I hope you're hungry, there's a lot of food here.'

'I could eat a scabby-headed wean.'

She gave a peal of laughter. 'I have no idea what that means, though I could take a guess. Do you know your accent gets broader and broader, when you talk about your dear green city?'

'You should hear me talking to my men at the yard.' Grayson puffed out his chest and pulled his shoulders back. 'It's a man's world, a shipyard. If every second word isn't an oath, they think you're a wee jessie.'

'I can't imagine anyone ever accusing you of being such a thing, though you're not at all as rough round the edges as you like to pretend. All this,' Constance said, nodding at the now full dining room, 'you know how to order fine wine, you aren't in the least bit intimidated by a French menu or superior waiting staff. And then there's Mr Urquhart, showing you that suite without a quibble.'

'He showed me the suite because I bribed him with five pounds, and because he is good enough at his job to be able to size people up in a matter of seconds. He knew I could afford it. Money talks, Constance, that's all.'

'No, it's not only money. You're so confident. You don't doubt that people will listen when you speak.' She had set her fork down, her pastry half eaten.

'What's brought this on?' he asked. 'Aren't you enjoying yourself?'

'Of course I am. It's nothing.' She picked up her fork again. 'This pigeon dish is delicious.'

'It's pâté, and whatever it is that's bothering you, it's not nothing.' He topped up their glasses. 'What happened upstairs between us, I know you felt it too. Am I presuming too much, when I say that we don't have much time together, so we should not waste a second of it?'

'You're not presuming.' She reached across the table to touch his hand, their fingers curling briefly around each other. 'You're right. Let's enjoy this moment and this wonderful food. After all, this might be my one and only chance to experience the best Edinburgh has to offer.'

'I reckon Mr Urquhart would tell you it's the best that Scotland has to offer, but I'm not much interested in Mr Urquhart's opinion. As long as you're enjoying it that's all that matters. I hope you're not full, though. There's still two more courses to come.'

'Roast goose. Peas with mint. Asparagus. Omelette with herbs,' Grayson translated as each dish was set down before them.

Constance, who had thought herself quite replete, found her mouth beginning to water. He served her himself, making a small, delicate plate of the omelette, peas and asparagus, making an effort to make it look appetising, reminding her of the care he'd taken when peeling an apple for her, the day they met. It didn't seem possible that they'd only known each other three days. If she was lucky, they'd have four more. He was right, there was no point in dwelling on what they could not have, she should enjoy what they did, and if that meant Flora must stay up all night to write, then that was what she would do.

'The omelette is delicious,' she said, taking a bite. 'Though you won't mind my saying, nothing tastes so good as a wee boiled egg fresh from your own hens.'

'You kept hens then, in Clachan Bridge?'

'We did, and we had our own cow, and a kailyard too, like every other cottage in the village.'

'So you were a crofter, as well as a schoolteacher?'

'Not really. I can milk a cow, make butter and crowdie, but the rest of it, actually planting out the runrigs and tending to the crops, we always paid some of the village children to do. My father earned a decent wage, and coin is hard to come by in places like Clachan Bridge, so we were never short of eager labour.'

'And the school you taught in, was it the laird who funded that?' Grayson had made short work of his omelette, and was now carving the goose which Constance, her own plate still half-full, regretfully refused.

'The old laird had the schoolhouse built when my parents first married, before I was born. I'm not sure where they lived while that was going on.'

'And the new laird, the improver who bought the estate, he continued to fund the school, then? Isn't that odd, given his plans?'

'I never have been able to decide whether it was good of him or cruel, to keep the villagers' hopes alive by maintaining the school.' Constance took a sip of wine. 'I knew from the start, because Robert told me, that he planned to give the whole estate over to sheep.'

Grayson set his knife down, reaching over the table to touch her hand. 'I shouldn't have asked. Let's talk of something else.'

'Actually, I don't mind. It's strange, isn't it? I keep trying to keep the past at bay, and it keeps fighting its way back into the conversation.' She took another sip of wine. 'I hoped, like we all did at first, that the laird would change his mind. Or rather, I hoped that Robert would persuade the laird to change his mind, because I assumed that he thought as we all did, that it would be a crime to turn the lands over to sheep.'

'But he could not?'

'He *would* not. He believed that sheep were the future. He reckoned the laird would give him a portion of the lands that were cleared, that he'd make a good living from it. I do him the credit of thinking that he didn't envision having to force the villagers out. He thought they'd see the sense of moving on. Nothing I could say would persuade him though. He actually thought I'd be pleased that he was providing a good future for us both. I couldn't marry a man as blind or selfish as that.'

'I should bloody well hope not.'

Constance forked the last, cold but delicious mouthful of omelette, frowning. 'I don't mean because of what he did. That was cruel beyond belief and unforgivable, but he was already not the man I thought I loved by then. I was forced to accept that he didn't love me in the same way. I didn't care about how we lived, how much land we had. I'd have happily lived in a simple cottage in the village with him. I wasted years of my life waiting for him, years we could have been happy, but he wouldn't have been—happy, I mean, not with me alone.' She pushed her plate away, shaking her head. 'What were we saying earlier, about telling each other what we didn't even know we were feeling? Sorry, I didn't mean to get so maudlin.'

'Blame the wine, and have some more, and don't apologise. We shall be each other's confessor.'

She smiled faintly, taking a sip of the very good wine, and pushing Robert to the back of her mind. 'Oh, well, in that case, I'll confess that when I was wee, I planned on having six children when I got married. Three girls, and three boys. I even had alphabetical names picked out for them. Ailsa. Bruce. Catriona. Dougal. Ewan. And Fiona. I was a very regimented thinker, even as a little girl.'

'Now you've got me wondering what you'd have done if you'd reached seventeen? A tall order but not unheard of.'

'That's a tricky one. I know, Quentin!' Constance exclaimed triumphantly. 'I know it's not in the least bit Scottish.'

'No, but it shows you were prepared for any eventuality.'

'All but the one I am faced with, which is no bairns of my own at all. Though it is a situation of my own making,' she added hurriedly, 'so don't be feeling sorry for me. One of the lovely things about being a teacher was spending time with so many bairns, and yet being able to pack them off to their parents at the end of the day.'

'I would have liked a whole houseful of weans, a consequence of being an only child, I reckon. I never had a number in mind as you did, and I certainly didn't have names at the ready, but—' Grayson broke off, shrugging awkwardly. 'I am lucky to have the two of them, and they would certainly not thank me now, for adding to their number.'

The waiter chose this timely moment to clear the plates, allowing them both time to lighten the mood. He returned almost immediately with two small silver dishes, setting one down in front of each of them. 'Lemon ice,' Constance said, with a sigh of satisfaction. 'My favourite, and I think I might have a tiny bit of room left for it. I'd never had an ice until I came to Edinburgh. Pearl is very fond of it.'

'It's certainly easy eating, if one has no teeth.'

'Oh, poor Pearl, I shouldn't have told you that. You mustn't think of her as an old crone, you know. I fear I've painted a false picture of her.'

'Then paint me a truer one,' Grayson said, handing his untouched dish of lemon ice over to her.

'Thank you, but why?'

'I don't really like ices.'

'No, I mean why do you want to know more about Pearl?'

'I want to know more about you.'

'You already know a great deal more than most.' Constance decided that she could, just manage to eat Grayson's portion of ice as well as her own, and picked up her spoon again. 'Pearl was my mother's friend, when they were growing up. She married a lawyer not long after my parents eloped, and came to live in Edinburgh. He did very well for himself, I think a combination of excellent connections and a flair for speaking, and was appointed to the bench quite young. He died about ten years ago, so I never met him, and that's when Angus came into Pearl's life.'

'There's no offspring, I take it?'

'No. She sent me gifts on my birthday every year when I was wee, and she visited us in Clachan Bridge a couple of times, but it was a long journey to make. She and my mother kept in touch though, writing to each other every month, and when we lost my mother, I took over responsibility for corresponding with her.'

'So she knew about the improving laird?'

'She offered both my father and myself a home, when it became obvious that we'd have to leave imminently. We planned to come to Edinburgh together, to look around for another school, maybe. I don't know. Obviously that didn't happen.'

'So Pearl took you in, and there you've been, the two of you and Angus, ever since. Has she given up her social life then, since her husband died? In my experience,' Grayson said, in answer to her surprised expression, 'a man does not make a success of the law without also being a success in society. Your Mrs Winston must have done a fair bit of entertaining when her husband was alive.'

'And she still does. She has her ladies of the law, as she calls them, for tea once a week. She doesn't like to dine out very often, and I wouldn't say Coates Crescent is a social whirl, but she's never short of company if she wants it. I can't imagine why you thought her a recluse.'

'Something you said, that first day. When we were walking back from Newhaven, I remember talking about whether we were likely to bump into anyone you knew, and you said that you had few acquaintances here. But you've lived with Mrs Winston for six years.'

'Oh, I see. No, Pearl isn't ashamed of me, and she doesn't keep me confined to the attic or the kitchens, when her friends call, it's just that I prefer not to—I'm the one that's not very sociable.' Constance pushed her unfinished second ice aside. 'That was absolutely delicious, but I couldn't eat another thing.'

Grayson drew her a look that made it clear he knew she was prevaricating, but to her relief, he chose not to push her. 'Do you want coffee?'

'No. It's getting late, and I've been away all day, I should be getting back to Coates Crescent. Angus will be wondering where I am.'

'Then I'll walk you back.'

Grayson handed over a bundle of notes to the head waiter without asking for the bill, earning himself what passed for a smile.

As they emerged into the foyer, Mr Urquhart abandoned another couple to wave them off, implying that he would not sleep a wink until Mr Maddox returned with his family next month.

'How will you explain the fact that you've left me back in Glasgow?' Constance asked as the descended the front steps of the hotel, back into Charlotte Square. 'Perhaps I'll be nursing a sick relative somewhere.'

He tucked her hand into his arm. 'It's turned into a lovely evening. Let's enjoy it. Will we take a walk around the square?'

'It's still busy, considering it's after six.'

'People like to make the most of the sun when it shines. It's the same back in Glasgow. The parks will be full of people taking the air, bairns screeching about, playing in the fountains.'

'No!'

Grayson grinned. 'Well, they can hardly jump in the Clyde, not in the city, it's filthy.'

'But didn't you say that they went—what was the phrase, down the water, on the River Clyde?'

'*Doon the watter.* I did. The Clyde estuary is almost the sea by the time you get past Greenock, so it's much cleaner.'

'And when you sail *doon the watter*, do you ever take a dip?'

'I dipped a toe in it once, and that was enough. The Mediterranean now, that's a whole different matter. The water there is like stepping into a warm bath.'

'You've travelled abroad! Oh, where—and when?'

'Before I was married, I spent quite a bit of time in the shipyards of France, Greece, Spain. I wanted to see how they built their ships, just to make sure that I could build mine better.'

Constance laughed. 'How wonderful. How lucky you are. Which country did you like best? What was the food like? And the people? Oh, goodness, and the language, how did you get by? I can't believe I didn't know this about you. Look, here is a vacant bench, let's sit down, and you can tell me all.'

'All? I take it you don't mean the nuts and bolts of shipbuilding?'

'If we had time, I'd be delighted to know that too, but for now just tell me—oh, describe each country to me.'

Smiling, shaking his head at her enthusiasm, he stretched his legs out in front of him and leaned back on the narrow bench.

He painted a vivid picture, of the colours and the scents and the sounds, of the dust and the heat, the strangeness of it all for a young man who had never been further than Lowland Scotland. He was not afraid to poke fun at his younger self either. 'The language might have been different, but shipyards the world over are similar, with any number of rites of passage,' he said. 'I remember the first time I went to visit my father at work, one of the other clerks sent me to the warehouse to get a long stand. After about half an hour of patient waiting the penny finally dropped. "Ach, don't worry son," my father said when I returned looking sheepish, "brighter folk than you have fallen for that one. Including me!"'

His arm was lying on the back of the bench as they talked. Constance edged closer to him, and his hand moved to her shoulder. Through her skirts, she could feel his leg pressed against her, reminding her of Newhaven, and the bench outside the inn, yet this was different. The charge between them, the acute awareness of each other was still intense, but there was a longing between them that hadn't been there before, a yearning to know, to be part of the other that wasn't physical. Was she being nonsensical? Yet as their eyes met and held, and silence hung between them, she could have sworn they were still talking.

He reached for her hand, remembering— which she had not—that they were sitting on a bench in the middle of Charlotte Square. 'Come on, you need to get back.'

She slipped her hand back into the crook of his arm, and snuggled as close as she decently could. 'If we cross here, we can walk along Melville Street, which will bring us out at the back of Coates. It's quieter.' Their thighs brushed with each step. 'How did you set about setting up your own yard? I'd imagine it is an expensive undertaking?'

'I worked for someone else at first. Then my parents left me a bit of money after they died in a cholera epidemic which swept through Glasgow.'

'You lost them both at once! Oh, Grayson, how awful.'

'It was quick, and they went together. It was a long time ago.' Though his voice told her that he was not indifferent.

She pressed his arm. 'All the same, it must have been difficult for you.'

'I threw myself into my work. I made the most of my parents' legacy, bought a small yard, and—ah, what can I say, Constance, I was a great success. I'm just brilliant at what I do!'

She laughed because he wanted her to, though the thought crossed her mind that work had consistently been both a panacea and a welcome distraction for him. They had reached the little gardens that formed the half-way point of Melville Street and she came to a halt. 'Coates is just a step away down there.'

Grayson put his arm around her shoulder. 'Look up. There are some stars peeking out.'

'When I first came to Edinburgh, I thought there were no stars. It took me ages to realise that they were there, but because of the lights it was too bright for me to see them.'

'When you're at sea, in the middle of the ocean, the stars are so bright you can read a book by their light.'

'I used to love to go outside in the winter on a clear night, and look at them. My father had a star map, and he could pick out all the constellations. Is it true you can steer a ship by the stars?'

'Trained navigators can, but I can't. There is a limit to my skills, I'm sorry to say.' Somehow, she had turned to face him. He put his arms around her, pulling her close. 'I've been wanting to do this all day. Just this.'

She laid her head on his shoulder, breathing in the warmth of his skin, feeling the rough wool of his jacket against her cheek, placing her hand on his chest over his heart. 'I didn't realise I was lonely.'

'Nor I.'

'You'll be heading back to Glasgow soon, now that you've done what you came here for.'

'Shush. I'm here now.'

Constance looked up, and as their eyes met in the dusk, it was no longer enough, just to be held. 'You're here now,' she said softly, 'and that's all that matters.'

Their kiss began tenderly, as their earlier kisses had, but soon their lips became urgent, their kisses heated. He tasted of wine. His cheek was rough with nascent stubble. They were in the shadow of the statue at the centre of the little garden, but anyone looking out of a window would see them, anyone passing by would notice. She knew this, but she didn't care. All she wanted was for their kisses to go on and on and on. His tongue touched hers. She pressed herself closer to him, wanting to feel him hard against her, shocked by the blatancy of what she was doing, and at the same time excited. When he would have stopped, a word of caution on his lips, she pulled him back, kissing him again, relishing the way her kisses knocked the breath out of him. His hand cupped her breast through her gown, under her shawl, and her nipples hardened, making them both moan.

But then he broke away, his breath fast, catching her hands when she would have pulled him back. 'If you kiss me again, I swear I'll pick you up and carry you back to Oman's Hotel, and tell Mr Urquhart that we have urgent need of the Caledonian Suite.'

'Oh, my goodness, can you imagine?'

He smoothed his hair down with the flat of his hand. 'I'd rather not. Come here, let me help you with those ribbons on your bonnet, they've managed to get into a right fankle. If anyone sees you like this, they'll think you've been dragged through a hedge backwards.'

'Is it that bad?'

'It's very bad, in a just-been-kissed-and-impossible-to-resist-kissing-again kind of way,' Grayson said, touching his lips to her forehead. 'Hussy!'

Constance giggled. 'You pay the most delightful compliments. Oh, dear, I really must get back, it's almost dark. Don't come any further, Coates is just there.'

'You're still free tomorrow, aren't you?'

'Definitely.'

'Good. I'll meet you outside the Custom House down in Leith at about nine, you'll need to walk Angus early.'

'Why on earth…?'

'It's a surprise. Will you be there?'

'I promise but I probably won't sleep a wink now.' Which was true, for she'd have to work into the night as it was. Constance stood on her tiptoe to kiss his cheek. 'Goodnight. Thank you again for a lovely day and a delicious meal.' Turning away, she walked quickly down Walker Street, refusing to allow herself to look back.

Chapter Seven

Anyone passing the Castle Esplanade yesterday would have been treated to an entertaining, if unedifying spectacle. Fifty burly clansmen marching 'up an doon and roon an roon' under the command of our own Grand Old Duke of York, MacDonnell of Glengarry. In Flora's humble opinion, the gentleman might have been better served trying to herd the sheep he prefers to populate his estates with, having packed his clansmen off to Canada and the four winds. Astonishingly, in the eyes of the law he has committed no crime, unless one counts being a bigger horse's arse than that belonging to your steed, as someone of Flora's acquaintance put it pithily.

One might come to the conclusion

*that grown men playing soldiers in their
best dressing up clothes would be more
suited to the schoolyard than the Castle Esplanade. One might very well be
right. If this is an example of the tartan 'pageantry' we can expect to endure during the King's visit, the least
their noble chieftain could do is order
his men to place their tongues firmly in
their cheek. What next? Highland coos
dancing a reel? It would be amusing if
it were not such a perfect example of
the contrast between the whimsical, self-
indulgent myth being portrayed in our
Capital City, and the stomach-churning
reality of life in the Highlands.*

Flora MacDonald, *New Jacobite Journal*

Friday, 12th July 1822

When Constance arrived in Leith just before
nine, the sun was already out, so she stood in
the shade of the Custom House, watching a
procession of clerks, masters and merchants
make their way briskly up the shallow flight
of steps and in through the massive doorway
which was flanked with double columns on

either side. What was the nature of their business in there? Grayson would know.

Where was he? Resisting the urge to check the clock again, she checked the buttons on her gloves instead and adjusted her shawl. It was new, made from sky-blue silk embroidered with snowdrops. It had been an early birthday present from Pearl, given before she departed for the Borders. It perfectly complemented her new blue gown, which she wished now, she had saved to wear for the first time. Mind you, if she'd been wearing one of her old gowns when they dined at Oman's Hotel, she'd have been mortified. Honestly! She had more things to worry about than a frivolous dress. But still, she couldn't help wishing her wardrobe contained more variety. Something more summery, with short sleeves. White muslin, or was she too old for that? Pale green would be nice, but it wouldn't go with her new shawl. And short sleeves weren't exactly practical. How many days in a year did they get like this?

Where was he? She felt as though she'd been waiting here an age. Perhaps he had changed his mind and wasn't coming. Checking the clock once more, Constance saw that it was only just nine, and before it began to chime, she heard her name being called, and her heart leapt, and she turned around to find Grayson smiling at her.

'I was looking the wrong way,' she said, unsettled by the wave of sheer joy that enveloped her. 'I thought you'd come from Leith Walk direction.'

'I had a bit of final business to attend to at the docks.'

'I see,' she said, though she didn't. His coat was dark blue today, his waistcoat the same sky blue as her shawl. 'Our clothes match.'

'You look lovely. I don't think I've seen that shawl before. Would you call that sky blue or azure? Or maybe it's cerulean?'

'Cerulean! Hark at the rough Glaswegian shipbuilder,' Constance said, laughing.

'The rough Glaswegian shipbuilder has a sixteen-year-old daughter who never has her nose out of those fashion-plate things. I like those wee flowers on your shawl. Are they snowdrops?'

'I have no idea, are they? It's a present from Pearl which I shouldn't have opened until my birthday. I'm worried I'll be too hot though, it looks like it's going to be a lovely day.'

'As it turns out, you'll need a shawl, where we're going.'

'Which is where? Is it Newhaven? I thought it might be since that's where we first met and…'

'It's not Newhaven. The point of a surprise, Constance, is that you don't know what it's going to be. Stop asking questions.'

'I can't help it. No one ever surprises me—not in a good way, I mean.'

'Don't worry, I'm pretty certain this will be a nice surprise.' Grayson took her hand, tucking it into his arm. 'If we cut through here by the side of Custom House we'll be at the Shore.'

'They're putting up scaffolding here. It will be the prime spot for watching the King land.'

'Hoisted flapping out of his barge like a monster cod,' Grayson said. 'I remember thinking that as I stood near here, just before I bumped into you.'

'Not even a week ago, can you believe it?'

'I have to keep reminding myself.'

They had reached the Shore, and came to a stop at the water's edge near a set of slimy stairs which disappeared into the water. The cries of stevedores and sailors carried over from the busy Queen's Dock, but here it was peaceful. The sun sparkled on the still waters reflecting the barges and the lighters. A gull landed on a mooring bollard and fixed them with a beady eye. A small wooden dinghy was being rowed under the bridge, making its way towards them.

'The current royal yacht the *Royal George* is a three-master,' Grayson said. 'Five years old, and in my humble opinion, well out of date.'

'Because she is not a steamship, I assume?'

'Naturally. She's a lovely ship of her kind, by all accounts, but she'll need assistance from a steam pilot boat to get her in and out of Greenwich. When she finally arrives here, she'll have to anchor in the Firth of Forth, out there, since she isn't manoeuvrable enough to come alongside at the docks yonder. Are you ready?'

'For what?' Constance asked, looking around her.

'To test your sea legs.' Grayson hailed the man rowing the dinghy, deftly catching the rope thrown from the little boat, dislodging the startled gull from the bollard to tie it up.

'We're going for a row in that wee thing?'

'A very short voyage, only as far as the Queen's Dock. We could walk, but this will give you the view the King will have when he arrives. Come on, take my hand, and Hamish here will help you in.'

Constance eyed the little craft askance. It seemed to her that the calm waters had suddenly become an Atlantic swell, for it was bobbing about alarmingly. There were only three steps visible. Clinging on to Grayson's hand, she descended the first two gingerly, then reached for Hamish's hand, feeling like a piece of washing strung out on a line. It was very, very slippery underfoot. She hadn't realised what a complete landlubber she was. Girding her loins, she took a leap into the boat, sending it rocking wildly and toppling into the seaman's arms. He staggered, but held the pair of them upright.

'I think you could say you're well and truly landed,' he said in a broad Glaswegian accent. 'Sit down there, hen, and don't move.'

Mortified, Constance dropped on to the wooden plank that served for a seat in the rear of the boat, watching as Grayson cast off, bringing the rope with him as he leapt agilely into the dinghy and Hamish picked up the oars.

'Move over a bit,' he said, slipping his arm around her. 'Don't worry, if we do capsize I'll save you.'

'You can swim, then?'

'Oh, like a fish.' He pulled her closer to him on the narrow bench. 'There now, you can relax and enjoy the view.'

'All very well for you to say. This is the first time I've ever been out on the water in my life.'

'You're joking? You've never even been out on a loch to catch trout?'

She shuddered involuntarily. 'We're not going fishing, are we?'

'I thought you liked fish. You enjoyed that stewed carp at Oman's.'

'On my plate, cooked, I am very fond of fish. Alive, flapping about with their scales and their tails and fins and those gill things they breathe through...' Constance shuddered again, screwing up her face. 'They terrify me. Please don't laugh, I know it's silly but I can't help it.'

'It's not silly. I'll let you into a secret. I'm feart of moths. It's the fluttering they make, the way they come at you in the dark, that horrible wee brush of their wings on your face. I can't stand it. God's honest truth, when one of them gets into the house, I have to fetch Shona to catch it.'

Constance giggled. 'I know you're exaggerating just to make me feel better.'

'We're not going fishing, I promise. Look back at the docks, and imagine what the crowds will be like when George arrives. There will be tartan hanging from every building, and heather strewn over all the cobbles. A tartan carpet for His Majesty to walk on, do you reckon? And the dockers, they're bound to turn out in kilts.'

'Mr Scott's pamphlet suggests a blue coat, white waistcoat and white trousers for everyday wear,' Constance said.

'I thought you were teasing me, when you said there was a dress code.'

'For the price of a shilling, you can read his epistle for yourself, in a day or two, when it's published.'

'But you've clearly already read it. How did you manage that? Do you have contacts you haven't told me about?'

Only one, Constance thought, cursing her slip. 'I've a friend who runs a bookshop,' she said, which was the truth of it. 'The world of printing and publishing is a small one. He had an early copy.'

'I'm relieved to hear you're not entirely friendless after all.'

'Pearl has an account with him. I think I told you that she reads a great deal.' She wasn't used to prevaricating. 'Mr Scott also recommends a shallow-brimmed hat decorated with a cockade in the form of a saltire. He assures his readers that the cost is not prohibitive.'

Grayson, to her relief, either didn't notice her discomfort, or chose to ignore it. 'Mr Scott would have us all decked out like sailors. Does he have similar advice for the ladies?'

'I'm not sure about everyday wear, but if they have the dubious honour of attending the Drawing Room at Holyrood, they are required to wear a gown with a train at least four yards long, and a headdress with a minimum of nine ostrich feathers. The world's ostrich population must be quaking in its boots.'

'They'll just put their head in the sand as usual. To be serious for a minute though, Walter Scott can't possibly think that people will follow his bidding. He's not designing costumes for the cast of a play.'

'Actually, I think that's exactly how he sees it.' Constance clutched the side of the boat as Hamish began to manoeuvre them towards a low jetty.

'We'll disembark here. It gets steep and a bit precarious further on, especially if you're wearing a dress.' Grayson took the rope, mooring the dinghy while Hamish held it steady before helping Constance out.

'Enjoy your sail,' the seaman called as he pushed off.

'What sail?' Constance asked. 'Haven't we just been on a sail?'

'That was just to whet your appetite.'

Grayson took her arm, steering her away from the edge of the jetty towards the main docks. The basin was filled with vessels jostling for space as a swarm of people loaded and unloaded the boats. Ships, she mentally corrected herself. 'Where are we going?'

'Inchcolm Island.'

'Island? But how…'

'In this little beauty. *PS Carrick Castle*. I've arranged for it to drop us off and pick us up later.'

Constance stared at the huge ship, dumbstruck. 'It's a paddle steamer.'

'She's not one of mine, I regret to say. She was built at another yard a couple of years ago, but she has a twin beam engine designed by Napier, who does some work for us, so she's not dissimilar to some we've built. What do you think?'

The *Carrick Castle* was the oddest shape, a

sleek, wooden-hulled boat with two enormous paddles, one on either side, that completely spoiled her lines, giving her an ungainly appearance. A tall red-painted funnel looked similarly out of place with its twin white hoops, sitting just in front of the paddle housing, as if it were an afterthought. Smoke was already belching from it. 'She looks enormous,' Constance said, quite overawed. 'Are we really going for a sail in her?'

'If we are, we'd best get aboard sharpish. I had a bit of a problem securing a berth for her at such short notice. That's why I was late this morning, and she needs to set sail in the next fifteen minutes.'

'You mean you arranged this just for me?'

'You told me you'd always wanted a trip on a paddle steamer, remember? Your wish is my command.'

'How on earth did you manage it?'

'I called in a few favours. I had hoped to arrange it for your birthday, but Sunday is a busy day for day trips, we're more likely to have the island to ourselves today.'

'I can't believe it. It's wonderful, Grayson. I'm speechless. Thank you.'

'You're more than welcome.' He saluted the

skipper who was standing on the deck. 'Come on then, let's get aboard.'

The gangplank dropped at a steep angle from the jetty down on to the ship's deck. Constance followed Grayson, clutching at the railings, taking careful sidesteps, trying not to look at the terrifying drop. The wooden struts under her feet were shifting. The ropes holding the ship were straining and creaking, as if the ship was eager to be away. The final step on to the deck was an immense relief, but she had barely taken it before someone started pulling the gangplank away. A huge blast from the ship's horn made her jump. The paddles began to turn, water sluicing from their slatted housing, and they were off.

'She's a working boat, designed to carry cargo rather than passengers,' Grayson said, helping Constance to the wooden bench which was bolted down in the centre of the aft deck. 'Luckily it's flat calm, for there are no safety rails. If the weather turns, there are cabins below the main deck fore and aft of the engine, but they're miserable, pokey wee places, and stink of engine oil, so we'll stay up here if you don't mind a bit of spray from the paddles.'

'I still can't believe it.' Constance, clutching

her shawl, was wide-eyed with wonder. 'I'm truly overwhelmed. You must have called in any number of favours.'

And dug deep in his pocket, but it was worth it just to see her face. As the steamer headed out into the Firth of Forth, Grayson found the blanket he'd stowed behind the seat, and tucked it around her knees. The sun was shining in a rare, true summer's sky. On the port side, they were sailing past the island of Cramond, the low tide exposing the causeway that joined it to the mainland. On the starboard side, the Fife coastline lay low and lush green in the distance. And beside him, Constance, her bonnet hanging from its ribbons around her neck, her hair blowing around her face, her expression rapt. A feeling of complete and utter well-being washed over him. He could sit here like this for ever.

'I don't want this ever to end,' Constance said, echoing his thoughts, smiling at him. 'I didn't realise paddle steamers travelled so fast.'

'Would you like to see the engine house?'

'I don't want to move right now. I feel so free. As if I've left everything behind me, and there's only you and me and the sea.' She laughed, lifting her face up to the sky. 'I know this is the Firth of Forth and not an ocean, and I know that there are at least two other men on this boat—ship!—but it feels as if we're alone.'

'There's the captain up there in the wheel-house along with his mate, and in the engine room there will be a stoker and an engineer.' Grayson took her hand under the blanket. 'But I agree, it does feel as if we're alone.'

Her fingers twined in his. 'Are the paddle steamers that go *doon the watter* like this one? Where do they sail from, is there a dock in Glasgow?'

'The Broomielaw, almost right in the centre of the city. There are any number of steam-ers, some this size, others much bigger. A few have their decks covered over to make a proper saloon with windows so you can take in the view in comfort, but most have open decks like this, and cover below which you'd only use if the weather was inclement. Apart from anything else, it can reek down there.'

'Rrrrreeek.' Constance leaned her head on his shoulder. 'How many people do they carry?'

'The likes of the *Carrick Castle* here will comfortably take about fifty, but there are oth-ers that will squash a few hundred on board.

In the summer, I've seen men leap the gap before the gangplank's even down. On a busy day at the Broomielaw, they'll berth two and three deep too.'

'And is it always busy, even in the winter?'

'Not with day trippers, but it's becoming the done thing among those who can afford it, to move their family to a house by the sea, and for the husband to spend his week in the city and get a ferry home for the weekend. Piers are being built all along the coast now, so they can be dropped off close to home.'

'Are you thinking of building yourself a pier, and buying a seaside home?'

'I like the notion of living by the sea, but it's not very practical. I've my business to look to, and my children in school.'

'Your daughter still attends school at sixteen?'

'She's a bright lassie, and she loves her books. They'll only keep her for another year though, and then…'

And then, he knew perfectly well, he'd have a battle with the Murrays on his hands, and another sooner rather than later, when Neil finished school. He was dreading it. He shouldn't have to fight to keep his children, not after all he'd done for them, and it stuck in his craw that it should even come to that. 'It's far too nice a day to be dwelling on my problems. Look, we're approaching the island, do you think you're up to taking in the view from the observation deck?'

Which was a grand name for a set of wooden stairs climbing to the narrow platform between the paddles, Grayson thought, helping Constance across the slippery deck. He clambered up the stairs behind her, trying not to be distracted by her shapely rear, and almost succeeded. The rhythmic thumping of the paddles and the vibration of the steamer's engine made the little deck shudder. He circled Constance's waist, pulling her up against him. 'You can feel the heart of the ship under your feet here.' He had to shout to make himself heard.

She clutched the flimsy railing, leaning back against him. 'It's so noisy.' Turning round briefly, he saw she was smiling broadly. 'I absolutely love it.'

The steamer could not berth at the island, for there was no proper jetty. Instead, a dinghy was lowered off the side of the ship, and as she was helped aboard, Constance understood the real reason for the little practice trip

earlier. She sat at the back—astern, Grayson
laughingly informed her, as he handed her
his coat to shelter her from the sea breeze and
took the oars. Her ears were still thrumming
from the sound of the paddle steamer's engine. Her hair was lank with the spray from
the paddles, her skin tight with the sunshine
and the salty breeze, but she had never felt
so well.

Grayson, she wasn't surprised to note,
rowed with a casual ease. She snuggled into
his coat. It was still warm from his body,
the wool slightly damp from the spray. His
legs were braced at an angle on one of the
wooden struts on the bottom of the boat. He
was wearing boots today, and breeches rather
than trousers. He had rolled up the sleeves of
his shirt. His arms were tanned. The sinuous
muscles rippled as he rowed. She watched, entranced, lulled into a pleasant state of dream-
like arousal by the rhythmic movement of his
arms, the oars skimming at an angle under
the water, the regular clunk of them in the
rowlocks, the tension in his braced legs, the
tilting of his torso towards her, away, towards
her and then away again. His hands would be
warm from the oars if they rested on her skin.
He had rough hands, calloused and scarred,

but they were always scrubbed clean, the nails trimmed very short. Their kisses would taste of salt. He would smell of brine and sunshine and sweat.

The bump of the boat on a wave made Constance jump in her seat. They were making a sharp turn towards a little beach. Grayson seemed to be concentrating on the manoeuvre. Her flushed face could easily be attributed to the weather. She tugged at the ribbon holding her bonnet around her neck, taking off her gloves to undo the knot, putting them inside her bonnet when she finally managed to remove it.

Grayson brought the boat into the shallows, jumping out to pull it up on to the beach, heedless of the effect of the salt on his boots. She stood up, but before she could begin the complicated business of clambering out of the boat, he scooped her up, lifting her clear, then letting her slide slowly down on to the sand, keeping his arms around her waist. 'Do you have any notion at all of what you do to me, when you look at me like that?'

'I was watching you row.' Her heart was racing. Warm sand, salt, and Grayson, that's what she could smell, and it was playing havoc with her insides. 'I was studying your technique.'

He smoothed a long strand of her hair from her cheek, letting his hand rest under her hair, warm on her nape. 'You're a terrible liar, do you know that?'

'I am.' She reached up to curl her arm around his neck. 'I do know that.' It was the way he looked at her, more than anything, that aroused her. As if he couldn't believe she was really there. And the way he always listened, no matter how trivial her remark, the way he gave her all his attention. 'I was thinking that you would taste of salt, if you kissed me.'

'And I was thinking that I had never in my life wanted to kiss anyone as much as I want to kiss you right now.'

Their lips met. He did taste of salt, and of tooth powder. Their kisses made her head spin. Last night, there had been urgency in their kisses, fire. Today was different. She didn't know how. She didn't care. She wanted their kisses to last for ever. She pressed herself against him, wanting every part of them to touch, to connect. She could feel his chest rising and falling, his breath fast like hers. His tongue stroked her bottom lip, drawing a moan from her. She pulled his face closer, her hand clutching at the tight muscles of his rear, her mouth opening, shaping to his. She felt as if she was melting. Her body was thrumming. She could feel the rigid length of his arousal pressed against her, making her insides twist and tighten with desire, but all she wanted for now was their kisses, more kisses, never-ending kisses. Kissing to make up for all the time they had lost, would never have. This was all she wanted. *He* was all she wanted.

She knew he felt the same. She knew it from the way he was murmuring her name over and over between kisses, as if he was afraid she'd disappear. She knew it from the way his hand always sought hers, pressing the clasped pair against his heart. Finally they drew apart, gazing into each other's eyes, smiling. Aroused, but not wanting to be sated, not yet.

'We've the whole day ahead of us,' Grayson said, as they watched the paddle steamer sail off, 'and we've not even left the beach and explored the island yet.' But still he didn't let her go. 'The way you look at me, no one looks at me like that. You seem to have taken up residence inside my head. I can't stop thinking about you, do you know that?'

'Yes, because I feel the same. Now show me this secret island you've brought me to. I live less than ten miles from here and didn't even know it existed.'

He laughed softly. 'Then prepare to be amazed.'

Chapter Eight

∽∾∽

Inchcolm was a long, low island roughly in the
shape of an elongated 'S' located less than a
mile from the Fife coastline. 'The name comes
from the Gaelic,' Grayson said. 'It means Co-
lumba's island, I'm told. That's Braefoot Bay
directly over there, Aberdour is just up the
coast a bit. This stretch of water is known as
Mortimer's Deep.'

'You've been doing your homework!'

'Do I go to top of the class, teacher? There
are a number of islands dotted around the
Forth estuary, but this is reputed to be one of
the most memorable.'

'Is it? Why?'

Grayson laughed, turning her around. 'Because of that.'

'Oh, my goodness!' Laughing, she gazed

up at the massive ruin. 'I didn't even notice it when we landed. What on earth is it?'

'An Augustine abbey built in the twelfth century. Shall we take a look?'

'Yes! What about your coat?'

'I'll leave it in the boat, it will be safe enough if I pull it up the beach a bit. Do you want to leave your bonnet?'

'And my shawl.' Constance handed it to him, tilting her head up to the sun while he attended to the boat. 'It's such a bonny day.'

There was a scrape of wood on the pebbly foreshore. 'You'll need to have a care not to burn.'

'I won't, though I'll probably get a few more freckles. You forget, until I came to Edinburgh I was a hardy wee soul from the Highlands who only ever wore a bonnet on a Sunday.'

'And who wandered barefoot in the heather,' Grayson said, taking her hand. 'Aye, right.'

She laughed, her fingers twining around his, enjoying the feel of her skin on his without her gloves getting in the way. 'Looking back, I wonder that my parents adapted to their way of life so well. My mother never talked of her family, but from the little Pearl has told me, I know that they were quite well off. She'd have had no experience of cooking or baking, never mind doing the laundry, yet I never once heard her complain. Quite the opposite, she and my father were very, very happy. Oh, my goodness, would you look at that?'

From the beach the abbey looked like a ruin, but now they had made their way around the roofless church, the full extent of the monastic buildings was revealed. 'It's absolutely magnificent,' Constance said, surveying it in awe.

A massive tower stood at one corner complete with battlements. A chapel, steep-roofed, hexagonal in shape, was built on to the tower and beyond it, the monastic buildings were constructed around a courtyard. There was a hush to the place, an air of peace and tranquillity that kept them both silent as they explored, astonished to find the cloisters intact, and any number of rooms, one leading to another. They were empty, their windows un-shuttered, but otherwise in perfect repair.

'You can almost imagine the monks sitting here, taking their porridge in the morning,' Constance whispered.

'Or drinking their beer,' Grayson said,

peering through one of the windows. 'You'd think a place like this would be full of ghosts, but you don't get that feeling, do you?'

'Do you believe in ghosts?'

He took her hand again as they made their way back outside, blinking in the sunshine of the courtyard. 'When you're gone, you're gone. I don't think the dead come back to haunt us, but I think their spirit lives on, in those they've left behind. I see Eliza in Shona. It's funny, you'd think it would be Neil, for he's her spit, but it's not about looks. It's the way Shona smiles sometimes, or the way she picks up a book, frowning at the cover before she opens it. The way she's lost to the world when she's reading, and you can say something three times over and she won't hear you.'

'That must be—strange? Difficult?'

'No, no it's not. I don't think Eliza is up there,' Grayson said, tilting his head at the cloudless sky. 'She's not looking down on me, keeping a watchful eye over us—I don't believe that. When she died, I wished I did think that, it would have provided some solace, but I couldn't persuade myself. What I do believe though, is she lives on in Neil and Shona, though that's such a bloody cliché.'

'Like most clichés, true enough though.'

'It's one of the reasons I wouldn't ever put a stop to Shona and Neil visiting their grandparents. Much as I'd like to. If only they could bring themselves to see that my children take their heritage as much from me as their mother, things would be a damn sight easier. But a Maddox from Govan cannot compete with a Murray from—' He broke off as they came to the edge of the courtyard, facing out on the other side of the island back towards Leith. 'Never mind. This place is much more extensive than I realised. Look, there's traces of a wall there, shall we follow it round, see where it leads?' He smiled down at her. 'Don't worry, I'm not going to spoil the day by being maudlin.'

'Nothing can spoil this day.' Constance lifted his hand to her lips, kissing his knuckles. 'Have you tried mending bridges with your wife's parents—did you say their name was Murray? I don't think you've mentioned it before.'

There was a brief silence. 'No, I haven't. Murray is the family name.'

Constance said nothing, puzzled by his tone, for he'd spoken the name as if it was significant. Did he imagine she might be acquainted with them?

'This looks as if it was the kitchen garden at one time.' Grayson pointed to a large flat swathe of land enclosed in a shallow wall. 'It's not for me to mend bridges. It wasn't me who burned them. I've done my best to appease them over the years, which is more than they've ever done for me. If they'd just let things be—but that's the one thing they can't do. It would have been better for all of us, if I'd married Bridie Gallagher, who lived in the flat next to my parents, though her father would have had something to say about that mind you. God feared him, rather than the other way around, and on the odd occasion I went to church, as far as he was concerned it was the wrong sort. Old Man Gallagher would have wanted to stick his oar in to how I raised my weans just as much, in his own way as L—as the Murrays. Life would be easier if marriage came without in-laws attached.'

And that, his tone made clear, was the end of the conversation about the Murrays. 'Have you any kin of your own?' Constance asked, deciding that it would be wise to take the hint.

'A few cousins, on both my mother and father's side. You look surprised.'

'You haven't mentioned them.'

'I employ three of them. The others, I see two or three times a year. We're not close, but we keep in touch, and it's good for Neil and Shona, to see that not everyone lives as they do.' The faint frown on his brow disappeared. 'It's awkward though, being the rich one in the family. My relatives are all hard-working and proud. They'll take a job from me, but nothing else. I get the feeling that they're always looking for evidence that I'm getting above myself.'

'You wouldn't fancy the monastic life?'

'I like my comforts, Constance. Porridge for breakfast and dinner I could cope with, even a vow of silence, but I draw the line at doing without this.' He pulled her into his arms, kissing her gently. 'Not yet, any road.'

The sense of an ending hovered between them. Grayson let her go. The ruined wall turned at a sharp angle. They followed it, past a cluster of outbuildings which might have been shelters for animals, to the next turn, where it led them back towards the beach where they had landed. 'What about you?' he asked, breaking the silence. 'Have you ever thought of seeking out your mother's kin?'

It was an obvious question, but an unwelcome one. 'Why should I, after the way they treated my mother?'

'You can't know that they all felt the same. There's maybe some who aren't even aware of your existence.'

'They are.'

'You sound very sure.'

'Pearl told them.'

'Of course, I forgot. She's visiting her own kin now, isn't she? Could you not have gone with her?'

Another obvious question. 'No. I'm not completely ruling it out, but it's not the right time.' She smiled determinedly. 'I wouldn't want to leave poor Angus. And besides, if I had gone with Pearl, we wouldn't have met.'

'Now that would have been a disaster. Here we are back at the beach, and rather conveniently, the sun's over the yardarm.'

'Is it? I've lost track of time. What's the significance of the sun being over the yardarm?'

He laughed. 'It's a nautical term, it means it's time for a drink. Look, here's a nice sheltered spot on the beach. We'll have the wall to our backs, and the sun is going round a bit so it will be out of our faces, and there's this rock to hide us from view if anyone else lands, though I doubt that will happen. Sit there, and I'll go and fetch our lunch.'

'Champagne.' Grayson announced as he turned the bottle and carefully eased the cork out. 'I prefer a claret myself, but I reckoned you'd never have tasted it before, and it's a day for treats. I hope it's still cold.' He poured some of the fizzing wine into two glasses, handing her one.

Constance chinked her flute to his. 'You're full of surprises! I had no idea you had smuggled a picnic on to the boat.'

'I hid it under the blanket.'

'Well thank you for a lovely and thoughtful almost-birthday. You've gone to so much trouble.' She took a sip, then sneezed. 'Bubbles! And it's freezing.'

'I put it in the water when I pulled the boat up.' He had already spread the blanket on the sand. Opening the wicker basket, he was pleased to discover that Oman's had not let him down. 'A terrine, baked chicken, some crayfish with a sauce, ham hough in a jelly, a smoked cheese and raspberries. Not bad, if I say so myself.'

'I love raspberries, they are so much more tart than strawberries.' Constance was setting out the food on the plates. 'This is a veritable feast. You're really spoiling me. I have never had a picnic on a beach before.'

'Another first, then. I don't think I've ever had a picnic like this either, not even when I was working in Marseilles. Do you want to help yourself?'

'No, you serve me please. You do it so beautifully.'

She was sitting with her back against the wall, her legs curled up underneath her. Her hair was a charming tangle, half down over her shoulders, wisps of it blowing over her forehead. He could swear there were at least a dozen more freckles on her nose. He thought them charming, but he knew better than to say so. He leaned over, unable to resist bestowing a brief kiss on her lips.

'You taste of champagne,' she said. 'I feel quite deliciously decadent. If I was a lady of leisure, I'd do this every day.'

Grayson handed her a plate with a small selection of each dish, and helped himself to the rest of the chicken. 'Even ladies of leisure can't command the Scottish weather. Picnicking in the rain and the wind isn't so much fun.'

'I suppose not. This terrine is absolutely delicious.'

'I'll have some in a minute.'

'You like to eat one thing at a time, and I like to have a bit of everything. We're different that way. And you don't like champagne, do you? You have hardly touched yours and I've nearly finished mine.'

'Have some more. There's a bottle of hock here, I'll have some of that instead. What else would you do if you were a lady of leisure, other than sit about on the beach?'

'Oh, I like to be doing something. In truth, I'm not cut out to be a lady of leisure at all.'

'But isn't that exactly what you are, apart from walking Angus and running errands for Pearl?'

Constance paused and took another sip of champagne. 'They both can be quite demanding in their own way.'

He always knew when she was prevaricating. It wasn't only that she looked away, the tone of her voice went just a wee bit higher. They were strangers that were about to pass in the night, Grayson reminded himself. Whatever she was holding back, she wasn't the only one. 'If I didn't have my children and my yard to look after, I think what I'd do is have a paddle steamer kitted out as my home from home, and take off, see how far it would get me.'

'How far would that be? I think you said that none had crossed the Atlantic yet?'

'Oh, I wouldn't want to go that far.' He took some terrine and topped up their glasses. 'Back to the Mediterranean, maybe. I'd sail around some of the islands. Sardinia, Crete, Corfu, Cyprus. Some of the smaller ones off Greece that I've never seen. The sun would shine all day. The sky and the sea would be the same colour of turquoise blue. The sands would be golden. Would you come with me?'

'In a heartbeat. Would we sleep on deck, under the stars?'

'Definitely. We'd fall asleep to the gentle lap of water against the hull, and we'd wake to watch the sun come up—and it would come up, every single morning without fail.'

'What about our crew, where would they sleep?'

Grayson laughed. 'Stop being so practical! You'll be mentioning mosquitoes next. Can I help you to some more to eat?'

'Just some raspberries, thank you.' Constance sat back, stretching her legs out. 'I wonder if the King will dine so well when he is in Edinburgh. One thing is for sure, he

won't be eating haggis or sheep's heid or—
what was that other thing?'

'Hodge-podge. I heard he has a taste for
Glenlivet whisky.'

*"The news has flown frae mouth to mouth,
the North for ance has bang'd the South. The
de'il a Scotsman's die of drouth, Carle, now
the King's come!"* I'm not sure if the "drouth"
referred to is Glenlivet, but it could be.'

'What the hell was that you were spout-
ing?'

Constance gave a peal of laughter. 'A poem,
written by Walter Scott himself, to welcome
the King. Though it's such terrible doggerel
that he's not actually put his name to it.'

'*"Carle, now the King's come."* What on
earth does that mean?'

'I'm not actually sure. Hail fellow, well
met, or something, if indeed it means anything at all. He could well have invented it.'

'I wish he hadn't bothered. I've never heard
such drivel.'

'It goes on for page after page. I'm not entirely sure what the point of it is, save to list
out the names of those and such as those who
will be standing in line to kiss the royal hand.'

'Sounds to me like Walter Scott kissing
the royal…'

'No! Do not dare say it.' Constance's eyes were alight with laughter. 'Especially not since I fear the royal rear will be on display in a kilt.'

'Enough, you're putting me off my food. Here, have the last of the champagne.'

'I've had far too much, it's going to my head, and it's warm.'

'Do you fancy a paddle to cool down?'

'Another first?' Constance drained her glass. 'Look away, while I take off my shoes and stockings.'

'If I absolutely have to.'

'You absolutely have to.'

The rustling of her petticoats was a torment. Grayson took off his boots and stockings, thinking to join her, but when he stepped out of the shadow of the rock to watch her walk barefoot down the sands, he changed his mind. She was dancing around every little pebble, her hand held out quite unnecessarily for balance. He looked on rapt, utterly endeared. She squealed when the first wave hit her, jumping back like a child, and he laughed aloud. Clutching her gown, she made a second careful foray into the water, standing calf-deep quite still, facing out to sea. Her hair had come completely undone.

Her dress, held out of the water, was pulled tight against her bottom. She stooped to pick up a shell or a stone, wobbled, recovered, turned around to wave at him, and he had that feeling that happened so very rarely, that he would always remember this, the perfection of the moment, the complete and utter joy of it, the sense that he was in exactly the right place at the right time.

Constance picked her way back across the sand. 'It was freezing, but wonderful. Here, this is for you.' She handed him the pink-tinged shell. 'Isn't it beautiful? Do you know what it is from?'

'A sea snail. Thank you.'

She sat down beside him on the edge of the blanket, digging her toes into the sand. 'I won't ever forget today.'

'Your feet must be covered in sand. Here,' he said, kneeling beside her, grabbing the linen cloth that had covered the food. 'Let me dry them for you.'

'I can do it myself.'

'I'm sure you can.'

Resting her foot on his knee, he began carefully wipe the damp sand from it, working between her toes, aware of her eyes fixed on him the whole time, of the silence between them that spoke volumes. When he was done, he kissed each toe and set about the other foot. He could hear her breathing. He had never been so deeply aroused, yet he didn't think that anything would come of it, would have been happy to go on like this, holding her feet on his lap, and nothing more. Save when he was done with her second foot she said his name, pulling herself up beside him, wrapping her arms around him, kissing him with such intent that it didn't even occur to him to resist.

He hadn't known that kisses could speak volumes, that so much could be said by simply looking into a person's eyes. He saw his own longing reflected in hers. Desire too, but it went deeper than that. This was right. It would be wrong for them to resist. The day had been leading up to this. The week had been leading up to it. Maybe even more than that.

They sank back on to the rug, kissing. There was no sense of urgency, only a sense of certainty. They would get there, but not yet. He kissed her eyes, and her nose and her cheeks and her mouth. He kissed her neck, and the skin behind her ears, and her mouth. She was running her hands over him all the time, slowly, not with abandon but as if she wanted to trace his shape.

He kissed the hollow of her throat, and the swell of her breasts above the neckline of her gown. He wanted to kiss her all over, but her clothes were too complicated, and he didn't want to stop to remove them. He pulled her on top of him, and she wrapped her legs either side of him, sweet torture dragging a groan from deep inside him. She ran her tongue over his bottom lip. He rolled her on to her back again, pushing her petticoats up, moving down between her legs. There were other places to plant kisses.

Toes again. Ankles. Pushing up the hem of her drawers, he kissed the skin behind her knee. Her eyes were wide open, watching him, questioning. It was clear this was another first, and he was glad of it. He pushed her skirts higher, pulling her towards him, and took her in his mouth. The first taste of her almost set him over. She gave a soft cry that became a whimper as he licked her. He took his time, teasing them both, dragging it out, taking her to the brink and testing his own control to the limit, but he didn't want it to end. She was saying his name, pleading with him, and he was so hard that it ached, but he ignored her pleas to go faster, going slowly, waiting, starting again, until it was too much for both of them, and she tipped over the edge, and he'd never, ever, not ever felt anything like it, watching her, tasting her, hearing her moans of pleasure.

And then kissing her again, frantic kisses now, as she pulled at his clothing, arching under him, as urgent for him as he was for her. 'Constance?' His voice was ragged with the effort.

'Grayson, for the love of God.'

He struggled free of his breeches, pulling her on top of him, seeing from her face that this was another first, but heedless now, wanting only to be inside her. When she took him, lowering herself down, her smile becoming powerful as he became helpless, he clutched at the blanket and prayed for control. She leaned over to kiss him hard, once, and then he lost himself as she lifted and thrust, hard, deliberate, slow when he wanted fast, watching his eyes, holding his gaze, until he begged her, and she heeded him, tightening around him, holding him deep inside her as he spent himself, wrapping her arms around him as he came, his face pressed into her shoulder to muffle his guttural cries.

It took him far too long to realise he was still inside her. Another age to regret it, cursing under his breath. 'I'm sorry. I shouldn't have...'

She kissed him, stopping the words. 'Don't. I'm past that. Don't worry.'

'But...'

'It's what I wanted.'

'And me.' He kissed her again, trying to ignore the dread that was slowly seeping into him. 'It's what I wanted too.'

It was late, the afternoon was over and the sun had lost its heat as they stood at the top of the tower, looking out at the Firth of Forth. The remains of the picnic was packed away. The hamper and blanket were stowed in the dinghy. They were both fully dressed. They were supposed to be watching out for the arrival of the *Carrick Castle*. Perhaps Grayson was, but Constance was hoping that the captain had forgotten all about them. She knew that if they left this island—*when* they left this island—it would be the beginning of the end.

They had made love. They couldn't blame lust, or abstinence, or the fates this time. They had made love, and they should not

have made love. It was out of the question.
Yet she couldn't imagine how they could have
not made love. It was how the day was destined to end. And now they both knew that
their time together was coming to an end too.
There was no going back, and no question of
going forward.

'There she is.' Grayson pointed at the little
dot approaching.

'I wish today would last for ever.'

He groaned, pulling her into his arms. 'So
do I.'

She wrapped her arms around his waist,
pressing her cheek to his chest, listening to
the steady beat of his heart. It wasn't beating
for her, any more than hers was beating for
him. In this moment, they belonged to each
other. But this wasn't the real world. Gently,
she disentangled herself from him. 'Best get
down, we don't want to keep them waiting.'

She sat behind him in the dinghy, watching
the island grow smaller as they drew away.
Aboard the paddle steamer, they agreed to
meet the next day to take a walk down to
Holyrood, each knowing that they could now
count the hours until there were no more
meetings. They sat silently together on the

deck after that, their hands clasped under the blanket, watching the sun going down.

Grayson put her in a carriage at Leith, telling her he preferred to walk off his lunch, and she didn't demur. 'Thank you,' she said as he helped her in. 'It's been a perfect day.'

He attempted a smile. 'Just a bit too perfect,' he said, closing the door and walking away.

Chapter Nine

Come one and all, says Mr Scott
And view the King's scarce-covered bot
For a penny more you can see the lot
Hail, now the King's come

The Highlands cropped of all its heather
So all can wear a jaunty feather
We can but hope for clement weather
Hail, now the King's come

Hail George the regal Jacobite
Strong of leg and pink of tight
Scotia bow before his might
Hail, now the King's come

The King at fair young maidens leered
While sycophantic clan chiefs cheered

*Meanwhile at home their lands were cleared
Hail, now the King's come.*

A poem by Flora MacDonald, inspired by the
work of Walter Scott

Saturday, 13th July 1822

Paul Michaels, the editor of the *New Jacobite Journal*, handed the poem back to its author, grinning. 'This is inspired. You've a real talent, it seems a shame that your work is not more widely read.'

'We'll have hundreds, thousands more readers in the next few weeks, you wait and see. The King's visit will provide no shortage of material like this. With Walter Scott more or less in charge of proceedings, Edinburgh will be decked out like a scene from one of his more melodramatic novels.'

Paul ran ink-stained hand through his short, frizzy hair. 'True enough. If Scott could have the castle painted tartan, he would.'

'I've written you an alternative parody version of his pamphlet too, the one that details the etiquette of behaviour and suitable attire. What do you think?'

He took the bundle of pages. She had

worked through the night to produce them in an effort to distract herself from the parting that was to come and the perfection of the day which had precipitated it with, it had to be said, mixed results. She was not in love with Grayson, she would not permit herself to be in love with Grayson, but she had flown precariously close to the flame.

'Constance?'

Paul was holding out her work, having clearly made no attempt to read it. 'I'm sure it's brilliant, but I have to ask myself if it's worth the effort and expense required to publish it. Look out there, at the people in the Grassmarket. You can't buy a bit of heather for love nor money in the city. They're all absolutely determined to embrace this royal visit.'

'That's all the more reason for us to point out the error of their ways.'

'We've been doing that for years now, my dear, and it's making little appreciable difference. I'm not sure we're ever going to turn the tide. Did you see the backlash against that article in the *Scotsman?* All they did was question, in the most subtle way, why the Scottish people should be expected to bow and scrape to the King, and they were ripped to shreds for it in the popular press.'

'So we're all to don our plaids and wave our flags and get down on bended knee when the King graces us with his presence. Patriotic obsequiousness is the order of the day, and that is exactly what the *NJJ* is going to strongly advise against.'

'Do you really think anyone will pay any heed? Hear me out for a moment,' Paul said. 'You're not going to like what I'm going to say, but I'm going to say it anyway. The fact is, the *New Jacobite Journal* has a readership smaller than the queue of ladies likely to attend the King's Drawing Room at Holyrood. Our readers have all got their hearts in the right place I'm sure, but frankly, Constance, they're the types who soothe their conscience by reading our journal, shedding a few tears, and then using it to light the fire the next morning.'

'Please don't give up, Paul. This is our best opportunity to make them see, to make them listen, to tell them what's happening.'

'My dear, most people simply don't care.'

'No, you're wrong. I *know* you're wrong. It's ignorance that's the problem, not indifference. We're a small press, we have so little reach. If the truth was exposed by the national newspapers, they would sway the hearts and minds of the general public, but it isn't being broadcast because...'

'Because those who own those newspapers are the very people who also own the land being cleared, or they are related to them. What's more, those people believe that it is the right thing to do, that the introduction of sheep represents progress.'

Constance got dejectedly to her feet, absently picking up a 'G' from the printing block tray, turning it over in her hand. 'People are obsessed with this royal visit. They will read anything and everything associated with it, including the *NJJ*. People who have never heard of us, Paul, will pick us up thinking that they're reading a description of— oh, I don't know, a levee, whatever that may be. We'll draw them in with mention of His florid Majesty, but they'll read on because they will be shocked, and angry and horrified when we reveal what is really going on in the Highlands.'

'You've a powerful and passionate way with words, it's one of your many strengths but they're being wasted.' Paul cursed under his breath. 'I'm sorry, I truly am. I know how much this means to you, but you've been writing for me for four years now and we're making no inroads. Isn't it time you turned your thoughts to pastures new, too?'

'I can't give up yet. I've come too far, I've sacrificed so much.'

'That's my point, Constance, this has been your life for the last four years. It's been all-consuming. It's not healthy. Even I have a wife and family to go home to at the end of the day'

'I'm not ready to quit yet.'

'No, but I'm afraid I am. There, I've said it. I've been taking a good long hard look at what we're doing here, and it's time for a change of direction.' Paul flicked open his dented snuff tin, taking a large pinch before wiping his nose with a large, ink-stained kerchief. 'Do you know, they're sending a squad of Bow Street Runners up from London to keep an eye on things, and I reckon the Home Secretary will send his spies here too, if Peel doesn't come himself. They want to ensure this visit's a roaring success.'

'Are you worried that they will arrest us?'

He laughed. 'They won't be concerning themselves with small fry like us. If the King's yacht is blown up, or the King himself is pelted with rotten eggs, it won't be our readers, but the Radical Army who are responsible. But it does show how seriously they're taking this visit. It's not only a matter of keeping the King well away from dabbling in foreign policy, it's an attempt to bring the whole bloody nation together.'

'By pretending that the King is some sort of new Bonnie Prince Charlie, you mean!'

'That's exactly what I mean. He's the first King to come here since the Young Pretender. You can bet he'll wear the kilt, and he'll play up his Stuart connection to the hilt. Whoever dreamed the idea up is a smart political operator. You can see it's working already. The city is raring to go, and preparing itself for a ceilidh that will last a fortnight. They're not interested in what's going on in the rest of Scotland. They don't want to know about a few crofters who can barely scrape a living from the land in the first place, being forced to make way for to sheep.'

'Paul! How can you be so unfeeling?'

'*I'm* not unfeeling. No one hearing your story could be anything but appalled, but my point is that no one cares to hear it. And as far as I'm concerned, right now there's other causes that I'd rather use my press to support.'

'You mean the Radicals?'

'They're gaining real strength. They want the right to vote, Constance. Ordinary men, who work in iron works and mills and docks all over the country, but most especially here in Scotland, are plotting revolution, and our Government is determined to put an end to it. That's what this royal visit is all about, at the end of the day. What better way to extinguish a revolt in the making, than to provide people with a monumental distraction.'

There was a light in Paul's eyes that she had not seen for some time. What he said made horrible sense. She had the sensation that the ground was being cut from under her feet. First yesterday—no, she wouldn't think of that yet—and now this. 'You said that you would give me until after the King's visit.'

'And I will, I owe you that much.' He sighed wearily. 'When Pearl Winston put us in touch, I couldn't believe my luck to have a real Highland woman, with first-hand experience, not just a social conscience. You've a pithy way with words that none of my other writers have, too. I feel guilty, at the pittance I've been paying you.'

'If I'd wanted to earn a fortune I wouldn't be a writer, and anyway you know very well it's not about the money for me. You gave me a purpose when I could easily have given myself over to despair. "Everyone gets hurt, but you can choose how much you suffer." I've never forgotten those words of yours.'

'Now don't get maudlin on me, young woman.'

'I'm not young, I'm forty years old on Sunday.'

'A babe in arms, compared to me,' Paul said, with a wry smile. 'And if I may say so, looking good for your years. I'm wondering if our Flora has maybe found a new Bonnie Prince?'

Found, and lost in the space of less than a week. Her cheeks flamed. 'Nothing and no one will ever get in the way of my work here.'

'As if I could ever doubt it. Go home, Constance, and think long and hard about what I've said. As soon as His Majesty heads back down south, it's over. It's time for both of us to move on to pastures new.'

The sun was hiding behind a thin layer of grey cloud today, making the vast edifice that was St Giles' Cathedral look even more forbidding, and very much in keeping with Grayson's mood. What a contrast to yesterday. He had spent a sleepless night, seesawing between remembered bliss and dread of what was to come. After yesterday, he knew leaving Edinburgh straight away was the wisest course of action, but the very notion of never seeing Constance again was impossible to contemplate. That fact alone was enough to make it clear to him that he was in deep waters. The letter which arrived this morning was a timely reminder—as if he needed one!—that it was time to end this little hiatus from the real world and go home. He wasn't ready to go home yet though. Tomorrow was Constance's birthday, which frankly, he thought she was getting out of proportion. But he'd promised her moral support and he couldn't let her down.

So he'd go on Monday. The decision made him feel considerably worse. Like St Giles', he'd seen better days, he thought sardonically. Auld Reekie's cathedral was, in Grayson's humble opinion, very much second best to St Mungo's medieval cathedral in Glasgow. The side of the edifice which faced on to the High Street leaned at a precarious angle. Until relatively recently, there had been a line of tenements and shops built close enough to hide this defect. He knew this from one of Walter

Scott's blasted novels, when the shops and the old tolbooth prison were described in, he had to admit, memorable and colourful detail. The novel was *The Heart of Midlothian*, not one of Neil's favourites, but Shona loved it. The heart-shaped mosaic the novel was named after was set into the pavement just a few yards away near the cathedral's west door. When they returned in August, the three of them could visit the main sites featured in the book. He should read it again before then, they'd like that. Or would Shona and Neil consider themselves too sophisticated for that?

With a sinking feeling, he sat on the steps of the cathedral and pulled out his daughter's letter. She couldn't wait to share the exciting news that her grandparents would be coming to Edinburgh for the King's visit. Word had reached them that His Majesty would be receiving the Scottish aristocracy at Holyrood Palace, and so naturally Lord and Lady Glenbranter didn't want to miss out.

Staring gloomily at the lawyers mincing to and fro across the square to the old Parliament buildings which were now the law courts, Grayson cursed the Murrays under his breath. At least there would be no room for them at Oman's on Charlotte Square. It would stick in their throat, knowing that their low-born son-in-law was residing there, rubbing shoulders with the Duke and Duchess of Argyll. Not that he would be doing any such thing, and even if he did, he'd be damned if he'd boast about it.

Would it be possible to avoid his in-laws then for the duration of their visit? Edinburgh was a notoriously small and tight-knit city. The bigger question was whether Neil and Shona would prefer to spend their time with their grandparents, and not their father. The answer to that was a resounding yes, for Lord and Lady Glenbranter would be bound to be invited to meet the King. There was no way he could deprive his children of the honour of accompanying them, no matter how dubious a privilege he himself thought it. Sickeningly, it was beginning to look like this visit wouldn't turn out to be the family holiday he'd hoped, but a series of treats for his children and their grandparents. Was this what the future held for him, relegated to the role of provider of funds and luxury accommodation? And currently, the procurement of bales of tartan. Knowing that the material was likely to be in very short supply, he made a mental note to do a bit of shopping sooner rather than later. A shopping list which would most decidedly would not include a plaid for himself.

Checking his watch, he saw that it was still fifteen minutes before he was due to meet Constance. It was she who had suggested they meet at St Giles'. She had business in the Grassmarket, she'd told him. With the well-connected bookseller? He'd walk down to meet her and surprise her.

He walked briskly down the steep incline of West Bow, coming to an abrupt halt as he reached the Grassmarket, taken aback by the clamour, which was raucous even for Edinburgh. Coaching inns lined one side of the wide thoroughfare. He'd arrived at one himself, but he had forgotten there was a cattle market at the far end. He'd never find Constance here. Deciding to make one quick circuit before cutting his losses and heading back up to their rendezvous at St Giles', he walked passed the White Hart and the Black Bull inns, where dray horses pulling carts loaded precariously with barrels fought for space with mail coaches and post chaises. Fighting his way across at King's Stables Road and the entrance to the market, he took a breather on the corner of West Port, and that's where he spotted her.

Constance was leaning against the railings of one of the steep sets of stairs that climbed up the outside of the tenements. A smaller building next to where she was standing housed a bookshop, with living quarters above it. He couldn't see her face, for she was standing side-on to the street, and something about her stance made him wary of approaching her. She was wearing a grey dress with a shawl of indiscriminate hue draped around her shoulders. Her gown looked to him far too warm for the muggy day, and it also looked, he had to admit, rather worn as well as outmoded. It hadn't occurred to him to wonder how she managed for money, but it must be a struggle for her. The arrangement with Mrs Winston sounded suspiciously like charity. What stopped her from teaching? One of the many things he'd never know about her now.

She was carrying a stack of papers, and rummaging about now, in her pocket in search of something. Inevitably, the papers fell to the filthy pavement. As she cried out in dismay, he ran to help her.

'Here, let me.'

'Grayson! Where did you come from?'

'I was early, I thought I'd surprise you.'

'Leave those. Please, I can manage. I didn't realise I—leave them!'

Her face was tear-streaked. 'Constance, what on earth is wrong?'

'Nothing.' She scrubbed her cheeks with her hand. 'It's nothing. I'm perfectly fine. I simply need to—give me those. I should have left them with Paul.'

'Your bookseller friend? What, has he let you have sight of another of Walter Scott's odes to tartan?' He meant it as a joke, for he couldn't put his arms around her, which was what he wanted to do. *'"Flora MacDonald's Alternative Etiquette Guide for the Inhabitants of Edinburgh Upon the Occasion of His Majesty's Visit,"'* he read. 'What is this? Who is this Flora MacDonald? It certainly can't be the woman who rescued the Young Pretender all those years ago, she is long dead.'

'It's a *nom de plume*. I meant to leave this document with Paul.' She grabbed the bundle from him and charged into the bookshop next door, emerging scarlet-cheeked and damp-eyed a few seconds later. 'Let's get out of here.'

'Constance.' He tried to take her arm, but she shook him off. 'For heaven's sake.' He caught her again, pulling her into the entrance of a close and wrapping her into his arms. She buried her face in his shoulder. Her silent sobs made his heart ache. Turning his back to the thoroughfare to shield her, he smoothed her back until she calmed enough to face him, handing her his handkerchief to mop her face.

'Thank you. I'm sorry. Paul said—but I know he's wrong, I *know* he is.' She folded his damp kerchief up and handed it back to him. 'You have no idea what I'm talking about, do you?'

'No, but if you want me to go and sort this Paul character out, I'd be happy to.'

She laughed weakly. 'I'm not sure precisely what you mean by sorting him out, though I can guess by the tone of your voice, and it would make me very unhappy. Paul is—I am—do you mind if we take a walk, it will give me time to recover.'

To Constance's intense relief, Grayson agreed. Her only consolation was that Paul remained unaware of the extent of her distress. She'd managed to quit the shop before her tears smarted. When she returned to leave her latest work, having inadvertently taken it with her in her distressed state, he'd been in the basement where the press was, so she'd left it on the desk in his office. She couldn't imagine what Grayson made of it. She had never planned to tell him, but she knew she wouldn't have the heart to lie to him, and right now, she really could be doing with a sympathetic ear. She was exhausted with the effort of keeping her secret, and if she could attribute her tears entirely to Flora, then all the better. Though she was fairly certain Grayson had guessed the depth of her feelings for him, and equally certain that she knew how he felt, it would be much easier for both of them if they remained unacknowledged.

Aware of him casting her sidelong glances as they climbed up West Bow, she ventured a smile. 'Slow down a bit, we're not trying to catch a mail coach.'

'A Highland lass like yourself should be used to climbing hills,' Grayson retorted, looking only marginally relieved.

'Would you be devastated to learn that I can't dance a Highland reel, for I've two left feet, and if you put a spinning wheel in my hands, I'd not know whether to play it or spin wool with it.'

'Please reassure me that you do know how to make porridge?'

'My one redeeming talent.' They paused for

a moment, surveying the crush of the Lawnmarket. 'My goodness, it's busy here, isn't it.'

'The world and his dog is heading down to the palace to take a look at the preparations, by the looks of it. Stay close, keep to the inside.'

The High Street gave way to the steep descent of the Canongate, which was lined on either side by the ubiquitous tall, narrow tenements of the Old Town. 'There's some parkland beside the palace over there.' Constance pointed. 'We can take a seat there. I can hardly hear myself speak for the noise of the traffic here.'

Her heart was thumping by the time they reached the welcome green space, Grayson leading the way to a grassy patch under a tree. 'This looks dry enough.'

She dropped carelessly down beside him, aware of his concerned gaze. 'Paul is a friend, but he's also my employer. I write for him. For the *New Jacobite Journal.*'

It was depressingly clear from Grayson's expression that he'd never heard of it.

'I'm Flora MacDonald. I mean, that's the name I use for my writing.'

'Flora MacDonald and the *New Jacobite Journal.*' Grayson's puzzlement was giving way to a deeper frown. 'You write political tracts?'

'I suppose you could call it that. Lately, I have been…'

'Taking the p—satirising Walter Scott? With materials supplied by your bookseller friend, I presume?'

'Yes, though that has only been my latest—Flora's latest tactic.'

'You've been writing these articles for a while, then?'

Grayson was tight-lipped, all trace of concern gone from his face, and there was no sign of the sympathy she had been longing for. 'Four years,' Constance answered warily. 'I know you've wondered at my lack of occupation.'

He swore viciously. 'Does your friend Mrs Winston know she's harbouring a rabble rouser?'

'I'm not a rabble-rouser!'

'Then what are you?'

Her courage faltered under that look he gave her. For the first time, she saw in him the formidable and ruthless Glaswegian shipbuilder. A stranger. As she stammered and stuttered her way through a precis of her four years as a political sketch writer, he said barely a word. By the time she had finished, she was wishing fervently that she had not begun in the first place.

'So what you're telling me,' Grayson said slowly, after an agonising silence, 'is that for the last four years you've been producing politically radical articles, but when the King visits you're planning on marking the occasion by writing and publishing genuinely treasonable articles? Are you out of your mind? Have you even considered the consequences? You could end up in gaol.'

'That is one thing I don't need to worry about,' she retorted, stung, 'because according to Paul, the only function my writing will serve is as kindling. Anyway, it's not treason to point out tragic truths that everyone is turning a blind eye to.'

'I can't believe what you've told me. I feel as if I don't know you. Constance, it's dangerous, you're playing with fire.'

'I don't care! Can you not see that these people need a voice? They are not peasants, too ignorant to know what is best for them as some say, or too lazy to work hard enough to make their lands pay. They are honest, hardworking people, who simply want to carry on crofting on the same patch of ground their families have occupied for generations.'

'But you have given them a voice, and what you're saying is that it's made no difference.'

'Then I need to try harder.' Hot tears stung her eyes. 'I'll prove Paul wrong. I'll find a way to make people listen. This visit…'

'Constance, this visit, as far as most people are concerned, it's the chance to dress up and have a bit of fun, that's all.'

'I thought you'd understand.'

'I thought—I wondered what you did with your time. I was baffled as to why you were so determined to hide yourself away. I couldn't fathom why you stayed in Edinburgh with Mrs Winston, and had no inclination to seek out your mother's relatives. And most of all, I couldn't understand why someone who so clearly loved teaching isn't a teacher any more. But I never thought for a moment that this would be the reason for all of it.'

'After what happened to me and what I witnessed, I had to do something. How can I go back to teaching while this is going on under our noses? I can't give up until I know I've done everything possible. Don't you see?'

He caught her hands, gripping them tightly.

'I can't bear the thought of you wasting your life like this.'

'I'm not wasting it and even if I was, it's my life to waste.'

'What will you do when the King has left Edinburgh and this journal you write for has been closed down?'

'I can't contemplate that at the moment. Look over there,' she said, a little desperately. 'Holyrood Palace has been going to rack and ruin for years, yet they're suddenly spending an arm and a leg refurbishing it from the public purse. Scotland must have a palace fit for a King, even if the King chooses to live and rule elsewhere.'

'Is that another scandal Flora MacDonald will highlight? I wouldn't like to be on the wrong end of your pen.'

'I can't tell what you're thinking. Usually I—but I can't. I thought you were angry, but now?'

He got to his feet, holding out his hand to help her up. 'Yesterday was perfect, wasn't it? We both knew we should have left it at that, didn't we? I did any road.'

She didn't want to see the look in his eyes. It made her heart feel as if it was being squeezed. She tried to capture his hand, but he shook his head, turning away. 'Tomorrow is my birthday. We agreed—you said—' She broke off, seeing the answer on his face. 'Why? Is it because you imagine that after yesterday I have expectations...?'

'No, it's because I've just realised that I might be the one developing expectations, and after what you've told me!' He swore again, softly and viciously. 'It doesn't bear thinking of.'

'I don't understand.'

'No, for I've made a point of not telling you,' he said heavily. 'Do you know, my first thought, when you told me about this writing of yours, was that you were putting yourself in harm's way.'

'I'm no more likely to end up in gaol now than I have been for the last four years.'

'My second thought was, that you were wasting your life. And my third thought,' he continued, before she could interrupt him again, 'was for how my association with you might impact on my family. My third thought, Constance, not my first. Until I met you, they've always come first. I can't have that.'

'What on earth has my work got to do with your family?'

Grayson shrugged impatiently, his expression troubled. Whatever he was working himself up to telling her, this would be their last conversation, and the fact that she couldn't bear to think about that, told its own story. 'I just wanted a bit more time,' Constance whispered.

'So did I.' He pulled her briefly into his arms, hugging her tightly. 'But it would be a mistake,' he said, releasing her. 'Look, I think we both need to calm down and regain some perspective. Why don't we take a walk over to the palace as we planned and have a look at what they're doing?'

Chapter Ten

Holyrood Palace lay in the imposing shadow of Salisbury Crags and Arthur's Seat. A two-storey gatehouse flanked by two huge towers with conical roofs led to the main palace building itself. The principal entrance was flanked by heavy stone columns, the doorway itself topped by the Royal Arms of Scotland carved into the stone mantel above, the whole topped by a clock tower high above which, two obviously new flags were flying. A constant stream of carts pulled up, laden with building supplies, floorboards and mouldings, glass, slate and iron. The clank of metal on stone echoed around the inner courtyard, as masons worked to make the main rooms watertight. There were a number of men wandering boldly about the rooftops, replacing slates and repairing guttering.

The whole proceedings were being supervised by one man clutching an extremely long list, standing atop two crates by the door. Pots of paint, rolls of carpet and wall coverings, stood in the shelter of one tower, while over at the other, a huge heap of mouldering tapestries and drapes, broken furniture and empty picture frames was growing larger by the moment. There were piles of rubble and tools everywhere, picks and rakes, hammers, chisels, and barrows.

Constance stood beside Grayson at the edge of the yard, their eyes fixed on the hive of activity, the tension between them palpable. Had he been implying he was in love with her? Her mind skirted away from confronting the possibility. He was leaving today. Their affair, if that is what it had been, was over. His going back to Glasgow would leave a chasm in her life. She had so quickly become accustomed to his company, to having someone to share her thoughts with, to laugh with, to simply *be* with. To imagine what could have been would be torture, plain and simple, especially since it could not be. He had his life. She had hers, and she would not think about what that would entail after the King's visit had ended.

'Sorry?' Constance jumped, finding Grayson's eyes not on the building works but on her face. 'I was miles away.'

'I was wondering if they were rebuilding the entire palace?'

'I don't know. It certainly looks like it, from here. I know they're making a receiving chamber out of what was the picture gallery, and presumably making some of the other main rooms fit to be used as antechambers. I have no idea what else they're doing, though it looks like they are also about to completely repave the courtyard. Oh, yes, and as well as ridding the palace of rats, they are evicting the people who have been staying in the grace-and-favour apartments. One of them is a veteran of Culloden.' She was babbling, but at least she was managing a semblance of a conversation, and Grayson seemed to appreciate it.

'It must all be costing a King's ransom, if you'll pardon the pun,' he said. 'Look, a new road is going to be built over there, according to the newspaper I was reading this morning. It will apparently shorten the King's journey from Dalkeith House, where he's staying for the duration, to Holyrood. They're going to install gas lighting the whole way too, and you can see, they've made a start on placing more lights around the palace. Even the man in the moon will know when the King arrives and all these are lit. More grist to Flora's mill, I reckon.'

'Perhaps, though you probably agree with Paul, that she'd be flogging a dead horse.' Utterly deflated, Constance turned away, heading back towards the bottom of the Canongate.

'You mustn't be thinking that I don't understand what's driving you.'

He offered his arm. She resisted for a fraction of a second before succumbing to the temptation to walk beside him. 'Then you'll know that I can't give up now.'

'I do know that, and I know I've no right at all to counsel you otherwise, though I want to. You're such a brave, strong woman. You've suffered so much, yet here you are, coming out fighting. Isn't it time you fought for your own interests, put yourself first for a change?'

'I could ask the same thing of you.'

'It's not the same thing.' They walked on up the hill, the noise from the palace receding. 'Maybe it is,' Grayson admitted grudgingly. 'Whatever, we've both made too many sacrifices along the way to change course now.'

At the Canongate Kirk, the burial ground opened out, giving a view over to the Greek folly atop Calton Hill. A few steps on, Grayson slowed by a coffee shop in the arcade below the row of tenements next to the kirk. 'Will we stop for some refreshment? I reckon I owe you an explanation.'

She nodded, casting him a nervous smile that almost stopped him in his tracks. She was bracing herself. As he was himself. The few customers were intent on their conversations or their newspapers, and the proprietor didn't bat an eyelid as he showed them to a quiet booth at the back of the room, while a maidservant brought them a pot of coffee.

'I had a letter from Shona this morning,' Grayson said, pouring two bowls of surprisingly fragrant coffee. 'She was asking me when I was coming home.'

Constance nodded, attempting a smile that she quickly gave up on.

He drained his coffee cup, topped it up and drank the refill back in one gulp. 'I'm not speaking only for myself when I say we got more than we bargained for, these last six days, am I?'

She stared down at her bowl, turning it around in her saucer. 'You know you're not.'

He longed to reach across the table and take her hand, but one touch would overset them both. 'What I'm about to tell you, is to ensure that when we part, we'll neither of us be in two minds.'

'No doubts, no regrets.'

'Precisely. What you need to understand, Constance, if you don't already, is that my children mean everything to me.'

She looked up at that. 'No one who knows you could imagine any different. It's one of the things I've admired about you from the first. You love them, pure and simple, and make no bones about it.'

Her words brought a lump to his throat. She hadn't touched her coffee. He poured himself the dregs. 'I'm not one of those fathers who thinks he knows best, and who wants to map out their lives for them. I want both of them to think for themselves, make their own decisions. Of course I'm not ready for them to grow up and leave the nest just yet, but I know that they will, so right now, what I want is to enjoy every moment I can with them, without suffocating them.'

He paused, because this was proving much tougher than he'd expected. Talking of his weans brought home to him just how strong his love for them was. His heart was racing. The coffee probably hadn't helped. 'I can see you're wondering what my point is, but bear with me. I told you that when Eliza died, her parents wanted to take Shona and Neil from me, thinking they could do better by them?'

'What I didn't tell you,' he continued when Constance nodded, 'is the reason they were so certain they could deliver on that promise. Murray is the family name. Eliza's parents are more usually referred to as the Marquis and Marchioness of Glenbranter. Eliza was Lady Elizabeth Murray, before she married me. She was their only child. As you can imagine they had big plans for her, since the continuation of the precious Murray family line was reliant on her future offspring and in particular her first-born son.'

Constance's face registered shock, but not recognition. 'Where are their lands—do they have lands?'

'In the north-east. I know very little about them, I've made it my business *not* to ask, but there's money, lands, and at least one castle which must be in good order since Shona likes her creature comforts. I never heard her complain of a cold bedchamber or worse, a cold breakfast.'

'You married into the landed gentry!'

'I married Eliza because I loved her, not because I hankered after high society.'

'I'm sorry. I didn't mean to imply—I am astonished, shocked that's all.'

'I kept it from you, deliberately, I'll admit that. I didn't want it getting in the way of our brief time together. You'd ask me all sorts of questions I couldn't answer, and more importantly I wanted a break from the reality of my situation. So, like I said, I kept it from you.'

'Are they improvers, these relatives of yours?'

'I don't know, and they're not my relatives.'

'Your son is the heir to a marquessate. Is he being groomed to be an improver too?'

'For—' Grayson broke off, shaking his head. 'This is why I didn't tell you. I knew it would be all you'd be interested in, and what's more that you'd be bound to assume the worst.'

'With cause. It's likely…'

'Aye, it's likely, but isn't it the law of the land to presume a person innocent until proven guilty, and not the other way around? I need a drink. A proper drink.' He hailed the waitress, ordering another pot of coffee and a whisky. 'Do you want one?'

'I'll take a brandy, thank you. I am afraid

that once again I'm going to spoil your notion of my Highland heritage,' Constance said when their drinks had been set down, 'by telling you that I can't abide whisky. It's the smell, it's like medicine.'

'Much-needed medicine in this case,' Grayson said, tilting his glass. *'Slàinte.'*

'Slàinte.' Constance took a tentative sip of her brandy. 'I had no idea you thought me tedious.'

'You know fine and well that's not what I meant.'

She took another sip of brandy. 'No, but you're about to pour your heart out to me, and I'm being tediously single-minded. I'm sorry. Please, tell me what it is you want to say, and I will try not to turn it into a political debate.'

'I suppose what I'm trying to say is that the Glenbranters want to take my son and daughter away from me, which is a far more heinous crime in my eyes than anything else they may do in the name of progress.'

'Don't apologise.' Constance tipped the remnants of her brandy into her coffee. 'A rough Glaswegian shipbuilder, and the daughter of a marquis. My God, no wonder they took agin' you.'

'They did, and then some.' Grayson followed her lead, tipping his whisky into his coffee. 'Back then, when I met Eliza, I was hardly a prize. I'd lots of plans and a great deal of ambition, but success was something I had yet to achieve.'

'I am embarrassed to admit that I imagined your wife to be one of those women who bend with every wind, and who thought herself rather above such mundane tasks as keeping house. I maligned her hugely. To have defied her parents and followed her heart must have taken an immense amount of courage. And demonstrates a profound love.'

'Oh, we considered the world well lost for love, right enough. We were besotted with each other.' He braced himself as he spoke, but the memory was hazy, the pain more like regret. 'As for her courage, it was short-lived. It stuck in my craw, though I never told her so, that she went running back to visit the minute she was summoned, and didn't even consider holding firm until her parents invited her husband to accompany her. There,' Grayson said, feeling rather sick, 'that's something I've never admitted to a living soul before, and I'm not proud of it. I thought she was being disloyal, but it would have been wrong of me to make her choose.'

'So you said nothing? Not ever?'

'She seemed happy enough with the situation, her parents doted on the children when they came along, and how could I complain, it would have been churlish of me, when she'd sacrificed so much to marry me.'

Constance frowned. 'She wanted for nothing when your business flourished.'

'I mean the life she was born into. The life that her parents want to give my children. Most people would consider being heir to a marquessate and all the lands and the castles and the connections that go with it as Neil is, a huge step up from being the son of a shipbuilder. Even a very rich shipbuilder. And then there's Shona. There's talk of a Season in London, which I gather would mean her attending a succession of parties in a series of fancy dresses in order to attract a queue of eligible young men keen to ask her to marry them.'

'My God, you make it sound like an aristocratic drover's market.'

Grayson gave a bark of laughter, but his smile quickly faded. 'The Murrays have thrown in a significant dowry to boot, to compensate for the questionable side of her parentage, I must assume. As if I can't afford to provide handsomely for my daughter. But my money, unlike theirs, is tainted by the fact I've earned it. As opposed to having extracted it from the peasants, before you say it.'

'I wasn't going to say anything of the sort. Go on.'

'As far as I'm concerned, it's an antiquated way of life that's dying out, and rightly so, but—parties, London, pretty dresses on the one hand, a title, a castle, endless heather-clad hills to roam on the other, you can see the appeal to a sixteen and a fourteen-year-old? Neil and Shona, when they come back from a visit to their grandparents, are always full of it, though they settle back down quickly enough, until the time comes for the next visit, and it all begins again. The Murrays are so bloody certain that what they can offer is superior to anything I can offer, and all I want is for my children to make their own minds up. So I steer a steady course.'

Grayson grimaced. 'I don't rock the boat, to continue with my seafaring analogy. It's worked so far. I've kept my promise to Eliza, and the Murrays know that. I've given them nothing to complain about, and there's nothing about me they can point the finger at either. I've never considered replacing their daughter, I've never wanted to. Most importantly, my children are happy.'

'And you intend to keep it that way. You needn't worry, I've no desire to take your late wife's place.'

'I'm not trying to quash your expectations, I know you have none. I'm trying to say that the pair of us have been wandering about in a wee bubble for the last six days, and what you've just told me brought me back to earth with an almighty bang. Since I met you, I've cared about nothing except seeing you again, counted the hours, for the love of God, when we've been apart. It's been wonderful, so wonderful that I've not given a moment's thought, after that first day, to what the world would make of us.'

'When you say world, you mean your children and their grandparents, don't you? My being such a fierce and vocal critic of their class was the final straw.'

'It's a class my children may choose to be part of, and if they make that choice, when they're old enough to make that choice, and wise enough, then I'll need to find a way to live with it. My point is, Constance, they have choices and I won't prejudice them. I wish it was otherwise but...'

'Don't say it, there's no need.' She picked up a teaspoon, stared at it then put it down again, making a point of meeting his gaze directly. 'You have sacrificed your life for your children. Why would you risk all that you hold so dear, for the sake of a woman you've known less than a week?'

'I can't.'

'No. And even if you could, I wouldn't have you do so. I've no more desire to force myself into a family that doesn't want me, than you have to take me on. I have my own priorities. You may call Flora's writing rabble-rousing, but to me…'

'It's something you need to do. You're being true to yourself, Constance. I wouldn't have you any other way.'

Her face crumpled. 'I wish you hadn't said that.'

It was like a punch to the gut. There, in that one sentence, in the face she was already hiding from him, frantically stirring her coffee, was all the proof he needed of her feelings for him. Grayson had to grip the edge of the seat tightly in order to stop himself from reaching for her, before taking a final swig of whisky-infused cold coffee to resist throwing caution to the winds.

'I was very happy,' Constance continued after a moment. 'At least, I was quite content before I met you. We've escaped reality for a spell and it's been lovely, but it's given us both a false impression. We think that we're...' It was her turn to finish her coffee, grimacing as she did so. 'When we look back, we'll both see that we were mistaken. We'll have some fond memories, but we'll be glad we were not so foolish as to believe what we're feeling now would last.' She got to her feet. 'You'll see, I'm right.'

He stared at her outstretched hand, for a moment unable to understand what she meant by it. No! The protest was so vehement, he was astonished that he hadn't shouted it aloud. What good would come of a protracted ending? She was right, and it was his own fault, for he'd given her no option. But to say farewell like this, in a public coffee house.

He got up, taking her hand. Their fingers clung. He wasn't sure if he could speak without his voice breaking. 'What will you do? I mean after—will you go back to teaching?'

'The battle isn't over yet, Grayson.'

'You don't win people over by preaching at them. They don't take kindly to having the error of their ways pointed out. If you must carry on this crusade, stop trying to reason with them, tug on their heartstrings.' He lifted her hand to his lips, turning it over to kiss her palm. 'I won't ever forget you. Say goodbye to Angus for me.'

'He'll miss you.'

A tear stole down her cheek. There was such yearning in her eyes, it was all he could do to prevent himself pulling her into his arms. Helplessly, he watched her turn her back on him, picking her way among the tables. Through the window he saw her, head bowed, heading up the Canongate. Then he slumped back on to the bench before waving the hovering waitress over and ordering another large whisky.

Chapter Eleven

The tale I am about to relate is not one of Mr Scott's confections, but the unvarnished truth of an event witnessed firsthand by Flora.

There once was a Highland village. Let's call it Clachan Bridge for the sake of argument, for that was its name, though it could easily have been a village in Sutherland or almost anywhere in the Highlands. Among the many cruel atrocities inflicted on its inhabitants while the land was being cleared to make way for sheep, one stands out for its heartless vindictiveness. As the cottages were being systematically burned, a young mother managed to drag the crib containing her newborn baby to safety in the nick of time. Seeing what she had done,

one of the factor's men strode up to the distraught woman and ordered her to remove the infant from the crib.

'We're under orders to torch all dwellings,' he sneered. 'I reckon this qualifies.' He then set fire to the crib.

'Where is my baby to sleep tonight?' the young mother sobbed.

'Under the stars with you,' the man replied callously, 'with a moss-covered rock as a pillow.'

The child died from the cold that night, and his mother three days later from a broken heart. They were buried together under a moss-covered rock. Remember this true story when you cheer the Staffords of Sutherland, Glengarry and their ilk, parading proudly in their plaid during the King's visit. The truth is not only stranger than fiction, it is infinitely more unjust and cruel.

Flora MacDonald, *New Jacobite Journal*

Leith Docks—Thursday, 15th August 1822

Constance huddled into the shadow of the Custom House, surveying the massed crowds waiting to welcome King George IV ashore with a mixture of astonishment, disbelief and disgust. Even though she'd watched the city fill to overflowing in the last month, she'd managed to persuade herself that there would be enough who felt like her to temper the whole-heartedness of the welcome. Yet here was what looked like the whole of Scotland decked out in its finest. And out there anchored in the Forth estuary could be seen the three masts of the *Royal George*, where the King would be donning his finery ready to disembark. A King who, the loyal *Edinburgh Observer* had claimed without a trace of irony, was a true Jacobite and royal Stuart. Aye right, as Grayson would have said.

Grayson. She ought to be used to the squeeze of her heart each time she thought of him. Her hand went automatically to the silver brooch depicting two figures in a small boat holding hands. She'd it worn every day since it was delivered to Coates Crescent on her birthday. There had been no message to accompany it. There had been no need for one.

Had her memories of Grayson become merely fond, in the month since she'd seen him? Had her feelings diminished, as she had so confidently predicted they would? Not a whit of it. No matter how many hours she worked, she had never been too tired to think of him. He'd been in her thoughts when she fell asleep and he was still there when she awoke. Everything reminded her of him, not least poor Angus. Walking the dog alone made her realise how lonely she was. Had she been content before, as she had claimed that last day in the Canongate coffee house? She was having to work blooming hard not to let Pearl see how miserable she was now, that was for sure. Absence, she could all too easily convince herself, had made her heart grow much fonder. Which was why she was here, hoping to catch a glimpse of him in the earnest hope that the reality would disappoint. And if it didn't, then seeing him in his chosen role as father would surely do the trick.

The unseasonable torrential rain which had forced the King to delay his planned disembarkation yesterday had given way to light cloud and patches of blue sky, and the gale had died down to a gentle breeze. Just as well, Constance thought darkly, for a display of just what, exactly, a Highlander kept under a kilt whipped up by the wind was most certainly not on Sir Walter's lengthy list of planned entertainments. Dear God, it was to be hoped the King would decide against the Garb of

Old Gaul in which to disembark. Smiling, she recalled Grayson's description of George being landed flapping like a monster cod from the royal barge to the Shore.

Grayson again! She had come early to secure this vantage point. Not only did it give her an excellent view of the landing point across the Shore, it gave her an excellent view of the reserved seats on the other side of the Custom House. She couldn't know for certain that he would be there with his children, but she knew him well enough. It was the best location, and he'd want the best for Shona and Neil. Eyeing the crowds, she wondered if she'd been overly optimistic. It was highly unlikely that she'd be able to pick him out among the throng. She was doomed to disappointment. But since she was here in her capacity as Flora to watch the shenanigans unfold, she might as well keep a look out for him.

It was, she reluctantly conceded, taking mental notes, a fine spectacle that Sir Walter and his band of merry men had orchestrated. Leith was alive with Highlanders, soldiers, dignitaries and tradesmen, all dressed in their finery, women bedecked in tartan sashes with tartan bows in their bonnets and hordes of children getting under everyone's feet. The denizens of Edinburgh and many thousands more were here in their Sunday best with their families and in some cases even their dogs, waving flags, brandishing tartan banners, cheering and smiling. The Highlands must have been stripped bare of heather right enough, for everyone wore a sprig of it—another of Sir Walter's decrees. Crowds were already lining the route the King would take, up Leith Walk to Picardy Place, where he'd be formally presented with the keys of the city. Would Grayson wait there, rather than make the journey to Leith? It was too late for her to change her plans now.

There were people clustered on the rooftops, hanging precariously out of windows, on makeshift platforms, clinging dangerously to the stone pier, all straining to be the first to catch sight of the royal barge. The air was filled with the discordant sound of several pipers playing different tunes, competing with the drums of the infantry regiments, and the trumpets of the cavalry. Dogs were barking. Bunting adorned the buildings and was strung across the streets. An armada of barges and pleasure craft crammed full of more spectators crowded the small crescent of the Shore where the drawbridge had been raised, and many more at anchor around the larger entrance to the harbour. Out on the Firth of Forth there were paddle steamers circling too. Was the *Carrick Castle* one of them? *Welcome! In our hearts you reign Sovereign!* proclaimed one garishly embroidered banner. Constance snorted in derision.

Out of the corner of her eye she noticed the occupants of the main stand were having to shift to accommodate a party of new arrivals. A disgruntled trio were being ousted from their prime seats. A boy and a girl were being ushered along to take their place by a tall leanly built man with close-cropped black hair tinged with silver at the temples. He was wearing neither hat nor gloves nor tartan, but a plain, well-cut black coat and trousers. He had a strong-featured face, the skin tanned, the deep-set grey-blue eyes crinkled at the corners, framed by dark lashes. She knew exactly where the lines of his tan stopped. Her fingers knew every callus and scar on his hands. The first time she'd seen him, she'd been sure they must have met before. Their eyes had met and she'd felt it like a shock, the jolt of recognition. *I know you.*

Grayson took his place between his son and daughter, both of whom wore a sprig of heather. He leant over the better to hear something Shona was whispering, frowning slightly, casting his gaze around. He wasn't looking for Constance, why should he be, but she sank into the shadows all the same. His daughter's gown was the latest fashion, white muslin by the looks of it, with short, puffed sleeves and a deep ruffle at the hemline trimmed with pale blue ribbon. Her shawl was pale blue silk to match the lining of her bonnet. The whole had an elegant simplicity that was testament to good taste and the money to indulge it. Grayson's daughter was not a beauty but she was striking, with glossy black hair and big, wide-spaced eyes under rather fierce brows and a generous mouth curved into a smile that was very like her father's. The boy, Neil looked younger than his fourteen years. Aside from the same fierce eyebrows, he bore little resemblance to either his sister or his father, slenderly built and fey-looking with a mop of light brown hair flopping over a high brow, a face that was all pointed chin and cheekbones. He was tugging at his father's coat, pointing out at the Firth, presumably at the King's yacht. Grayson was nodding, listening intently to whatever the boy was saying when Shona said something that made them all laugh.

They were happy. Grayson had told her so numerous times, and here was the evidence. There was no need for Constance to feel excluded, because that would be to imply she had ever been included. There, seeing them had done the trick. She wouldn't waste any more time pining after what she couldn't have. Now she could concentrate on absorbing the spectacle unfolding in front of her. Flora's heart-rending tales still needed some ballast, and heaven knows, there was plenty here.

She tore her eyes away from Grayson and his family The procession of dignitaries was unravelling as the clock ticked and the King still made no appearance. A number of the horsemen had dismounted. Did they realise they looked, in Grayson's words, like a bunch of eejits, these men in their tasselled boots and their Spanish cloaks, surrounded as they were by the sea of faux Highland warriors in their plaids wielding their rusty claymores? What were they supposed to represent? Walter Scott's notion of heraldry, doubtless, but they looked to Constance like a troop of minstrels in search of an audience, or the lost cast from one of Shakespeare's more obscure plays. Their steeds were similarly, preposterously decked out with rosettes and braiding and tassels. On the other side of the Shore, archers and lancers and constables vied for space. The noise was enough to give anyone a megrim, with trumpets and cornets vying with bagpipes and drums, none of them in tune or even playing the same refrain. No wonder the King had decided not to come ashore. If she was George, she'd be contemplating turning tail and heading back to England.

She was considering turning tail herself, when a gun was fired from the *Royal George*, and all other noise ceased. The retort from cannon fired from strategic points across the city echoed out, and the cheering began. Excitement in Leith was at a visceral fever pitch when the King finally appeared on the deck of the yacht. He was not wearing a kilt, but a nautical uniform of some sort, presumably an admiral, since this was the highest rank in the navy, as far as Constance knew. The crowd surged around her, mercifully obscuring her view as he was lowered into the barge with its sixteen oarsmen, which then began to make its way to the harbour entrance, followed by a number of smaller official boats. Standards were raised as the royal barge passed each stage of the long procession to the jetty, and pipes wailed. It was almost half an hour before His Majesty was helped ashore, his crew standing with their oars upright, the King leaning heavily on one official, his feet barely making contact with the flower-strewn red carpet before another official flung himself on to his knees and kissed the plump royal hand. Though he was a great deal fatter than she'd imagined, the King had a certain statesman-like dignity, Constance reluctantly conceded, and a surprisingly charming smile. She wondered what he was making of the spectacle put on for him.

Walter Scott had staged a pantomime of gigantic proportions, and she'd had her fill of it. In the midst of the thronging crowd, she had never felt so alone. Was she the only person in Leith not overcome with hysterical excitement and sheer joy to be in the royal presence? No, there was one other who she was certain would be feeling the same. One other who would appreciate the preposterousness of it all.

Grayson was staring straight at her. Their eyes met, and her heart leapt, and for a long,

precious moment it was as it always was between them.

There you are.

Here I am.

Her hand was involuntarily reaching out
towards him when she caught herself. She
was a forty-year-old spinster without a home
to call her own, whose only paid employment
was coming to an end in a matter of weeks.
And here she was staring longingly at a rich,
successful, self-made man and his handsome,
happy family, like some wee orphaned waif
with her nose pressed against the window of
a toy shop. Mortified, tears stinging her eyes,
Constance turned away.

Shona and Neil were in their element, their
eyes out on stalks as they gazed in awe at the
spectacle of massed pipe bands and marching
bands, and the officials in their finery prancing about like roosters, and the hawkers selling heather and flags and meat pies and wee
drams, and tartan bloody everything. Grayson was bored and on edge.

It was daft of him to imagine that he might
bump into Constance. Even if she was here,
looking for fresh material for Flora Mac-
Donald, he'd never pick her out in this crush.

He shouldn't even be looking for her, yet he couldn't seem to help himself. Not a day had gone past since last he saw her, that he had not thought of her. The pain of missing her was almost physical. For days, when he first got back to Glasgow, he'd tried to persuade himself he was suffering from gut ache. Too much rich Edinburgh food, probably. Or maybe it was Constance who was too rich for his blood. Hurling himself into work hadn't helped, and doing his best to enter into his children's enthusiastic preparations for this visit had made it much worse, for then he had Flora's sardonic commentary in his head, vying with Shona and Neil's excited speculation.

He was being daft to think he'd see her, of course it was, even though the chances were she was here, watching the mayhem unfold, maybe looking for the *Carrick Castle* in the crush of boats out on the water. It was a waste of time, looking out for her, and what the devil good would it do anyway, if he did happen to see her? He should be enjoying himself, chuffed to bits to be sitting here with his offspring, for they had elected to be here with him and not with their grandparents who were up at Picardy Place waiting to witness the King being given the keys to the city.

'Because I want to see the King actually set foot on Scottish soil,' Neil had declared this morning.

'And because I know the trouble you've gone to, to get us a good view,' Shona had added.

He *was* pleased as punch to have satisfied his children, but he couldn't care less that he'd got one over on the Murrays. In fact, he'd been hard put to not to feel guilty, seeing the disappointment writ large on Lady Glenbranter's face this morning, when she'd called at the hotel only to be informed that the seats she had reserved for the children weren't required. She'd come without her husband. That hadn't surprised him.

A gun went off out on the Firth and was answered by a cacophony of cannon.

'The King is coming,' Shona said, clutching his hand. 'Look, they've raised a flag.'

Neil, consulting a dog-eared booklet, began to read out the order of ceremony. Judging by the jostling for position, it was going to be more like disorder. Some of the officials, in their outlandish velvet and gold outfits were struggling to get back on their horses. One of the archers had fallen into the water, and was in danger of upsetting the dinghy he was clinging to. The cobblestones were still soaking from the rain which had fallen relentlessly since Grayson and his family had arrived in Edinburgh two nights ago. The appalling weather had forced the King to delay his landing, but the winds had died down today, thanks be, given the number of men there who were dressed in flimsy plaids.

Flora MacDonald would have a field day, parodying all this. Grayson had managed to lay his hands on a number of back issues of the *New Jacobite Journal*. Constance's alter ego had a vicious pen and a knack of seeing past all the pomp and ceremony right to the hypocritical heart of this royal visit. Reading her work should have helped reconcile him to the necessity of their parting. If Lord Glenbranter, God forbid, ever got hold of the *New Jacobite Journal*, he'd have an apoplexy. If he discovered that his low-born son-in-law had been consorting with such a revolutionary, nothing would stop him in his efforts to prevent his grandchildren from being contaminated. But Flora's writing simply evoked the author. Recognising his own words in the piece about Glengarry, Grayson had been forced to stop reading for a moment, missing her so much he felt physically sick. Her humour was so black that it was difficult to see sometimes, but what she'd been writing of late—now that was in a different league entirely. No one, reading those gut-wrenching stories of Highland dispossession could fail to be moved, surely. No wonder she found it impossible to keep quiet about what she'd seen. Had her evocative tales found a bigger audience? He couldn't bring himself to believe it. It must be breaking her heart. It was breaking his, thinking of the waste of her talent and her time and her passion.

Was she here, wincing at the skirl of the bagpipes and wrinkling her nose at the smell of wet wool? He and she were probably the only pair of people in Leith not wearing tartan or heather. How long did it take, for the love of God, for one fat man to get off his yacht, into a barge and on to the shore? There would be all sorts of speeches to welcome the King, according to Neil's programme of events, and then the parade would take itself off up Leith Walk. He could take a walk to Newhaven when it was over if he fancied torturing himself a bit more. Just as well really, that he had Neil and Shona with him, champing at the bit to follow the procession back to the city.

The King's barge was finally being tied up, and someone was precariously balanced, one foot on the jetty the other on the edge of the barge, to help him out. His son informed him that the King was wearing an admiral's uniform, and his daughter pointed out the diamond-encrusted brooch as the Order of the Thistle, but the hairs on the back of Grayson's neck were standing on end. Looking across the sea of faces, he spotted her, and though she was a good twenty feet away, their gazes locked and his heart leapt. As she turned away, he was already on his feet. Belatedly remembering his children, he commanded them to stay strictly put before pushing his way to the end of the row, leaping down from the platform and giving chase.

'Constance!' He caught up with her at the front entrance of the Custom House on Commercial Street, where they had met the day they sailed to Inchcolm Island. 'Constance!'

She turned. For a long moment they simply stared silently at each other. Then their hands found each other. They stood there together, ignored by the jostling hordes, utterly rapt in a world that was quite their own, and everything he'd been telling himself over the last month, about their parting being for the best, about how impossible it was even to think of seeing her again, of how he'd stop missing her in time, all of it, he knew with crystal-clear clarity in that moment, to be completely ridiculous. 'Constance,' he said softly.

She gave a start, tugging her hands free, breaking the spell. 'You'll be missing the speeches.'

'Will I? Thank heaven for small mercies.'

'You can't leave your children on their own.'

'They'll be fine, for a few moments. I can't believe you saw me in this vast crowd.'

'I wasn't spying on you, I—well the truth is, actually I was.'

'I'm glad. I was looking out for you. I kept telling myself there was no chance, but I kept looking all the same.'

'I knew where you'd be.'

'I was where you told me to be.'

'Because it was the best spot. I wasn't planning on tracking you down.'

'Constance, just shoosh. I'm glad you did.'

She nodded, her smile tremulous. 'I know, but you should go. As soon as the speeches are over, it will be mayhem.'

'I've been reading Flora's work in that journal you write for. Some of your older writing and your most recent articles too.'

'Paul said they'd bring a tear to a glass eye.'

'I don't know about that. They damn nearly brought tears to a rough shipbuilder's eyes.'

'"Stop trying to reason with them, tug on their heartstrings." That was what you suggested, and that's what I've done. Not that it's making much difference. You're probably our only new reader.'

'You should write a book instead.'

'Maybe I will, when this is over. You really should get back to your family.'

'I've missed you, Constance. I save things up to tell you, and then you're not there and there's no one else to tell.'

'Don't. We agreed...'

'Do you think I don't remember every word of that last painful conversation? It doesn't make any difference though. My head tells me we did the right thing, but I don't want to listen to my head. If it's different for you just tell me. I'd be glad to hear it, in fact. Eventually, I'll be glad too.'

'I'm afraid I can't oblige. It's not remotely different for me. I came here today thinking that if I could see you with your family—who you really, really should be getting back to—then it would cure me of missing you. I wanted to remind myself of how impossible it all still is, but when I saw you, I didn't want to hear what I was telling myself.'

'Would it be terribly wrong of me to ask to see you again, while I'm here?'

'Yes, but if you don't ask me I'll be bitterly disappointed.'

'Then you will? If you can find the time, that is, what with your writing and your duties to Mrs Winston, assuming she's back?'

'She is. Would you like to join Angus and I for our walk tomorrow morning?'

The relief he felt was frightening, so he decided not to think about it. 'The usual time?'

'Same time, same place. Now go, please.'

She gave him a shove. He threw her a smile over his shoulder then ran, pushing his way through the crowd, arriving back at the platform just in time to see the King's carriage drive off. He waved at Shona, who was looking anxious.

'Where have you been?' she asked, when the pair of them joined him on the street.

'I saw a friend and went to say hello. It would have been rude not to.'

'What friend?'

'Would you look at that, I don't think I've

ever seen so many carriages in a procession like that. And what regiment is that following on behind, Neil?'

'They're dragoons.'

'Shall we join everyone else and make our way back up to the city, or do you want to wait until the crowd goes down? Shona, what do you want to do?'

'Neil wants to walk behind the procession.' She took his arm, put her other through her brother's. 'I didn't know you had any friends, Pa.'

Chapter Twelve

Friday, 16th August 1822

When Constance arrived at the park Grayson was already there, as he always used to be, stowing his notebook and pencil in his pocket, as he always did.

'Still working every spare minute, I see,' she said. She laughed as the terrier yapped frantically for Grayson's attention. 'Angus has missed you.'

'Angus can wait.'

'He can.' She dropped the lead and stepped into his arms, burrowing her face into his chest. He held her tightly and she closed her eyes, breathing in the scent of his soap and his linen. It felt so right, but then it began to feel oddly awkward. 'Angus's turn now,' Constance said, breaking free.

Grayson knelt to scratch the terrier's head, then picked up the lead. 'Will we walk?'

'Did you follow the procession yesterday? I hear the King won the hearts of all by returning the keys to the city when he was handed them.'

'I don't give a damn about the King.'

'He's spending the day with his friends at Dalkeith House. I doubt there can be a ptarmigan left in the Highlands, for so many have been shot and sent as gifts for the pot. And grouse. It's as well we're past the Glorious Twelfth, or he'd be obliged to content himself with...'

'Hodge-podge and sheep's heid. What's wrong, Constance?'

'I don't know what we're doing here. We said our goodbyes, and we both know there's no question of any sort of future for us, so— what *are* we doing, Grayson? Torturing ourselves?'

'Is that what it feels like? The last thing I'd ever want to do is hurt you. Should I go?'

'No. That would be worse. Wouldn't it?'

He laughed, then sighed. 'I'm not sure of anything any more. Look, here's our usual spot, shall we sit down?'

'The grass will be damp. It's rained almost

non-stop since you left. No, don't give me your coat to sit on, you'll ruin it.'

'I care only marginally more for this coat than I do for the King. Come here and sit down beside me and let's try and see if two intelligent, middle-aged people can make sense of what they're doing.'

'You'll probably get more sense out of Angus.' Constance lowered herself carefully on to the coat, grimacing. 'My knee.'

'What's wrong with it?'

'Gout, probably.'

Grayson gave a snort of laughter. 'It will be dropsy next, by your next birthday, you mark my words.'

'I bumped into my bedpost in the dark, if you must know. I was working late, and my candle blew out, and—well, you can imagine.'

'Would you like me to kiss it better?'

His smile was teasing, wicked, warm. Constance forgot to feel awkward and remembered how it had been between them from the beginning, as if they could read each other's thoughts, as if they had known each other all their lives, as if they were meant to be together. 'Yes please,' she said.

He laughed. And then his smile faded as their gazes locked and their fingers twined and they leaned into one another, and their lips met and clung for a long moment while their world resettled. And then they kissed. Their kisses were gentle and tender. They were soothing, reassuring kisses, without any other intent. The passion that was always there between them smouldered in the background of those kisses, but they were not the kind of kisses to stoke the fire. Constance had tried so very hard not to put her feelings into words. Those kisses made the words unnecessary. When they finally drew apart, her lashes were wet with tears.

'I can't bear to make you cry,' Grayson said, kissing her lids. 'I should go, I'm being selfish.'

'I don't want you to go. Since you went away, it's not only the Edinburgh skies that have been grey.'

'I wouldn't have put it that way, but couldn't have put it better.' Grayson twined his fingers around hers, pressing a kiss to her knuckles. 'The days seem driech, even when the sun is shining. Not that it has, much, since we're having a typical Scottish summer.'

She laughed weakly. 'I've certainly been under a cloud. Poor Pearl keeps asking me if she's done anything to offend me. She has been my only friend, save for Paul, for so long, and I struggle to give her the time of day at the moment. I feel so guilty, it's not her fault that she's not you.'

'Yesterday, Shona asked me why I'd run off, and I said I'd spotted a friend in the crowd. "I didn't know you had any friends," she said to me. It hadn't even occurred to me until she said it, that I don't. I've lots of business acquaintances, but I don't have any friends as such. Out of the mouth of babes, as the saying goes.'

He plucked a long blade of grass and began to twist it round his finger. 'You can't miss what you don't have. I didn't know that I was lonely. I didn't realise that I was missing someone to laugh with, to talk to until I met you. Proper adult company, not my children, but someone who I can talk to about— anything really, save work and my children, I suppose. I enjoy your company, and I'm lonely without it. Your conversation isn't the only thing I miss about you,' he added, with a devilish smile, 'but believe it or not, it's the main thing.'

'I do believe you because it's exactly the same for me.'

'I shouldn't be relieved to hear you say so, but I am.'

'So what are you suggesting, Grayson, that we become friends? Correspond? Meet occasionally for coffee and cake?'

'I'm saying we *are* friends. I suppose I'm saying that there's not actually anything wrong with me having a friend. Quite the contrary. Even the Murrays couldn't object to that.'

'Until they discovered that I'm not only a female but a rabble-rouser to boot. I think you might find it difficult to explain me away as your friend, then.'

'Ah well, as the saying goes, God loves a trier. It doesn't alter the fact that what I told Shona yesterday was the truth.' He cast the blade of grass away and squeezed her hand. 'We *are* friends, aren't we?'

'Best friends.' Who most likely would never see each other again, after today. Constance pushed the thought ruthlessly to the back of her mind. 'Talking of friends, Pearl has invited one of hers to come and stay for the second week of the King's visit. What about your children's grandparents, have they arrived yet?'

Grayson grimaced. 'They're here all right, staying at Oman's in Waterloo Street.'

'Which is only the second-best hotel in Edinburgh.'

'So Neil made a point of telling them, for he was well primed by that Urquhart fellow. The Murrays left it far too late to rent anything more than a bedchamber, no suite with a sitting room, and worse still, their servants have been boarded elsewhere.'

'A victory for Clan Maddox then?'

'Not really. As the old man made sure to point out, money can buy a superior hotel room, but only breeding can secure an audience with His Majesty.'

'Charming. Does that mean you've actually spoken to them? I thought your plan was to avoid them at all costs?'

'That was a misguided plan.' Grayson stared down at their clasped hands, frowning. 'That last day, you asked me if I'd ever tried to mend bridges with them, and I told you that it wasn't up to me.'

'You said it wasn't you who had burned them, I remember.'

'Which is true.' He sighed. 'But it now strikes me as being a bit petty on my part. And when you asked me if they were land improvers too, and I didn't even know that much, I was more than a bit ashamed. It's been seventeen years, maybe nearer eighteen, since Eliza and I were married, and she's been gone for eight of them. I know I've changed, but whether they know that, and whether they care or not, I've not a clue. For the last eight years, they've been trying to lure my children away from me, and I've been burying my head in the sand, trying not to rock the boat and hoping everything will turn out for the best. I'm a practical man, a problem solver. A bridge builder not a bridge burner, if you like. I've realised that ignoring the situation isn't going to resolve anything.'

'You've clearly been doing a lot of soul searching since I last saw you.'

'That's what tends to happen, when you meet someone who turns your nicely ordered life upside down and disrupts your sleep into the bargain.' His smile was strained. 'I don't approve of the world the Murrays inhabit, where your bloodline matters more than whether or not you're a decent person. I don't like their attitudes, I heartily dislike the way they look down their noses at anyone who doesnae speak with a fancy English accent, who has made their money by hard graft, and who doesn't need a servant to wipe his—' He broke off, shaking his head. 'You get my drift.'

'And I couldn't agree more.'

'Aye well, that's the problem. Most people wouldn't agree, and though I hate to say it, I can actually see that there's advantages to be had, in having the right name and background, and the connections that go with it. I've never made any attempt to force my children down one path or another. If they choose to be part of the Murrays aristocratic world, I'll have to live with it, but I want them to have the choice, and I want them to be the ones to decide what's best for them.'

'Isn't that what all of you want, both you and their grandparents?'

'You'd think so, wouldn't you? I've hoped so for the last eight years, but I'm not so sure now. I've been far too passive, this is too important a matter for me to sit back any more, doing nothing but hope, so I'm going to have to find a way of making them listen to my point of view.'

'Which means you'll have to mend fences? That is a very noble thing to do, when they must know you could simply cut the connection.'

'It's not noble, it's the right thing to do, and I'd never cut them off.'

'No,' Constance said, smiling, 'because you're much more of a gentleman, in my humble opinion, that Lord Glenbranter will ever be.'

'I think you're perhaps just a wee bit biased. It might be the right thing to do, but I can't say it's a task that's filling me with delight. *She's* not so bad, but he's a curmudgeonly old bugger. And that,' Grayson said, rolling his shoulders and stretching his legs out in front of him, 'is more than enough of the Murrays for now.'

'You're not the only one who has used their sleepless nights to do a bit of soul searching, you know,' Constance said. '"What will you do, after?" you asked me that last day. I didn't want to hear the question, never mind answer it, but unfortunately, everything my best friend says to me sticks in my head.'

'And have you come up with any answers?'

Constance shook her head. 'It feels like giving up, to look for a teaching post. And I'm not ready to give up, even if Paul is. I still feel like I have unfinished business.' Constance squeezed his fingers. 'I'm forty years old, I've at least another twenty years ahead of me.'

'Ach, you're not even halfway through.'

'Thank you for my lovely birthday present, by the way. It's perfect and I wear it every day. You'll tell me I'm daft, but I like to imagine that by doing so I have you with me in spirit.'

Grayson shook his head, smiling sheepishly. 'I don't think you're being daft at all. I carry this about with me all the time. Do you remember giving me this?' he asked, pulling something from his pocket.

'Inchcolm, the pink shell! How could I forget?' She smoothed her hand over his cheek, leaning in for his kiss. 'You have no idea how much I've missed you, and how often I've told myself that it will get easier in time.'

'Oh, believe me, I have every idea.'

'What are we to do? All the reasons we had for parting are still there. Nothing has changed.'

'One thing has, for me. I can't imagine my life without you. And yet that is precisely what I must do.'

'Oh.' A lump rose in Constance's throat. She tried to swallow it, blinking furiously to prevent herself crying. 'Sometimes when you say exactly what I have been thinking, I wish you hadn't. I can't bear to say goodbye again.'

'Then we won't. Not yet, any road.' Grayson

frowned. 'The King is here for a fortnight. It's my chance to see if I can forge some sort of relationship with the Murrays, and it's Flora's last chance to win hearts and minds through the *NJJ*, but—what do you think, Constance? Can we manage to find a morsel of time to spend together while all that's going on?'

'You were looking forward to spending the better part of this fortnight with Neil and Shona.'

'If I'm to build bridges with the Murrays, I'll need to show them that I'm willing to share my children with them. I'll be honest,' Grayson added ruefully, 'if being with them requires me to sit through another day like yesterday, I'll be happy to bequeath that dubious honour to them. What do you think?'

'I know what I want.'

'Aye, that's the easy part right enough. Come on, Angus is stirring, that's a sure sign we've been sitting here long enough.' He got to his feet with his usual enviable ease, holding out his hand. 'Are you sure you don't want me to kiss that knee of yours better?'

'I can think of much more interesting places for you to kiss.'

'What was that you were saying, about wishing I did not say what was on your mind,' he said, wrapping his arms around her. 'One of the other ways I while away the sleepless nights is by torturing myself, imagining just that.'

'Let's see if the reality is better,' Constance said, putting her arms around his neck.

Their lips met. Their tongues touched, and this time their kisses were passionate. Far too passionate for decency's sake. 'Angus,' Constance said, her breathing ragged.

'Angus might be old and toothless, but I bet he's had his moments.' Grayson picked up his coat, shaking it out. 'You were right about the rain, this is soaking.'

'You'll catch a chill if you put it on.'

'Good, I need something to cool me down. The things you do to me, woman!'

'You do them to me too. I'm not sure that friends are meant to kiss like that.'

'We're best friends, remember?'

'Ah, so *best* friends can kiss.' Stooping, Constance gathered up Angus's lead. 'Will you walk with us tomorrow morning?'

'Definitely, I wouldn't want to disappoint Angus.'

'What have you planned for the rest of the day?'

'I'll find that out when I get back to the hotel and wake up my slug-abed son.'

* * *

Having fed and watered Angus, Constance was surprised to find Pearl waiting for her in the morning room. 'You're up and about early.'

'I thought I'd join you for morning coffee. Did you and Angus enjoy your walk? Where did you go?'

'Oh, the usual place. You know Angus, he's a creature of habit.'

'Like me. And you too. In fact I've been thinking my dear, that we are all of us rather stuck in a rut.'

'Have you? What has brought this on?'

'You've not been yourself this past while. Don't think I haven't noticed.' Pearl was a small, round apple-shaped woman with a fluffy halo of silver curls above a plump-cheeked countenance designed for smiling. Today however, a frown drew her delicately drawn brows together. 'You are remembering,' she said, 'that my friend Isabel is arriving next week.'

'I hadn't forgotten. I thought we could give her the blue bedchamber.'

'I don't want to talk to you about the house-keeping arrangements, Constance.'

'That sounds ominous. What *do* you want to talk to me about?'

Pearl set her coffee cup down, shaking her head at the offer of a top up. 'Isabel is one of my oldest friends, as you know. She's fallen on rather hard times since her husband died. Unlike my dear Kenneth, who left me very well provided for, poor Isabel is having to cut her cloth to fit considerably reduced circumstances.'

'I see. You'd like to offer her a home, is that it?'

'I'd like to see if we would suit, yes.'

'Of course. My staying here with you was always meant to be a temporary arrangement.'

'No, no, my dear, you've got hold of the wrong end of the stick entirely. I'm not about to throw you out on to the street. There's no shortage of rooms in this house, though I do think—perhaps I will take another cup of coffee after all, if you would be so good. Thank you.'

'I know I've been poor company this last while.'

'I've not seen you so unhappy, Constance, since those dark days when you came here from Clachan Bridge. Oh, my dear, I am so sorry.'

'Sorry?' Constance tried not to panic. What had Pearl seen or heard?

'He told me himself,' she said.

'What? Who?' Grayson didn't know Pearl. 'Who told you what?'

'Why Paul, of course. He told me that he'd spoken to you about shutting down the journal, and that you had taken it very badly. He followed you out to make sure you were all right.' Pearl pursed her lips, shaking her head. 'He made some cryptic remark about Bonnie Prince Charlie doing his work for him. Do you have any idea what he meant?'

'About Bonnie Prince Charlie?' Constance busied herself with her coffee spoon. 'Just a silly joke between us, that's all. Pearl, I'm so sorry I've been such a wet blanket.'

'My dear, *I'm* sorry that you can't see it's for the best. Forgive me for being frank, but I think you need to start thinking about life beyond Flora.'

'So you agree with Paul, then?'

'Oh, Paul! How do you think I became acquainted with Paul Michaels? He was up in court before my husband twenty years ago, being sued for libel by some prominent figure whom he had offended with his views. My husband happened to side with Paul on that occasion. Paul is a good man, Constance, and heaven knows his heart is in the right place but he's a political butterfly. It's in his nature always to be on the lookout for a new cause to support, a different battle to fight. Never mind what Paul thinks, it's what you think that matters. You're still a relatively young woman. You have many years ahead of you.'

Years to be spent without Grayson. To her horror, Constance found herself on the edge of tears. Her encounter with him had been so wonderful. After all these weeks of being so miserable and missing him so terribly, it was such a joy simply to be in his company, but what now? Weren't they simply putting off the inevitable, by continuing to see each other? When the King left, so would Grayson, and the agony of missing him would begin all over again. Was it better to store up a few more memories, or were they, as she had suggested, simply torturing themselves? What they were really doing, was burying their heads in the sand like the poor ostriches providing the feathers for the ladies who were attending the King's Drawing Room. They couldn't keep on blithely ignoring reality because they didn't want to face it.

'What is it, my dear?' Pearl levered herself with difficulty out of her chair to join her on the sofa. 'You really must stop blaming yourself. You have done all you can. Your latest Flora pieces have been excellent, and so heartwrenching.'

'Thank you.' Constance sniffed. 'I appreciate you saying that, but they are clearly not wrenching nearly enough hearts.'

'It's not that people don't care, my dear, it's that they don't believe there's anything to be done.'

'So the Highlands will be stripped of people and inhabited by sheep, and no one will lift a finger to stop it?'

'Sheep make money for the landowners and crofters do not. I do worry about all those poor dispossessed souls. Half of them probably don't even speak English.'

'Out of sight, out of mind,' Constance said bitterly. 'That is why they are shipped off to Canada.'

'Perhaps they make a better life for themselves there. It is possible. No wait,' Pearl said, putting her cup down decisively, 'before you treat me to a lecture, let me speak.'

'I don't pontificate—do I?'

'I'm afraid so, but it's so very clear that

you speak from the heart that I don't ever feel as if I'm being lectured. If females could serve as politicians, you would have my vote. If I had a vote. My goodness, can you imagine how the world would change then?' Pearl smiled wryly, shaking her head. 'However, we have to make the best of the world as it is, warts and all, and it's time that you accepted that, I'm afraid. You are an idealist my dear, this will be difficult for you to hear, but sometimes we have to accept that a battle simply can't be won. You've fought the good fight. It's time to admit defeat and move on. Which brings me to the main point of our little chat. Isabel, my friend, isn't coming alone next week. She's going to be accompanied by James Fraser and his wife.'

'Fraser,' Constance repeated, slightly stunned by Pearl's home truths. 'That is my mother's maiden name.'

Pearl beamed. 'James is your first cousin, most anxious to make your acquaintance and to do what he can to make amends for the way his family treated your parents. His father was your mother's brother, your Uncle James. Now *he* had known of your existence, and of your situation since you first came to me, but wanted nothing to do with you. Young

James knew nothing of this, and it was only when your uncle died a couple of months ago, that I felt I could tell him when I was back home in July. He's desperate to meet you.'

'Is he?'

'Oh, very eager indeed. I understand completely why you had no interest in meeting the family members who treated all of you appallingly. Forcing your mother to choose between them and the man she loved, as if there was ever any chance Anne would opt for them. Then when you were born not a word, and when Anne died too—unforgivable. But James is different. A new generation, Constance, a fresh start. Have I done wrong in inviting him?'

'No, of course not, but—I'm sorry, Pearl, this is so much to take in.'

'A fresh start, Constance, that's what you need.' Pearl patted her hands. 'I don't want to steal his thunder, but I think your cousin and his wife have a proposition for you that you might find attractive. There's no imperative for you to accept it, I would happily have you stay here for another six years or another twenty, but I can't see you being happy with that prospect. You like to be doing something constructive, and you like to dance to your own tune. I wasn't surprised when you broke your engagement to that man Lockhart. You're not cut out to be someone's wife, any more than you're cut out to be a mere lady's companion. Once Paul has stopped publishing your work, one genteel old lady or even two, if Isobel comes to stay, won't keep you occupied. There now, I'll say no more. Wait until James Fraser and his wife get here. Take the time to get to know them both. Hear them out and think about it, that's all I ask, for your parent's sake. And for mine.'

Chapter Thirteen

Saturday, 17th August 1822

'Shona and her grandmother are off to visit a friend out at Cramond,' Grayson said, 'and Neil is accompanying his grandfather to the levee at Holyrood, after which the old man wants to introduce him to some of his friends. So I wondered, after we've walked Angus, if you were free to take a walk up Calton Hill with me?'

Constance had leapt out of bed this morning, eager to embrace the day, ridiculously excited about meeting Grayson. On the way to the park, her spirits had plummeted. She ought to tell him that they were making a mistake. But seeing him leaning against the tree, putting his notebook in his pocket, his smile reflecting her own simple delight, she had decided that really, it would be wrong not to make the most of what they had. It wasn't as if she was taking up precious time he might spend with his children either, so her conscience was quite clear. She smiled. 'I'd like that very much.'

'What about your knee?'

'Oh, it has been miraculously cured overnight, even without healing kisses.'

'Excellent.' Grayson took Angus's lead in one hand, and Constance's hand in the other. 'What the hell is a gentleman's levee, do you know?'

'A procession of men queuing up to kiss the King's hand, I think. Your son is going to be very bored.'

'That's excellent news. The last thing I want is for him to get a taste for high society.'

'Why let him go then?'

'He was desperate to meet the King, and I was desperate to spend a decent bit of time with you. The fates were conspiring to bring us together again.'

'And the sun is determined to shine on us too.'

But as they began their usual circuit of the parkland, Constance's mood began to darken again. 'I told you that Pearl has someone coming to stay next week, didn't I?'

'A friend, you said. What's the problem with that? Won't it mean you'll have more time to yourself?'

'No, quite the opposite. She's not coming alone.' She tugged the dog's lead. 'Angus isn't in the mood for his walk today.'

'That suits us fine, doesn't it? Let's get him home, and you can tell me what's bothering you.'

'When I got back to Coates yesterday, Pearl was already out of bed and waiting for me.'

'That sounds ominous.'

'Don't worry, she doesn't know about you. I thought at one point—but I was wrong, she was talking about Paul.'

'Ah, I see.'

Constance was forced to laugh. 'No, you don't but you will.' She wouldn't tell him that Paul had seen them together, it would worry him needlessly.

'I hope so. What was it Pearl wished to discuss with you that is making you so down in the mouth on this lovely day?'

'She—how do you say it, she burst my bubble. Essentially, she told me that I was a hopeless idealist who had to face up to the fact that despite my best efforts, my race was run. Her solution was to foist me off on to a cousin who, she says, has some sort of proposition for me. A cousin who I didn't even know existed, I might add.'

'Away!' Grayson exclaimed. 'I've never met the woman, but I know she's only ever had your best interests at heart. Wasn't it she who introduced you to Paul Michaels?'

'Yes, and since then she's been biting her tongue, waiting for me to realise that I'm wasting my time.'

'No, Constance, that's not fair. If she'd said so a year ago, would you have listened? You'd have told her you'd prove her wrong, wouldn't you?'

'But I haven't proved her wrong. Quite the reverse.'

'Not for the want of trying. God love you, you're still trying, and you won't give up will you, not until you're forced to.'

'Pearl thinks the same as you, that you can't stop what people see as progress.'

'What matters most is that you've tried,' Grayson said gently. 'You had to try and you have to keep on trying until you feel there's nothing left for you to do. You wouldn't be able to live with yourself otherwise.'

His words brought her to the verge of tears again. She was *not* going to cry. 'You know me too well.' She forced a watery smile.

'And so does Pearl. It's clear she loves you, Constance, and respects you too. Her keeping her thoughts to herself all this time is testament to that.'

'She says I'm an idealist, who has to dance to my own tune. That makes me sound horribly selfish, as well as possibly deluded.'

'You want to find your own niche in life. That's not selfish, it's admirable.'

'Admirable but deluded all the same, for what I want is to put an end to the Clearances.'

'Maybe Pearl's right then, and you need to find another way to change the world.'

'I could pretend I'm a man, and become a politician.'

'I'm biased of course, but I much prefer you as a woman.'

'When my cousin comes to stay next week, my time won't be my own, Grayson.'

'Then we should, as the saying goes, make hay together while the sun shines. Which it is, look.'

'It is. Here, give me Angus. Wait here for me, I'll only be ten minutes.'

* * *

It was probably just as well, Grayson thought as he waited on Maitland Street at the end of Coates Crescent, that their time together was going to be limited. When he was with her, all was well with the world, but when he wasn't, it was blindingly, depressingly clear that the situation was impossible. Constance was a distraction from his real purpose here in Edinburgh. He had enough on his plate, mending fences with the Murrays and spending time with Shona and Neil. Though now he came to think about it the two things were all tangled up. Today, for instance, it wasn't as if he was sacrificing time that should be spent with his family to spend it with Constance. He was at a loose end, she was at a loose end. Some time together was good for them both. A way for them both to let off steam. A rare moment in between all the other calls on their time, when they could be themselves. It was such a relief to be able to talk to her again, to laugh with her again. His best and only friend.

He smiled to himself. Who was he kidding? Yet he could think of no other more apt label to describe their relationship. His smile faded. They couldn't ignore the real world for ever. A few snatched moments over the next couple of weeks was all they would have. Would it be best simply not to have them? No, he wouldn't be able to resist seeing her, he knew that. Much better then, to do precisely what he'd suggested, and make hay while the sun shone. Not that it was shining particularly brightly today, actually.

He ignored the soppy way his heart leapt at the sight of Constance hurrying towards him, minus the toothless wonder that was Angus. 'The sun has changed its mind,' she said.

'Talking of light shows, did you see last night's illuminations?'

'Walter Scott's latest extravaganza. I heard the guns and rockets, but since Pearl can hardly walk the length of herself, and Angus was hiding under a bed, I decided to stay indoors.' She made to put her hand on his arm, then changed her mind. It irked him that they had to be discreet, he didn't like the implication that they had something to hide. 'You, I am sure, were walking the streets until the wee small hours with your children.'

'You're right. We were out until almost midnight, wandering around. There were candles in almost every window, and all sorts of displays on the public buildings with various symbols pledging allegiance to Georgie Boy. Crowns and thistles and royal arms, flags and shields, stars and a few designs that I couldn't make head nor tail of, but which my erudite offspring informed me were scenes from Scott's novels.'

'Your children enjoyed themselves, then?'

'Neil loved it. Shona thought it all clever enough, but ultimately a terrible waste of candles, and she was worried the noise was keeping people awake who had work to go to in the morning.'

'She sounds like a very practical young woman. Very like her father.' Constance slid him a sidelong glance. 'And in her looks too, I thought her very like you.'

She was clearly uncomfortable voicing even that much of an opinion. He didn't know what to make of it himself. His children were part of his other, real life, yet he was curious all the same. 'And what did you think of Neil?'

'I only saw them from a distance. They are clearly brother and sister, though they are very different.'

'They have their moments. Shona's so used to being the older sister, she's finding it difficult to adjust to Neil developing opinions of his own.'

'I thought you looked very happy together, the three of you. Comfortable with each other.'

'We spend a lot of time in each other's company.'

'I only saw you for a few moments and from a distance, but that was obvious. You…'

'I what? Go on.'

She bit her lip, frowning. 'It's not only that they so obviously love you, it's that they are completely at ease in your company. In my experience which, I'll admit is limited to living and teaching in the Highlands, fathers are all too often distant figures to be respected and feared, not teased and consulted, and with such affection.'

There was a lump in his throat. Devil take it, he was in the middle of Princes Street. 'Thank you,' Grayson said gruffly. 'I expect it comes of them having no mother, that makes us so close.'

'I think it comes simply from you being a father who actually sees them as people in their own right. People who might have opinions, I mean and heaven forefend, thoughts and ideas of their own. Who even encourages independent thought, as my own father did.'

'A high compliment indeed.'

'You're not like him in any other way.'

'I'm relieved to hear that.' He smiled at her, squeezing her fingers. 'Thank you. I mean it.'

'Yes.'

'I can see from that troubled look that what you really mean is yes, but...'

'You are such a complete little family, the three of you, and you've been like that for so long now, it's impossible to see how anyone else would fit in without seeming like an intruder.'

There was nothing to say to this. He was never so completely himself as when he was in Constance's company, but when he tried to imagine her even introducing her to his children, his mind skittered to a halt. He'd be on tenterhooks and so would she. Shona and Neil would be—what, confused and uninterested at best, and openly antagonistic at worst. No, there was absolutely nothing more to be said on the subject.

'Would you look at this traffic,' he said instead, inanely. 'There's carriages end to end all the way along Princes Street.'

'There must have been an accident.'

But as they reached the junction of Waterloo Place and Regent Bridge it became apparent that the cause of the increasing mayhem was not an accident, it was the sheer volume of gentlemen attempting to get to the levee at Holyrood. Shielding Constance from the crowd, Grayson stared appalled at the onlookers blatantly peering into the stationery carriages, and the hawkers forcing their baskets of heather and tartan rosettes through the open windows. One persistent man selling pies was actually opening a carriage door exposing the occupants inside, four men sitting ramrod straight for fear of crushing their antiquated black silk breeches and coats, their hair stiff with powder.

'I don't think any of that lot will risk eating a meat pie. That bloke's on to plums,' Grayson said sardonically. 'Would you look at them, they're like waxwork effigies awaiting their doom. I'm half wishing that I'd escorted Neil myself to meet his grandfather. Mind you, the old man acts as if he's got a poker stuck up his rear most days.'

'Was your son's hair powdered?'

He laughed. 'Not bloody likely. I can hardly persuade Neil to run a comb through it at the best of times. No, it was certainly not powdered, nor was he decked out in black silk.

He'd have looked like one of those wee lads they pay to walk in front of a hearse.'

'I believe the rules at the levee are very strict. He may be refused entry if he's not appropriately dressed.'

'That's his grandfather's problem. I've high hopes, now I've seen that lot, that my son will decide he's happy to be refused entry. If we cross here, we can walk through the burial ground and cut on to Calton Hill halfway up.'

'How do you know that?'

'I had a bit of time to myself on my last visit, you might recall. There's a great view from up there, you can see right down to Leith. If it's too steep a climb for you I can always give you a coal carry.'

'I can tell from that wicked look in your eye that I'm going to regret asking. You surely don't mean that you'll heave me over your shoulder like a sack of coal?'

'It's much more fun than that. You jump on to my back, put your arms around my neck and your legs around my waist.'

Constance burst out laughing. 'Tempting as the offer is, I think I'll preserve my dignity.'

'Spoilsport. Come on then, at least give me your hand.'

'Are you going to tow me? I'm quite capable of getting to the top myself, you know.'

'I simply wanted to hold your hand.' He pulled her close, planting a kiss on her lips. 'And to do that, too.'

'We're in a graveyard, Grayson!'

'The inhabitants are in no position to object. There are some notable people interred here. That massive mausoleum there contains the mortal remains of David Hume, if you're interested.'

'I've heard his name, but I have never read any of his work.'

'Nor have I.'

'What does this obelisk commemorate?'

'The Chartist Martyrs.'

'More radicals,' Constance said, frowning at the inscription. 'Paul says that there is a Radical Army of men who are intent on causing a revolution if they are not given the vote. He says that one of the reasons the King is here in Edinburgh, is to distract people from their cause.'

Grayson shrugged. 'If it is, then it's working. Can we forget about what Paul says and enjoy the day? Come on, let's go up to the observatory, we'll get a bird's eye view of the procession down to Holyrood from there.'

* * *

They were on the path leading to the top of the hill, dominated by the tall tower of the Nelson monument. Some of the bonfires which had been lit to welcome the King were still burning, kept going by the people who had set up temporary homes in tents on the hill for the duration. The path took them around the green-domed observatory building and past the odd, half-finished edifice that was supposed to resemble some ancient Greek temple. Clambering on to the plinth, they both caught their breath at the view of Leith, the Firth of Forth and the Fife coast beyond.

'Is that Incholm?' Constance asked, pointing.

'I reckon.'

'Pearl says I have a tendency to lecture.'

'The world needs idealists like you to tell pragmatists like me what needs doing.'

'But I haven't even done that, have I? I've pointed out the injustice of what's happening, I've pointed out the hypocrisy of what is going on down there in Holyrood, but I've not said what should be done to remedy it all.' She sighed wearily. 'Because progress can't be halted. There will be more Highlanders in

Canada soon, than there are left in the Highlands. And as Pearl pointed out, half of them only speak the Gaelic.'

'There you are then,' Grayson said, 'there's your next quest. Set up a school to teach them English.'

'I'd have to sail to Canada.'

He slipped his arm around her waist, pulling her close. 'There's no need for that. Teach them before they sail. In fact, set up your school in Greenock or Port Glasgow, and then you'll be located where your Highlanders sail from, and by a happy coincidence, not too far from me.'

'You don't need me to teach you English.'

'No, I just need you.'

He helped her down from the plinth and they walked slowly around to the other side of the hill and the view over to the Old Town.

'You shouldn't have said that.'

He grimaced. 'I know.'

'We're fooling ourselves, aren't we? What was it you said the other day, about two middle-aged intelligent people trying to make sense of their situation? We're not being very sensible, are we?'

'When I'm not with you, I'm very sensible, and I tell myself that we're wasting our time.

Worse, we're making what's to come a lot more painful. But then I see you and all that goes out of the window.'

'I know. When I'm with you, I can make myself believe anything is possible, but when I think it over, I can't make sense of any of it. We can read each other's thoughts, but we couldn't be more different. I'm fighting to change the world, you're fighting to keep your own wee world just the way it is. Introducing me into that world, it would be like firing one of those rockets from last night. Your children would resent me, your in-laws would think me a revolutionary, and you...'

'Don't say I wouldn't want you.'

'No, but you don't want a wife, Grayson and even if you did, I'm about as different from Eliza as it's possible to get.'

'I don't want to replace Eliza.'

'I know that.'

He shook his head impatiently. 'That's not what I meant. I don't want another Eliza. I have changed so much since she died that if we met now, I don't know that I'd even like her very much, let alone fall in love with her.'

'So what are you saying?'

He cursed under his breath. 'I don't know. I feel like we're going round in circles. I don't want this. You don't want that. Maybe all the fates intended for us was a brief liaison, and here we are, desperately trying to turn it into a lifetime.'

'And failing to find even a starting point.'

'Aye. And yet when I look at you, I swear to God, my heart actually flutters.' He put his arms around her waist, pulling her close, and she smoothed her hand over his cheek.

'And when we're like this,' Constance said, 'it feels like nothing else in the world matters.'

Their lips met in the most bittersweet of kisses. It was destined also to be the shortest. A loud wolf whistle brought them to their senses. Grayson released her, smiling sheepishly. 'Fate, in the shape of that grubby wee lad in tartan trews over there is giving us a wake-up call. You know what, I'm sick of talking about all this.'

'There's nothing to talk about.' She slipped her hand into his. 'Why don't we just enjoy the day?'

'That is a very good idea.' They stood together, watching the long snaking line of carriages stretching from Princes Street in the west, the beginning of Regent Row in the south, and over in the east at Abbey Hill, begin to move. The gates of the palace must have been opened, for a throng of people could be seen moving into the yard, a blur of black, scarlet and tartan milling around. Sun glinted on the vast array of weaponry sported by those who had opted for Highland dress, and those who had been set to guard the King while he submitted his hand to the caress of hundreds.

'Do you think that they actually kiss the royal hand?' Constance asked, wrinkling her nose.

'If they do, I don't fancy being at the back of the queue.'

'It will be a very long queue. There must be hundreds of people down there.'

'A good few will be hingers-on. Courtiers, the proud Highlandman's retinue, servants, coachmen and footmen,' he elucidated.

'Hingers-on,' Constance repeated. 'I sometimes feel I'm learning a whole new language, talking to you. I shall offer to teach Glaswegian in my school, as well as English.'

'There's something to be said for that. You could teach them the lingo and give them some advice on life in the big smoke at the same time. There's a big difference, I'd imagine, between living in a cottage with a kail-yard, and living up a close in a tenement.'

'It's a good idea, but unfortunately I have no idea myself of how to live up a close in a tenement.'

'I'll tell you, and you can tell them.'

The tinny sound of the trumpets announcing the King's arrival distracted them, followed by what could have been a band playing the national anthem. The crowd in the palace yard surged towards the doors and slowly, over the next hour, disappeared in one door and out of another.

'How long do you think he's giving each person?' Grayson asked.

'It can't be more than a few seconds.'

'Time for a bow and a scrap and a slobber and not much more. What's the point of it?'

'To have your name on the roll call that is to be published tomorrow. To be able to say that you were there?'

'But to what purpose? It's not as if there's time for anyone to have a quiet word in the royal ear. Could you do me a wee favour, Your Majesty, and grant me a royal charter for my sporran-making business, that kind of thing.'

'Could you do me a wee favour, Your Majesty, and tell the Marquess of Stafford to stop burning his tenants out of their cottages.'

'Stafford? You used that name in your last piece—or rather Flora did. Who is he?'

'His wife is the Countess of Sutherland. It was her factor, Patrick Sellar, who started the trend for clearing the land, and James Loch who carries it on to this day. Loch and Stafford are probably down there, kissing the King's hand, as we speak. The number of tenants they have dispossessed makes the Clachan Estate Clearances look half-hearted.'

'I'm planning on finding out what is happening on the Glenbranter Estates.'

'Don't do that, Grayson, it's hardly conducive to your ingratiating yourself with your in-laws.'

'I've no plans to ingratiate myself. I want us to understand one another, and to accept that we all want what is best for Neil and Shona, even if we can't necessarily agree what that might be.'

'But if you start asking them about improving…'

'I'll ask them for their views, and I'll listen to them. I'm not going to open the conversation by asking them if they've burned any of their tenants out of their homes recently.'

'If they are improvers though…'

'What? Would that mean we can't be friends?'

'No!'

'But if I take the stance that it's their land, that they're not doing anything illegal even if it is immoral, what then?'

'If it were not for Shona and Neil, would your stance be different?'

'If it were not for Shona and Neil, I'd not be asking them.'

'No, of course you wouldn't, why should you, it's none of your business. Why are you asking them, then?'

'Those lands will belong to Neil one day. It might be too late by then, of course, but at the very least, I can make sure my son understands that being a landowner is as much about the people who live on it as it is about making a profit from them. You see, Flora might not have stopped the Clearances, but she's changed this man's thinking.'

'Thank you, but please think carefully before you speak to them. You want to persuade them you're a sensible, loving father with his children's interests closest to his heart, not a revolutionary intent on destroying their way of life.'

'I thought you'd be pleased.'

'Flora would be. I'm speaking to you as Constance.' She squeezed his hand. 'Who more than anything wants you to be happy.' Because she cared for him, more than anything else. It was too frightening a thought for her to give it room. 'Look down there, I think the King is leaving already.'

'You are a remarkable woman, Constance. I wish…'

'Don't say any more, please, Grayson.'

He flinched, but nodded. 'An hour,' he said after a tense moment's silence, 'that's all I reckon the King's been at the palace, not much more. An hour to be kissed what, a hundred, three hundred, four hundred times?'

'Judging by the crowd, more like a thousand.'

'A thousand kisses in an hour. That's a challenge I'd be more than willing to take on.' He kissed her swiftly. 'But for now, I'll have to content myself with one.'

Chapter Fourteen

Tuesday, 20th August 1822

'I am *so* glad to be back, Pa.' Shona strode into the sitting room of the Caledonian Suite, pulling the white ostrich feathers from her hair.

'Two hours it took that French hairdresser your grandmother sent to create that coiffure, and you've destroyed it in less than two minutes.'

'The feathers made my head ache. We had to sit in the carriage for *hours* before the King even arrived, and when we finally got to the palace, would you believe there were no facilities in the waiting room?'

'Facilities?'

'She's referring to chamber pots,' Neil piped up. 'When I went to the palace with Grandfather, they were located behind a screen in the waiting room.'

'When you went to the palace, there were no ladies present. All the gentlemen escorts and the footmen were in the same waiting room with us, so even if there had been a screen with—with facilities, I would not have dreamed of using them.'

'Your train would have got in the way too,' Neil said, grinning.

Shona swiped at him with a feather. 'Make yourself useful and fetch me a lemonade. I'm parched.'

'Please?'

'Please, darling Brother, fetch me a lemonade. And Pa, you'd best pour a sherry for Grandmother, I think she'll need it.'

'Your grandmother is here?' Grayson jumped to his feet. 'Where? Why didn't you say?'

'We dropped Grandfather off at the other Oman's, but Grandmother said she wanted to speak to you, only when we arrived, she met someone she knew. I expect she'll be up soon.' Shona dropped down on the sofa. 'I'm exhausted. And I'm famished. May we have dinner early, and invite Grandmother? Please, Pa. When Grandfather isn't here to talk over her and put her down, she's actually good company. You may even discover—heaven forefend—that you like one another. Will you ask her?'

'Ask her what?'

'Lady Glenbranter.'

'Mr Maddox. May I come in?'

'Of course. Would you care for a sherry, or a cup of tea?'

'I'd actually prefer a whisky if you have such a thing. What an ordeal. Did Shona tell you how long we had to wait?'

Grayson handed her a crystal glass of whisky. 'Glenlivet, which I'm reliably informed is the King's favourite. Would you like a little water in it?'

'I never dilute good whisky.' Lady Glenbranter tossed back the golden liquid in one swallow and held out the glass again. 'I would be most obliged if you would pour me another, thank you.'

'I'll join you, if I may.' Like Shona, Lady Glenbranter wore a silk gown and long white gloves, though she had detached the obligatory lace train. She was a woman who would more likely be referred to as handsome rather than beautiful, with a strong nose and a decided chin, though her soft brown eyes and sculpted cheek bones, and her smile, when she deigned to use it, reminded Grayson of Neil. And of Eliza, of course.

Grayson poured the drinks, chinking his glass to Lady Glenbranter's before sitting opposite her in the chair next to his daughter. 'So, was it worth the wait?'

'His Majesty, for reasons beknown only to himself, was dressed in the uniform of a field marshal,' Lady Glenbranter said.

'With a white sash and a huge diamond brooch,' Shona chimed in. 'He was so *old,* Pa, and so fat. I do believe he was wearing rouge too for his face was a very unnatural shade of pink. We had to walk for miles through so many different rooms before we were finally in the waiting room, and then when our names were called, one of the helpers, I forget what they were called…'

'Lords-in-waiting.'

'Yes, that was it. Well, he spread my train out behind me and then Grandmama and I were positively hurtled into the Drawing Room. We had to curtsy so low I was almost kneeling on the ground, and then we had to bend over the King so that he could kiss us and then we had to make another curtsy, and leave the room walking backwards, which let me tell you is very difficult, with a train.'

'I'm sure it is. Did the King actually kiss you?'

Shona giggled. 'To be honest, it was all such a blur that I can't remember anything except making a huge effort not to screw my face up for he smelled odd, and I wanted to laugh, because it was all so strange, with everyone taking it so seriously. Did he kiss you, Grandmama?'

'Certainly not. I made sure to keep a bit of air between us.' Lady Glenbranter shuddered. 'So unhygienic. The whole thing was a waste of a day, if you ask me, but my husband was keen to have our names on the list of attendees, and at least now both Shona and Neil can say they have met the King.' She took a sip of her whisky, making an approving face. 'Shona, I wish to have a word with your father.'

'That's nice. I was saying a moment ago, that we should invite you to dine with us, Grandmama. Will you?'

'I would like a word with your father in private, my dear.'

'But Neil is fetching me a lemonade.'

'Drink it in your room while you get changed.' Grayson pulled his daughter to her feet, kissing her cheek.

'But Grandmama will prefer...'

'Your father and I are perfectly capable of having a civilised conversation together without your supervision, Shona. Contrary to your expectations, I'm not about to bite his head off and I am sure he will return the promise.'

'I promise,' Grayson said, waiting for Shona to close the door before taking his seat again. 'I am grateful to you and Lord Glenbranter for making the effort to include Shona and Neil in your royal engagements.'

'It is magnanimous of you to say so. May we speak frankly, Mr Maddox?'

'It is always my preferred approach. I wish you would call me Grayson.'

'Mr Maddox. I will not pretend that I have ever been anything other than unhappy that Elizabeth married you. You will think me antiquated, but I firmly believe that a union between two people from such very different walks of life is doomed to failure.'

'Ours did not follow that pattern.'

'No. If Elizabeth had lived, however, it may have been a very different matter. My daughter never once expressed any regret. I will go as far as to say that Elizabeth loved you until the end, but she was not entirely happy.'

'I was aware of that.'

Lady Glenbranter's brows shot up. 'You were? She was most insistent that you were not, and equally insistent that she had never discussed the matter with you.'

'None the less. I knew Eliza very well, Lady Glenbranter. She was my wife. I know she never quite reconciled herself to what she had chosen to give up. She loved me, I loved her very much, but she couldn't quite bring herself to try to merge her two worlds. Not that she received any encouragement from you to do so, mind.'

'You are referring to the fact that we never invited you to Glenbranter when she and the children visited?' Her Ladyship finished her whisky. 'As a matter of interest, would you have come?'

'For Eliza's sake, yes. Though to be honest, I'm not sure how it would have helped,' Grayson said frankly. 'I've no more interest in being part of your world than you have in being part of mine.'

'You are quite correct. We understand one another perfectly.'

'The problem is…'

'The problem is that Shona and Neil belong to both.'

'Your husband would not concur with that view, I reckon.'

'My husband doesn't understand that there is one significant obstacle to having Neil and Shona live with us permanently. No, I don't mean you as such, Mr Maddox. I mean the love your children have for you. They would be very unhappy if forced to choose. I see I have surprised you.'

Grayson laughed. 'Trust me, in a very positive way.'

'When my daughter died, I expected you would marry again. It's what most widowed men do, when they lose their wife early and are left with young children.'

'It never occurred to me to do such a thing.'

'You would not take the help I offered.'

'Forgive me, Lady Glenbranter, but the help you offered was to take my children away from me.'

'The offer was made with the best of intentions. You were a young man with a growing business.'

'My business has never got in the way of my duties as a father.'

'It is greatly to your credit, Mr Maddox. You must rid yourself of the notion that I am your enemy.' Lady Glenbranter's smile was rigid, but it was a smile. 'We are on the same side when it comes to the children.'

'I would very much like to believe that.'

'I understand your scepticism, but it's the truth. I am exceedingly fond of Shona and Neil. You have proven yourself an excellent and loving father, and one who has, moreover, always put his children first. There have been times over the years when we have been less than considerate, Mr Maddox, but you have refrained from retaliating. You have never prevented us seeing our grandchildren and that means a great deal to me. To us, I should say. A very great deal. Lord Glenbranter and I are very grateful for your forbearance. Thank you.'

'You are welcome.'

'Well now, I think we have made excellent progress.' Lady Glenbranter set her glass down decisively. 'You and I will never agree on what is best for Elizabeth's children, but I think we can agree that the decision can ultimately rest with them. In truth, I doubt that Shona would permit it to be otherwise. She is a very decided young woman.'

'I'm afraid she takes that from me.'

'I will be indiscreet and confess that I

rather admire her for it, though her grand-father considers it a most unfeminine trait.'

'Does he point this out to her?'

'Oh, yes.' Lady Glenbranter smiled grimly. 'Every time he does, she tells him that he is quite right, and changes the subject. It is a very effective technique.'

Grayson gave a bark of laughter. 'I'll keep a look out for it in case she tries to use it on me.'

'I am glad we had this little chat. I won't stay for dinner, if you don't mind, my husband is expecting me.' Getting to her feet, she extended her hand. 'Let us call a truce on our battle of wills, Mr Maddox, and see if we can work together a little better in the future. Neil in particular is at a volatile age. He needs stability. Let us see what we can do to make sure he doesn't feel as if he's at the centre of a tug of war.'

'Well!' Shona burst into the sitting room as soon as Grayson had shown Lady Glen-branter out. 'I suppose I should be flattered that Grandmother thinks she doesn't need to worry about me, only Neil.'

'You were listening!'

'Oh, Pa, what on earth did you expect? We both were. For goodness sake, you and the grandparents haven't spoken in for ever. Then we come to Edinburgh and you practically throw me and Neil into their company, which you have *never* done before. And then Grandmother actually deigns to pay a call on you. We had no choice but to listen. It was obvious that something was afoot'

'We thought you were intending to give us away,' Neil said, joining them.

'What!'

Shona glowered at her brother. 'We thought you were making arrangements for us to go and live with the grandparents.'

'Why on earth would you think such a thing?' Grayson stared at his offspring aghast. 'It's the very last thing I would ever want to do. You're everything to me, you two.'

'We know that, silly.' Shona threw her arms around him. 'We never doubt that for a moment, do we Neil?'

His son shrugged awkwardly. ''Course not.'

'Come here.' Grayson sat down on the sofa, patting the spaces by his side, putting one arm around each of his children when they joined him. 'Firstly and most importantly, I love the pair of you very, very much. Is that clear?'

When both nodded, he managed a ragged

smile. 'Secondly, your grandparents love you too. Yes, understood?'

More nods. His heart rate began to slow to normal. 'Now here comes the trickier bit. Your grandparents have some very fixed ideas about what they want for you.'

'Grandfather says I'm going to be a marquess when he dies,' Neil said morosely. 'Do I have to be, Pa?'

'Your grandfather isn't likely to die for a long time yet, Son.'

'He says I need to go to a proper school, where I'll meet the right people.'

'Does he, now.' Was this the stability Lady Glenbranter intended for Neil? No, he couldn't believe she'd have beaten about the bush if that had been her only goal. 'If you were listening in to my conversation with your grandmother, you'll know that what we've agreed is not to make either of you do anything you don't want to do.'

'So I don't have to go to a different school?'

'Oh, for heaven's sake, Neil!' Shona exclaimed. 'I wish I had your dilemma. Grandfather doesn't think girls should go to school at all. He says it's a waste of time and money, filling our heads with ideas when we should be at home sewing samplers.'

'And Shona asked him if he knew what a sampler was, and he went all red, Pa.'

'You decided against the tactic of telling him he was quite right, and changing the subject then?'

'If you use the same tactic every time, you'll get caught out. Grandfather's old-fashioned and he doesn't half like the sound of his own voice, but he's not daft.'

'Nor am I. You are teetering on the edge of being impertinent, Miss Maddox.'

Shona kissed his cheek. 'Sorry, Pa.'

He laughed. 'I'm not endeared.'

'No, of course you're not, that's why you're smiling that soppy smile.'

'Please can we go down to dinner now?' Neil said, 'I'm so hungry I could eat a scabby-headed wean.'

'I hope,' Grayson said, 'that you don't treat your grandparents to too much Glasgow patter. We'll go down to dinner in a minute, but I want to be serious with the pair of you first. Will you tell me why you thought that I wanted you to go and live with your grandparents?'

Shona stared significantly at Neil, who stared down at his feet. 'You've been really grumpy,' she said.

'Not grumpy,' Neil said. 'Sad.'

'Sad?'

'Not sad as such.' Shona chewed her lip. 'More just sort of fed up.'

'How long have I been just sort of fed up?'

'Weeks?' Shona looked at Neil, who nodded. 'And then we came here, and you wanted us to spend more time with the grandparents. We thought you were fed up with us.'

His first feeling was one of immense relief that they hadn't discovered the real reason for his mood. It had occurred to him, much too late, that Neil and Lord Glenbranter could have been in one of the carriages en route to Holyrood the other day, when he and Constance had walked up Calton Hill. He'd dismissed the notion as highly unlikely, but this was a warning to him to take more care. Or stop seeing her completely. He swore under his breath. For the love of God, he had a much more important matter to deal with now.

'I was actually fed up with me. But now I've come to an understanding with your grandmother I feel much better. Are you convinced now, that I'm not fed up with you and never will be?' he asked, receiving two very decisive nods.

'Well then, I'm glad you were listening in

to that conversation with your grandmother, though you know that you shouldn't have. Will we get ourselves down to dinner now, and you can tell me what you'd like to do to-morrow?'

Wednesday, 21st August 1822

'But that's excellent news,' Constance said when Grayson had finished telling her of Lady Glenbranter's visit the previous day. 'It's exactly what you hoped to achieve.'

'Provided I keep behaving myself. There's a bit of me that thinks she's got a nerve, you know. Well done, Mr Maddox—she refused point blank to call me Grayson. You've been a good boy for the last eight years. Provided you don't misbehave, then we'll get on fine.'

'She didn't really say that?'

'As good as. I don't mind, really. It's not that I have any plans to misbehave.'

'Keep an even keel and don't rock the boat.'

'Aye, that will be my epitaph. Will we sit?'

'Have you time? I thought you were going to Cramond with your children?'

'I've half an hour or so. I wanted to see you.'

'That sounds rather ominous.' Constance

sat down beside him on their usual spot. Angus was already curling himself up for a sleep.

'I got a bit of a fright, when Lady Glenbranter left. Shona and Neil had been listening in on the conversation. They thought it was leading up to my sending them off to live with her.'

'What! Oh, Grayson, where did they get that idea from?'

'I'll tell you.'

He did, and Constance listened, appalled. 'How long had they been keeping all that to themselves?'

'Do you know, I've no idea. I was horrified.'

'I'm not surprised.'

'I thought at first that Neil had seen us together.'

'From the carriage on the way to the levee.'

'You thought of that too?'

'Afterwards.' She winced. 'Not at the time.'

'No, me either. When I realised that Neil hadn't seen us, I was mighty relieved.'

Her heart sank. 'We shouldn't see each other again, should we?' She'd meant it to be a statement, but somehow it came out as a question.

His hand found hers. 'I don't understand

why it's not easier. I've got what I wanted, as far as my children are concerned. Why isn't that enough?'

'It's human nature to want what you can't have.'

'Is that really what you think keeps us coming back for more, Constance, even though we know we shouldn't, even though we've told ourselves countless times that we shouldn't?'

He looked straight into her eyes and she knew then, exactly what it was that kept them coming back. Why they couldn't stay away from each other. She knew with utter certainty what it was, and she knew that he felt it too, and she knew it would be absolutely fatal for either of them to admit it.

She disentangled her hand from his. 'My cousin and his wife arrive today. I'll soon find out what this mysterious proposition is.'

Grayson got to his feet. 'I'm not a procrastinator or a ditherer. When I make up my mind to do something, I do it. If I could persuade myself that being with you was wrong, it would be easier. I feel like I'm stringing you along.'

'You're not! I promise you, you're not. I feel the exact same. I don't know what to do for the best,' Constance said wretchedly. 'I know that when you go back to Glasgow it will be over, I do know that. There's a clock in my head counting down the days already. It will be down to hours before we know it. Should we cut our losses now, today? Spare ourselves more pain?'

'I think the answer to that is a definite yes. There's not actually anything to discuss, is there?'

'No, there really isn't.'

They stared at each other in shock. Then Grayson nodded and made to go. 'I forgot. You asked me to find out if that woman was at the Ladies Drawing Room. The Marchioness of Stafford. She stayed at home, apparently, back in Sutherland.'

'Thank you.'

'You're welcome.' He waited a moment, shook his head, turned his back and walked away.

Chapter Fifteen

Flora is reliably informed that the Count-ess of Sutherland, otherwise known as the Marchioness of Stafford, was not in attendance at the Ladies Drawing Room on Tuesday. Was she indisposed or too ashamed to show her face? Ah, but shame implies an element of humanity, and when you have heard my tale, I defy you to credit the lady with even a shred of that emotion.

Are you sitting uncomfortably? Then I'll begin. A few years ago a debilitat-ing crop failure struck parts of the far north-east of our country. Whole commu-nities were starving. But fear not, gentle reader, for who rode to their rescue but none other than the Countess of Suther-land, providing essential famine relief to her tenants.

What's this, Flora, I hear you say, singing the praises of a landowner? Ah but my story has a sting in the tale. The grateful tenants were astonished to discover that the cost of the food provided was added on to their next year's rent. What's more, those who couldn't afford the extra charges were summarily evicted from their homes.

Talk about giving with one hand and taking away with the other! Is the Countess under the illusion that she can play God? No, there is no need to answer that question for you and I know, dear reader, that most estate owners believe they have the power of life and death over their tenants. One can only hope that they will eventually be forced to give an account to a higher power for their despicable actions. Flora trusts He will be equally merciless on the guilty.

Flora MacDonald, *New Jacobite Journal*

Thursday, 22rd August 1822

Wednesday had passed in a blur of activity that prevented Constance from thinking. Pearl and Isabel closeted themselves away for the better part of the day, leaving her to entertain her cousin and his wife. James and Edith Fraser were a charming couple about her own age, delighted to make her acquaintance, eager to bury the past and equally eager to see Edinburgh *en fête*. It would have been a bittersweet experience for Constance filled with memories of an identical stroll with Grayson, as they walked the length of the High Street and the Canongate down to Holyrood, had not her new relatives been so entranced by all they saw and so full of questions.

Their proposition was revealed over dinner and discussed in detail for the rest of the evening. By the time she retired, Constance's future was all but decided. She lay awake, trying to persuade herself that it was a relief, feeling utterly numb.

Knowing full well that Grayson wouldn't be in the park the next morning, she was none the less enormously disappointed to be greeted by an empty space under the tree where he ought to have been. It wasn't that they had anything more to discuss, but she had wanted to tell him her news. That was what she told herself any road, as he would say. She wanted him to know she had a future planned.

* * *

The day turned driech and miserable for the King's Grand Procession from Holyrood to the castle. Pearl and Isabel waved Constance, James and Edith off as soon as breakfast was over. Thinking to avoid the crowds, she took them the route in the shadow of the castle along Lothian Road, through the market at King's Stables Road, which was closed for the day and into the Grassmarket. There was a terrible crush. The noise of carriage wheels and horses' hooves on the cobblestones made her head ache. She was hard put to maintain her smile, and immensely thankful that there was so much going on to distract her relatives.

The best place to stand was at the top of West Bow, where it opened out on to the Lawnmarket. Looking up, hundreds of people could be seen hanging over the Esplanade, and a frightening number clinging to the rocks below the castle itself. Arriving out of breath at the top of the hill, they were confronted with hordes of people fighting for position, climbing up on to the precarious-looking temporary platforms. Flowers, sodden with the rain, decorated the many benches, and flags hung limp from every building. No one wanted to give way. The air was redolent of damp tartan and wet horse. Surgeons and sailors, grocers and gardeners, porters and printers, clerics and candlemakers, all gathered in their designated areas. Clusters of children from orphanages and schools sat resolutely cross-legged as others clambered over them. A choir was performing in one wynd, the now ubiquitous bagpipes were whining from another. And the rain fell in a steady drizzle.

'I think this is as good a viewing position as we're going to get,' James said, shepherding his wife and Constance under the shelter of an awning.

'How on earth did you persuade them to make room for us?'

Her cousin smiled. 'I happen to be acquainted with His Lordship over there.'

The man James indicated was tall and sparse, with a shock of white hair and a short pointed white beard, a hawk-like nose and a heavy frown. He wore a pair of tartan trews with a short black coat. A very expensive ceremonial sword hung from a belt at his side, and the pin in his bonnet winked with jewels.

'Who is that?' Constance asked.

'His estate has lands adjoining ours, so I suppose you could call him our neighbour. To be honest, Constance, we don't see much of him and are happy to keep it so. A very proud man, the sort who likes to compare blood-lines to ensure his is superior, you know? The bigger portion of his lands are in the north, where he spends most of his time. I will introduce you to his wife when she arrives. She took an interest in our little project, and will be pleased to know that we are now in a position to progress it, thanks to you. Ah, there she is. And that must be her grandchildren. Lady Glenbranter! I say, over here, my lady.'

With a sickening lurch in her stomach, Constance stood behind her cousin as Grayson's dead wife's mother was ushered under the covering, holding out her hand in greeting to James. She had the impression of an elegantly dressed, stern woman with an unexpectedly warm smile. Constance managed to mumble a greeting. As she made her curtsy, she received an uninterested nod from Lord Glenbranter. Grayson's children both smiled politely, but their eyes were on the crowd shaping and reforming itself in the Lawnmarket as stewards urged people to make way for the procession.

'My son-in-law,' Lady Glenbranter said to James. 'Mr Maddox, may I present our neighbour from our property in the Borders, Mr James Fraser and his wife, Edith. And this is—I beg your pardon, I didn't quite catch your name.'

'Miss Constance Grant,' James said, beaming. 'My cousin, and I am delighted to say, the new head teacher for our school.'

'Miss Grant.' Grayson took her hand, his fingers twining automatically in hers. Their eyes met. He looked as shocked as she.

'Do you know each other?' James asked.

Constance snatched her hand away.

'A teacher, you say?' Grayson asked.

'Indeed, indeed.' James beamed. 'Our school serves a number of the local villages. Of late, we've had quite a few displaced Highland families moving into the area, and the language is proving a bit of a hurdle for them. To discover that my very own cousin is not only a teacher but a Gaelic speaker! Well, Mr Maddox, I call that serendipity, don't you?'

'If Miss Grant thinks so?'

'She does,' Constance managed to say, unable to meet his eyes, seeing her own torture reflected there. 'I have agreed to journey south with my cousin next week. I think it—it is a most timely offer. Don't you agree, Mr Maddox?'

Grayson nodded slowly. 'Most timely. I...'

'Pa, come and see this.'

'Excuse me.'

No! Anguished, she watched Grayson rejoin his children. They were standing only a few feet away. She could hear every word. Witness every gesture. Shona and Neil were children to be proud of, but they were not her children. Even if she and Grayson could find a way to be together, even if by some miracle his children welcomed her with open arms, would she be content? No. Being a mother to someone else's children was not enough. James was giving her the opportunity to shape the lives of whole generations of children, many of whom were innocent victims of the Clearances. That would be her mission, her legacy.

And yet, there remained the small matter of Grayson. Now she was so utterly and completely certain he would never be *her* Grayson, she could admit that she loved him. Watching him made her heart ache with longing. No one understood her as he did. No one knew her as he did. He was the other half she didn't know she had been missing. But they were destined never to be together.

She had lost so much in her life. It had

taken her years to patch herself back together after leaving Clachan Bridge, but she'd managed it. If she hadn't bumped into Grayson that fateful day in Newhaven, she would be trembling with anticipation and looking forward to the new chapter of her life which awaited her in the south. An opportunity to help the very people whose shoddy treatment she had been shouting from the rooftops. It would have been so much worse if there had ever been any hope of something more significant between them, but there never had been. She loved Grayson, and now she had lost him for ever, but he had never been hers to lose in the first place. She'd saved herself that pain, at least.

Grayson listened to Shona and Neil prattling away. He answered their questions. He smiled at them. He looked where they pointed as the procession began to make its painfully slow way past. An advance guard of yeomanry led the way, the heavens opened, various bands struck up, and the crowds cheered. His children waved the flags he'd purchased at ridiculous expense for them. Lord and Lady Glenbranter stood stiffly side by side. Constance's relatives pointed and waved. They seemed an affable couple. He was like an overgrown puppy, but not an ounce of bad in him, as the saying went. The wife looked like the ballast, the sensible head. Good people. Constance would be with good people. Family. Doing work that would satisfy her conscience too. It was ironic that the very thing they'd joked about her setting up on Clydeside so she could be near to him was coming to pass. She'd be happy. He prayed she'd be happy. It was what he wanted for her more than anything. He loved her so much.

He loved her. Cries of *'God Save the King!'* echoed and resounded as the royal equipage approached. A covered carriage, Grayson noted, with three men in it, all ridiculously overdressed. A woman standing next to him swooned into the arms of a happy gentleman. Shona and Neil were hoarse with shouting. Was this it? Was this how it ended?

His eyes met Constance's, and it was like the first time and every time since. That jolt inside that told him, this was who you've been looking for without even realising it. That feeling. *I know you.* Another place and another time, they'd have been able to admit it from the start. They were made for each other. But this wasn't another time and another place. He loved her, but he had loved his family first.

The crowd surged forward, and he managed to reach her side. 'Constance, do you think we could see each other...'

'One last time?'

'Say goodbye properly. Not like this.'

'Yes. Please.' She smiled at him then. 'We owe it to ourselves.'

'Yes.' He found her hand, squeezed her fingers. 'Tomorrow. I'll meet you where it all began, yes?'

'Yes. It seems fitting.'

'Pa!'

He turned away. When next he was free to look for her, Constance was crossing the street behind the tail end of the procession with her cousin and his wife.

Friday, 23rd August 1822

Grayson was waiting, at the end of the harbour in Newhaven when Constance arrived. He was wearing a dark blue coat and grey trousers. No hat. No gloves. The sun was out, sparkling on the incoming tide. He had been staring out at the sea, but as she approached he turned around, his eyes never leaving her as she made her way along the rough stone jetty to join him.

'Here you are,' he said, holding out his hand. 'I worried you would think the better of it.'

Constance stepped into his arms. 'We need to say goodbye properly. Doing it here brings us full circle. We won't be able to tell where we began and where we ended, it's just us.'

Grayson pulled her tightly to him, his arms around her waist. She closed her eyes, resting her cheek on his chest. 'You know I love you,' he said. 'I think I fell in love with you the moment I set eyes on you, right here.'

'I love you so much too,' Constance answered. 'You know that, don't you?'

'I do.'

She lifted her face and their lips met. Their kisses spoke for them as they always did, for the first time making no attempt to hide their feelings. She brushed his cheek, running her fingers through his short-cropped hair, pressing tiny kisses to his mouth, telling him she loved him in between. He smoothed her hair, his fingers stroked the warm skin at the nape of her neck as he returned her kisses, telling her how much he loved her, that he would always love her, always. Then they stood, side by side, hand in hand, and watched the tide creep into the harbour.

'There is some sort of military parade being reviewed by the King today,' Grayson said, when she asked him about his children. 'I asked the Murrays to take Neil and Shona to it. They'll see them safely back to the hotel for me.'

'I had no idea that my cousin knew Lord and Lady Glenbranter.'

He laughed softly. 'I could see that. Your cousin seems like a good man.'

'Yes. I'm very fortunate.' She told him of her cousin's plans as they made their way back to the main road, and the inn where they had first taken lunch. Their table was waiting for them, she wasn't surprised to see.

'Bread and cheese and coffee,' the landlady said, setting down the tray. 'Nice to see you again, I remember you from before. You were indisposed, Mrs....'

'Maddox.' Oh, if only!

'No tot of rum?' Constance teased when the landlady had bustled off.

'I didn't want to break with tradition.' Grayson made up her plate for her, cutting the cheese into slivers, fanning the apple slices out. 'Will it satisfy you, what your cousin is offering?'

'It will be a new beginning. I can't stop the improvers, but I can help their victims. It's a chance for me to prove that an idealist can make a practical difference.'

'We joked about it, on top of Calton Hill, do you remember? You teaching English to Highlanders.'

'Of course I remember. When James explained his idea, it was the first thing I thought of. There are not so many of them, where I am going. The dispossessed, I mean.'

'Will you be happy there? Content with your lot?'

She turned on the bench to face him. 'I'll make sure I am content. As to whether I'll be happy—I intend to try. You've taught me that I'm capable of being happy. I don't plan on spending the rest of my life being unhappy. I've had enough of that. I plan to make the most of what I have.'

'That is a very good plan.'

'Another lesson I've learnt from you.'

'I'll take my own advice, then.' Grayson drank the last of his coffee. 'I almost came to the park on Thursday morning. Even though we'd said goodbye the day before, I almost came. There was a bit of me that still couldn't accept the fact that I wanted two completely opposing things which were irreconcilable. I couldn't live without you. You couldn't live with me. We'll find a way to make the impossible possible, I told myself, because I wanted to believe that, because I wanted to see you.'

'What stopped you?'

'Neil. "Are you sloping off and leaving us to go on one of your mysterious early morning walks again?" he asked. So I took him out with me, in the opposite direction from the one I wanted to travel. And you know, Constance, for a moment, just for a moment, I cursed him because I'd already set my mind on seeing you again.'

'I knew you wouldn't come, but I still hoped.'

'Your cousin James has inadvertently put an end to any lingering uncertainty. Now you have pastures new to go to, it makes everything clear cut and definite.'

'Yes, but it's not only that. It was seeing you with your family yesterday. Being forced to stand right beside you, watching you all together, it made me wonder what on earth they would make of me, if you introduced me into their lives? What would I make of them?'

'If I didn't know you better, I'd think you were scared of them.'

Constance crumbled a small chunk of bread into crumbs. 'Not afraid of them, afraid of failing you. I'd be terrified of making them unhappy, and you in the process. I'd be afraid of discovering that we'd made a mistake, and then of losing you. I'd be very scared that if I lost you in that manner I wouldn't recover a second time.' She pushed the crumbs into a heap on her plate. 'You're not mine to lose. That's what I realised yesterday when I saw you with your children. If you were mine, and I lost you, I couldn't bear it. I've lost too much already. And so have you.'

'I know that. It's part of it, of course it is. When Eliza and I married, we took a real chance on our feelings for each other. When she died, we were all devastated—I mean the Murrays too. Eight years on, and we're finally all hopefully moving towards some sort of happy medium, a compromise we can all live with. I'd be off my head to risk upsetting the applecart all over again. Even if you would take me on, which I've known all along you wouldn't.'

'I've never said that, I've never been in a position to. There was never any question of what my feelings for you were, Grayson.'

He grinned. 'Nor mine for you. Have you had enough to eat?'

She looked down at her half-eaten meal. 'I've had more than enough food, and more than enough talking. Let's stop discussing what is already decided, shall we?'

'What would you like to do instead?'

'End this exactly the way we began it. It's what we both want, isn't it? Nothing less feels appropriate.'

'Are you sure?'

'When I'm with you like this, just you and I, I'm always sure.'

'I wonder what the landlady must think of us?'

Grayson locked the door, leaning against it. 'She'll think, and most landladies are shrewd judges of character, that we are two people who thought that they were well past the age of falling in love. Who weren't even looking for love, and yet who tumbled headlong into it in a matter of moments. Two people who were made for each other, but who found each other in the wrong place, at the wrong time. So now they're saying goodbye. They won't forget each other, not ever. But they'll try to be happy without each other, because if they don't they'll have wasted something precious. That's what she'll think for it's the truth of it, isn't it.'

'The God's honest truth.'

He crossed the room and into her open arms. There were tears on her cheeks. His own heart was full to overflowing. For a moment as he held her, he thought that this had been a mistake, but then she lifted her head, smiling at him through her tears, and she kissed him.

'I love you,' she said to him. 'I love you so very much.'

'I love you too. I just love the bones of you.'

The first time they had been in this small back bedroom in a fisherman's tavern they'd been hurried, desperate for fulfilment and embarrassed afterwards by their brazen lust. On the beach at Inchcolm they had made love passionately. Now, on the last occasion they would make love, they took their time, wanting to savour every moment, sear it into their memories to be cherished for ever. He pulled the pins from her hair. Removed his coat. His waistcoat. He turned her around to peel off her dress, kissing every inch of her skin. Her neck, her shoulders, the line of her spine. His shoes and stockings were next, then his shirt.

She kissed his throat. Her tongue flicked over his nipples. He kissed the swell of her breasts above her corsets, then the valley between them, when he had unlaced her. His trousers were next, and his drawers. She knelt before him kissing his belly, the top of his thighs, then pressed tentative kisses up the length of his shaft that nearly sent him over.

Her chemise and petticoats let him spend an age on her breasts, and he'd have spent an age more if she'd let him. But she said his name like a plea, and he couldn't resist her. Naked, they fell on to the bed, their kisses frantic now. She sat astride him, taking him inside her slowly, her eyes fixed on his, watching him, gauging him. He stroked her as she began to move, wanting to feel her coming around him, her harsh moan, the pulsing of her climax bringing his on, sending him over the edge and into the sweetest of oblivion.

She held him deep inside her until it was over, and then she fell on top of him, kissing him gently. Her skin stuck to his, slick with sweat. He rolled her over, curling into her back, one arm around her waist, pressing his mouth to her damp neck.

'I love you,' he said.

She wriggled against him. 'I'm going to ask you to prove it again soon, I warn you.'

He laughed, his chest rumbling against her back. 'I'll do my best, but you'll have to give me a moment to recover. I'm not a young man any more, remember.'

It took much less time than she would have thought possible. His light caresses became more purposeful. She could feel his arousal hardening against her bottom as he teased her nipples. And then it started again. More slowly this time, but the conclusion was the same. For a few blissful moments they were one.

It was dusk outside when they finally left the bed. That first time, she had been embarrassed by her underwear, by her almost forty-year-old body, by the lust which had propelled them from the harbour to this very bedchamber in the space of a couple of hours. Except it hadn't been lust, it turned out, it had been love. This time, there was nothing between them save a tender caution as they helped each other dress. It was such a fragile feeling, this sense of peace, of fulfilment, that they had managed to forge. They didn't want to shatter it. She would not count the moments, she would savour them.

They walked together the same route they had walked that first time. The twilight was damp, smoke-tinged, for there had been yet more salvos and rockets and cannons fired as the King's visit drew inexorably on to its own conclusion. They walked close together, Constance's hand on Grayson's arms, their heads bent towards each other, oblivious of their surroundings. At Picardy Place, the platforms set up for the key-giving ceremony had been dismantled, and they changed their route, opting for Queen Street rather than Princes Street.

The gardens had been taken over as a camp site for troops of Highlanders. There was a clatter of carriages coming down the hill from George Street. 'The Peers' Ball is taking place in the Assembly Rooms tonight,' Constance said.

'The Murrays will be there.'

Grayson wouldn't release her when they reached his hotel at Charlotte Square. 'I'll walk you all the way back,' he said, 'this one last time.'

They took the route they'd followed another

night, after they had dined together. 'No stars tonight,' Constance said when they stopped, of one accord, at the little garden in the centre of Melville Street. 'Let's not drag this out, my darling. It's too painful as it is.'

One last kiss. Then one more. She turned away, but he pulled her back for one more. 'Promise me you will be happy,' he said.

'I will try.'

One more kiss, and then she took off, running as fast as she could, until she reached the door of the town house at Coates. Light shone from the drawing room. Angus came toddling to meet her as she opened the front door, but he gave up following her as she fled, up two flights of stairs to the sanctuary of her bedchamber. She cast off her gown and her corsets, but didn't change into her nightclothes. The scent of their lovemaking was on her chemise and her skin. Pulling the pillow to her, Constance lay awake for the rest of the night, determined not to cry.

Chapter Sixteen

Monday, 26th August 1822

'Goodness, Pa, you do scrub up well,' Shona said as Grayson entered the sitting room of their hotel suite. 'I'm so glad you agreed to come with us. The dancing will cheer you up.'

'Do I need cheering up?'

'You could give a wet blanket a run for its money. You look like you've lost a sixpence and found a penny, as Mama used to say.'

'So she did. I'm fine, Shona, I'm just…'

'Tired. So you keep saying.'

'It's that wee bed in my room, my feet hang out the end.' Grayson took a seat. He had spent most of the last two nights in here, watching the city lights through the windows, wondering what Constance was doing. It was a foolish occupation and fruitless, for he'd never know, but it was the only one he seemed capable of at the moment. Day and night, she was permanently in his thoughts. He had given her up for the sake of his children, but he was finding his children's company almost tiresome at the moment. It was grossly unfair of him. It had been guilt that made him surrender to Shona's pleas that he escort her to this damned ball, but having agreed, he should at least make the effort to put up an appearance of enjoyment for her sake.

'You scrub up very well yourself, young lady, if you don't mind me saying,' he said, forcing a smile. 'Another new gown?'

'I could not wear any old rag to a ball attended by the King.'

'I wasn't aware that you possessed any old rags. I hope you're not expecting His Majesty to ask you to dance.'

Shona made a face. 'I sincerely hope he does not. There is only one gentleman I'm interested in dancing with, and he will be by far the handsomest in the room.' She stood on tiptoes to kiss his cheek. 'I mean you, just in case you're wondering.'

'The pleasure will be all mine. I'm such a terrible dancer, it certainly won't be yours.

Thank you,' he said, taking the glass of whisky his daughter had poured him. 'What's this for?'

'Brace yourself. I need to tell you something.'

'What have you done?'

'*I* have not done anything.'

'The what has Neil done?'

'Neil hasn't done anything either, for once. He doesn't know about this. I've been waiting to get you to myself to speak to you.'

'Sit down then, and tell all.'

'I can't sit down, I'll crush my gown. May I have a sip of that?'

'Absolutely not.'

'Grandfather lets Neil have a wee dram. He says it will make a man of him.'

'I'll be having words with your grandfather about that.'

'He doesn't drink it, you needn't worry. He pours it away when Grandfather isn't looking. He doesn't like the smell.'

'Like medicine,' Grayson said, thinking of Constance. Again.

'Pa!'

He blinked. 'I'm sorry.' Shona was chewing her bottom lip, a sure sign that she was worried. 'What is it, Shu-shu?'

She smiled at his use of her baby name,

but she didn't stop chewing her lip. 'You know Mr Urquhart? The man who owns the hotel?'

'He runs the hotel. It's owned by Mr Oman and his wife. What about Mr Urquhart?'

'He said the oddest thing to me, the other day.'

Shite. Grayson took a swig of the whisky. 'What exactly did Mr Urquhart say?'

'He asked why my mother wasn't with us.'

Double shite. He took another swig of whisky. 'How odd.'

'It gets odder still. I told him that my mother was dead. He said that he was very sorry to hear it, and asked me if it was an accident.'

'Right.' Grayson finished the whisky and reluctantly decided against another. Tonight of all nights, he wasn't ready for this, but it had to be dealt with. How he was going to deal with it was another question. He had never lied to his daughter. 'You told him it wasn't an accident, I presume?'

'I told him that she died of a long illness which is what you always say. He said she'd looked very well when he saw her last month.' Shona met his gaze unflinchingly. 'Here. That she had dinner with you.'

'Right.' *Right, what?*

'So did you have dinner here with a strange woman?'

'She's not strange, Shona, and it's not at all what you're thinking.'

'I don't know what to think.'

'I suppose it's too much to ask that you forget all about it?' One look from his daughter made him hold his hands up. 'No. Fair enough.'

'Is that all you can say?' Forgetting her concerns about crushing her ball gown, Shona sat down beside him. 'Is she your friend? The one you saw in Leith the day the King arrived?'

'She is. She is my—we were very good friends, Shona.'

'Were?'

'I'll not be seeing her again.'

'Why not? Wouldn't we like her?'

'I don't know. I've never considered it.'

'Perhaps you think she wouldn't like us?'

'She has other more important concerns. Plans. Work. She's no time or inclination to be cultivating my offspring.'

'Well, that's a relief, for I am not in the least bit in need of being cultivated. Nor is Neil. We are fine as we are, thank you very much.' Shona pursed her lips. 'What I want to know is, are you intending to marry this secret friend of yours?'

'No!'

'Then is this lady your mistress?'

'Shona!'

'Because if she is, you had best make sure Grandmother doesn't find out. That is a very rude swear word.'

'You didn't hear it.' He got to his feet, deciding that another whisky was definitely in order, his head reeling. 'Would you mind if I married again at some point?'

'Yes, I would. I don't want another brother or sister.'

'There's no question of that.'

'Good, because the very idea of you—' She broke off, screwing up her face. 'Ew... Also, I don't want some stranger telling me what to do. I can choose my own clothes, I have my own friends, and we already have a housekeeper. So you don't really need another wife, do you? *Are* you thinking of getting married, Pa?'

'No. I wasn't. Haven't. Does your brother think the same as you do?'

'Oh, Neil would be horrified. Why did that woman pretend to be my mother?'

'She didn't. Mr Urquhart assumed we were married, and we thought it amusing, so we didn't correct him.'

'It's an odd sort of joke. If you did want to get married again and if you did pick a suitable woman, it wouldn't be fair for me to tell you not to, even if I didn't want you to, would it? I mean I'm sixteen, I've got my life ahead of me while you—I mean you are nearly fifty.'

'I'm forty-three.'

Shona shrugged. 'What I'm trying to say is, that I don't want you to be lonely.'

'In my dotage.'

'I didn't say that!'

'Come here a moment.' Grayson gave his daughter a hug. 'Thank you for telling me all this. It can't have been easy for you.'

'No, it wasn't but—well, you're our Pa and you've done everything for us and I know we're sometimes selfish but we love you and we just want you to be happy.'

'I love you both with all my heart and I'm very proud of you. Now, enough of this mutual admiration society. Go and get your cloak, and we'll go. We don't want to arrive after the King. It's not only rude but probably treasonable.'

* * *

The Assembly Rooms on George Street were illuminated with gas lamps for the occasion of the Caledonian Hunt Ball. The building, rightly revered as one of the finest in the New Town, was in the Greek classical style, the arcaded facade adorned with four columns supporting an imposing pediment. When Constance arrived on foot with James and Edith, there were queues of carriages and sedan chairs all the way from Charlotte Square, disgorging a steady stream of grandly dressed passengers. Tartan was, inevitably, very much on display once more. Several of the ladies wore plaid sashes over their evening gowns, and a good many of the gentlemen were in full Highland regalia. Their armour would clank, Constance thought irreverently, when they danced, and their ceremonial swords would be a positive danger to life and limb. A number of gentlemen were in dress uniforms bedecked with orders and medals, and a number were in court dress, for goodness sake, with powdered hair.

'If he is not careful, that gentleman will be mistaken for a footman,' Edith said to her. 'And goodness, would you look at that one.

He could arm a battalion.' She took Constance's arm as they joined the crowd in the entrance way. 'I'm really glad you agreed to come with us at the last moment. I'm not really one for this sort of thing, but James is a real social creature. I much appreciate you keeping me company. Oh, my goodness, look at the crush.'

The entrance foyer was crowded. They left their cloaks in the ladies' retiring room and Edith assured Constance once again that the borrowed evening gown of gold silk suited her perfectly, and that she personally preferred the more sombre emerald-green for herself.

A sweeping staircase with encircling arms led up to a spectacular glass dome in the roof. Leaving James to seek out an acquaintance, Edith and Constance took a leisurely stroll around the building. The ballroom at the front of the building, its walls hung with mirror glass, had been transformed into a throne room, the windows draped in blue velvet trimmed with gold, and a throne set on a dais at the far end. A second, smaller ballroom was similarly decked out, thought it lacked a throne. There were two supper rooms clad floor to ceiling in tartan which would clash horribly with the tartan-clad attendees, Constance thought. Flora could fill an entire issue of the *NJJ* with the sheer overstated and unnecessary extravagance of the whole affair, if she chose.

In the drawing rooms and withdrawing rooms, there was an abundance of flowers, their fragrance adding to the perfume of the ladies, and the more earthy scent of sweat mingled with candlewax and the ever-present aroma of damp tartan. The card rooms were hushed, the gentlemen already at play huddled over the baize tables. Constance and Edith quickly withdrew.

Returning to the ballroom half an hour later, they were just in time to witness the King's arrival. George, thankfully, had decided against the too-short kilt and pink tights which had been the subject of much derision in the press. Instead, along with the courtiers who surrounded him, he wore a blue coat with red cuffs and collar which did nothing for the frighteningly florid puce of his complexion. His breast glittered with diamonds as he made his stately way to the top of the room and graciously took the hand of a very pretty young lady for the opening reel. Gow's Band had been instructed to play only music that the King decreed to be 'national and characteristic.' Constance, a veteran of many Friday night village ceilidhs, watched the whirl of tartan on the dance floor, recognising neither the steps nor the tune.

Turning to speak to Edith, she discovered that they had been separated by the King's grand entrance. How she would find her again in this crush, she had no idea. The best policy, she decided, would be to stand out in the foyer by the stairs. She pushed her way through the crush to do so, relieved to breathe a modicum of fresh air. And there he was, dressed in plain black evening clothes, standing quite alone.

Grayson. She didn't say his name aloud, but he looked up all the same, and their eyes met, and immediately they began to make their way towards each other.

'You're the last person I expected to see mingling with the hoi polloi at one of the King's soirées,' he said.

'I'm here as a favour to Edith. Wild horses wouldn't drag me here otherwise.'

He smiled and her heart turned over. He took her hand and she followed him without a thought for anything or anyone else. A door he opened at random gave way into a room filled with shelves of glasses. 'I don't give a damn why you're here, I'm just delighted that you are. I've missed you.'

'It goes without saying that I have missed you too, terribly. Has it only been two days?'

'Three. It feels like a year.'

'Three.' She smiled. 'Is that really all?'

'I am also here under duress. I promised Shona I would be her escort tonight. She seems to be growing up under my nose.'

'She sixteen, Grayson. A young lady, not a girl.'

'A young lady who knows about you.'

'What! How?'

'Urquhart. The one person it never occurred to me to worry about. It was a strange conversation. She doesn't want me to marry. Neil would be outraged. She's appalled at the very notion her father might want a wife in any real sense, but she'll grant me that I might be lonely in my old age.'

Constance laughed. 'So if we deck ourselves out in lambswool and buy a couple of bath chairs, then we might earn her blessing.'

'Aye, I know, it's ridiculous. Are you still all set to head south with your cousin next week?'

Constance slipped her hand from his, her smile fading, the elation she'd felt when she saw him seeping away. 'Nothing has happened to change my mind, if that is what you're asking.'

'The school we talked about in Glasgow though, wouldn't you be just as happy teaching there?'

'It doesn't exist.'

'Not yet.'

'Please don't. I can't bear it. We shouldn't be having this conversation, there's no point.'

'Constance…'

But she ignored him, pushing her way past him, out on to the first-floor landing. There was a retiring room somewhere, but where? To her dismay, she found herself in a large drawing room. To her further dismay, it was occupied by Lady Glenbranter, Shona and Edith. And to her horror, Grayson came storming in after her.

'Constance, I…'

'Grayson!' She waved him frantically away, but it was too late. All three pairs of eyes had turned towards them.

'Pa?'

'Mr Maddox! Miss Grant?'

'Cousin Constance?'

No one said anything as a bemused silence filled the air. 'It's her, isn't it?' Shona said, speaking first, her tone outraged. 'That's her. Miss Grant. Your friend from Leith. The one Mr Urquhart said—' She broke off under the harsh gaze of her father's appalled stare.

'Excuse me, I really must go,' Constance muttered, mortified.

But Grayson caught her as she made to flee, with the oddest smile on his face. 'You're quite right, this is indeed my friend from Leith, Shona, though she's actually from Clachan Bridge in the Highlands, and she's not only my friend. She's my best friend.'

'Best friend!' Lady Glenbranter exclaimed. 'She's a woman!'

'Very perceptive of you,' Grayson said. 'What you don't know is that she happens to be the woman I love.'

'No, Grayson, don't. You can't.'

But his smile rooted her to the spot. 'I can. I have to say this, because it's so blindingly obvious. We've said goodbye so many times, because we've convinced ourselves there is no other way forward. The only thing we've proved is that we simply can't say goodbye. So why not try to make it work instead? Do you see what I'm saying, Constance? My darling, instead of telling each other that it's impossible for us to be together, can't we try to achieve the one thing we both want more than anything, and make it happen?'

'But we've said our final farewells.'

'Yes, and the moment we saw each other, we were instantly wrapped in each other's arms.' Casting a harried look at their dumbstruck audience, he pulled her over to the corner of the room. 'I know you think this is a bolt from the blue, and it is. I never for a moment imagined when I came here—but seeing you again, I realised it might just be that simple. Let's stop being determined to live apart and start attempting to live together.'

Another hurried glance over Constance's shoulder showed him Shona in earnest conversation with her grandmother. The Urquhart story. He would deal with that later. Now all that mattered was explaining his revelation to Constance.

'We've been looking at things the wrong way round,' he said. 'Through the wrong end of the telescope, to use the maritime metaphor. We've been focusing on what we might lose, what we're risking. Your independence. My relationship with my children. I'm not minimising the risks. There's an awful lot at stake for both of us. It requires a huge leap of faith. But just think, Constance, what we might gain.'

'At a cost. Such a cost. Too much of a cost.'

'Is it? We don't know for certain. That's what dawned on me when I saw you again to-night. Neither of us knows what the outcome will be if we try to make a life together, but I do know I'll regret it for the rest of my life if we don't at least try. I admit I'm scared of what that might mean. It would require compromise from you too, which you'll admit is not one of your strengths.'

'But I'm already compromising by giving you up.' She clutched at his hands. 'I'm not sure what you're asking.'

'I'm asking you to marry me. Let's make a life together. A new life together.'

'But your children…'

'Will have to learn to get used to the idea. So will the Glenbranters. Why should we be the only ones willing to compromise, to sacrifice a little for the sake of some one else's happiness?'

'You make it sound simple.'

'I know it's not, far from it. But I've made so many sacrifices already, I'm damned if I'll make the biggest sacrifice of all, the chance of happiness with you, and I'm damned if I'm prepared to spend the rest of my life missing you. What do you say, Constance? Shall we try for a happy ending and to hell with the consequences?'

'I'd rather try for a happy beginning, middle and end. My head is whirling.'

'Then don't answer now. We'll leave our audience in suspense.'

'I'd forgotten all about them.' She forgot about them again, looking into his eyes. Here he was, her other half. Surely it was worth any amount of compromise and struggle, if they could find a way to be together? 'What if we discover it's a mistake, it's simply not possible?'

'Then why don't we put that to the test? What if we agree that we're not getting married, not just yet, and see if we can't iron out those so-called insurmountable obstacles. A year, that should do it, shouldn't it? In a year, all being well, I'll ask you to marry me.'

'Or not, if we fail.'

'But then at least we'll know. Then there won't be any doubt. We'll be able to walk away knowing that it couldn't work, rather than wondering. I love you so much, Constance.'

'I'd like to say that's all that matters.'

He pulled her into his arms. 'Right now, it is,' he said.

He kissed her, and she kissed him right back, with gusto, utterly oblivious to the very audible outraged gasps coming from the other side of the room.

As all good things must—depending on your point of view—the King's visit has come to an end. And so, dear reader, has the tenure of the New Jacobite Journal. *Flora has, quite literally, nothing more to say, save to thank you for supporting her efforts to give a voice to those with no voice of their own.*

Ultimately, we might have achieved little, but at least we ensured that someone bore witness to the suffering of the disposed in the Highlands, and to the identity of their oppressors. I sincerely believe that history will judge this shameful chapter in Scotland's history harshly. I am proud to have played a small part in ensuring that truth will eventually prevail, even if justice proves to be more elusive.

Like my namesake, having enjoyed

brief notoriety, this Flora intends to slip into obscurity, a mere footnote in our nation's history.

Flora MacDonald, final issue of
New Jacobite Journal, 30th August 1822

Chapter Seventeen

Glasgow—Monday, 14th July 1823

'Happy birthday, my darling.' Grayson strode into Constance's study bearing a parcel.

Shoving her chair back from her desk, she leapt to her feet. 'It's arrived!'

'Quite literally hot off the press.' He held it out of her reach. 'Kiss first.'

'You had a kiss first thing this morning, same as every morning.' She tried to reach for the parcel. 'An awful lot more than just a kiss, if I remember correctly!'

He caught her by the waist, kissing her soundly. 'I can never, ever have enough of your kisses. You take my breath away.'

'You say the loveliest things. Now please may I have my parcel?'

'Here you are.'

Her fingers were shaking as she struggled with the knot in the string. As it pulled tight she groaned in frustration, finally pulling it free by brute force. The brown paper opened to reveal a book bound in blue cloth with gold lettering. She traced the title reverently. 'I can't believe it's real.'

'All your own work. I am very proud of you, Constance.'

'It probably won't sell well.'

'Probably not,' Grayson deadpanned. 'That first run of five thousand copies will lie mouldering in all the bookshops which have ordered it.'

'Five thousand! That many?'

'Remember, it's being sold beyond these shores, in bookshops in England and as far away as Canada too.'

'Paul has worked a miracle.'

'No, you have. It was your work—or Flora's if you like—which caught the eye of Harriet Siddons, the lead actress from the Theatre Royal, Edinburgh. Your work which inspired Mrs Siddons and her husband to put on those melodramas based on Flora's Highland tales which proved so popular. Paul had the business sense to publish the plays alongside a selection of Flora's best pieces, which was probably the best move he's ever made. People can't get enough tales of Clachan Bridge.'

Constance ruffled the uncut pages of her book, lifting it to her nose and inhaling. 'I worry that I've trivialised it all by turning it into a story.'

'What you've done is document a way of life that is being systematically destroyed. What is in this wee book is a story of the simple beauty of the Highlands, of the harshness of the environment and the proud people who lived there. It's an ode to a dying way of life.'

'That is lovely, but I happen to know that you are quoting from Paul's advertisements.'

'It doesn't mean it's not true. It's a shame we won't see it in the bookshops until we come back.'

'Are we really going away for two whole months? What about our chosen mode of transport, is she ready?'

'The cabin interiors were completed last week. I didn't tell you, because I wanted today to be the first time you saw her since you launched her hull.'

'Two whole months of sleeping under the Mediterranean sky, just you and I.'

'You and I and the crew and the mosquitoes. But no children, neither my two nor your schoolroom full in the Borders, and not an interfering grandparent in sight.'

'Shona is so excited to be taking over some of my classes in James's school, now that I'm going to be opening our own when we come back. What a transformation in her, in one year.'

'In no small part down to you.'

'You should be very proud of her. She is a fine, independent young woman.'

'Who is very childishly excited about being your bridesmaid later. Thank goodness one of my children holds you in as high esteem as I do. She speaks Gaelic like a native too, now.'

'That's thanks to her grandmother, I can't take any credit for that.'

'That's a talent the old bat kept well hidden.' Grayson rolled his eyes. 'I'm glad the pair of you hit it off, but that woman makes my hackles rise every time we meet. Within a week she was calling you my dear Constance, but I'll remain Mr Maddox until the day she parts company with the earth.'

'There is every chance I'll be relegated to Mrs Maddox after we've tied the knot.'

'In about two hours' time. Pearl and Isabel got here safely, I take it?'

'They're putting up at a hotel in the town. I couldn't persuade them to stay here.'

'I can't believe it's finally really happening.' Grayson pulled her into his arms. 'You're not having second thoughts, Constance?'

'No. Are you?'

'Never, about what I feel for you. Not once.'

'That's never been the problem. It's Neil, isn't it?'

'Who else! I'd feel an awful lot happier if he was staying with the Murrays while we are away.'

'His grandfather won't have him on the estate, now that he's decided he wants nothing to do with it.'

'Typical, isn't it. For years I didn't want him to have anything to do with the place either. Then when I met you, I started worrying that my son was going to inherit acres of sheep-filled moors that had been stripped of their crofters. Ironically, when it turns out that old man Murray is one of the few decent landlords in the north, my son suddenly decides that he's going to—actually, I've lost track of what it is he says he's going to do.'

'He's fifteen. His head's all over the place.'

'I know. He's unsettled.'

'We can't assume we're to blame for it,'

Constance said, setting her book down and taking his hands. 'Lads are like that at his age. There's every chance he'll grow out of it.'

'You realise there's a chance he might not turn up today. It's not you he's furious with, it's me.'

She couldn't argue with that, for she had witnessed too many of the battles between father and son over the last year. Constance's heart sank. 'Are you suggesting we postpone our special day?'

'No. What I want to do is shake some sense into him.' Grayson shrugged impatiently. 'He didn't say he definitely wasn't coming to the ceremony today, which I take as a good sign. He's a really gifted draughtsman, Constance, but of course he won't let on to me that's where his interest lies. I'm hoping that Hamish will sort him out while we're away. And when we come back and move into the new house, hopefully Neil will see that as a fresh start for himself too. In the meantime, I'm going to have to trust in Hamish to keep him under his wing.'

'Hamish is great with Neil.'

'He's indispensable to me too, now that I've cut back on my hours at the yard. Best offer of employment I ever made, was to that man.'

'And you had no idea that he was anything other than a poor down-on-his-luck fellow Glaswegian when you hired him and his dinghy that day.'

'What a day that was. *Are* you happy, Constance?'

'I never knew I could be so happy.'

'Nor I, my darling, but I can wait a little longer if you are having doubts?'

'I have worries, and we still have plenty of problems to solve, but I don't have doubts. I've stopped trying to change the world and turned my mind to shaping the future. I might occasionally come second in your priorities sometimes, just as you are in mine, but I know I'm never second-best, and I hope you know the same.'

'I never doubt it. I've missed you madly, while you've been away setting up that school of James's.'

'I couldn't let him down.'

'Of course you couldn't. I'll doubtless miss you just as madly when we come back and you get stuck into establishing your own school here. But I wouldn't change you for the world. I love you so much, Constance.'

She twined her arms around his neck, reaching up to kiss him deeply. 'I love you too. I can't wait to promise I will love you for ever.' She kissed him again. 'And ever.'

'For evermore,' Grayson said, planting one final kiss on her lips. 'My constant Constance.'

* * * * *

Historical Note

The Scottish Clearances marked the mass dispossession of land and displacement of population in the Highlands and rural Lowlands during the late eighteenth and early to mid-nineteenth century. In a nutshell, the landed gentry forcefully removed crofters who had farmed the lands for centuries, replacing the people with more profitable sheep.

Though James Loch and Patrick Sellar are often reviled for being the architects of the Clearances on the Sutherland lands, the situation is—of course!—much more complicated. However, Constance's experience in this book is not exaggerated. The events which unfolded at the fictional village of Clachan Bridge are lifted from real-life examples, as are those she describes when writing as Flora.

If you're interested in reading more about this troubled and complex period of Scottish history I can recommend T.M. Devine's *The Scottish Clearances*—or, for a more colourful if somewhat biased account, John Prebble's *The Highland Clearances*.

There was no such publication as the *New Jacobite Journal*. Surprisingly little was made of the Clearances in the contemporary press until John Delane of *The Times* published Charles Spence's accounts in 1845.

King George IV arrived in Leith on the twelfth of August 1822 for a two-week-long visit that allowed Sir Walter Scott to re-imagine the myth of the Highlander. Edinburgh was decked out in tartan and heather, and any number of rites were invented and enacted, which were subsequently adopted as ancient traditions by the Victorians.

Though I've altered the July timeline in my book slightly to suit my story, the August dates and the events mentioned are all historically accurate. I owe an enormous debt to John Prebble's colourful account of what became known as *The King's Jaunt*. I haven't had to invent a single colourful detail. Among other things, George really did wear pink tights because his kilt was too short. And the rain, a topic prevalent in a number of my books, really did fall like stair-rods almost every day.

Grayson's ships are Clyde-built. I live on the Clyde, as you'll know if you follow my early-morning posts on Twitter, and I have strong personal links to the shipbuilding industry there. Grayson is not my first shipbuilding hero either. If you like your heroes self-made and a bit rough around the edges, you can check out my other two in *Strangers at the Altar* and *Unwed and Unrepentant*.

I've taken a few liberties with the timing of the introduction of steamships. The *Carrick Castle* was actually built in 1870. I chose to feature her because she sailed on Loch Goil, near my own home.

Grayson does *not* speak like a Regency hero. I have no idea what a rough Glaswegian would have sounded like back in 1822, so I've made him sound like a contemporary Weegie. I had fun with his language. I know… I know…it's anachronistic—but it's *my* book!

There's a *lot* more history in this book that I don't have the space to go into here. For more details of sources, and blogs connected with my research, check out my website. Any mistakes are all my own doing.

COMING SOON!

We really hope you enjoyed reading this book.
If you're looking for more romance, be sure to
head to the shops when new books are
available on

Thursday 17th September

To see which titles are coming soon, please visit
millsandboon.co.uk/nextmonth

MILLS & BOON

Coming next month

CHRISTMAS AT COURT
Blythe Gifford

'You are to be betrothed on Christmas Day.'

Alice paused, struggling to understand. Her parents had told her this season at court would be important for her future. That was the reason they had allowed her to come alone. They must have known.

She lifted her chin. 'To whom?'

'To John Talbot, son and heir of the Earl of Stanson.'

Had she seen him at court? It did not matter. It was not her place to object.

'When do I meet him?'

The Queen raised her eyes and looked behind Alice. 'Now.'

There, at the door, stood the man she had taken for a messenger only a few hours ago.

He looked not at all pleased.

*

Sir John stepped into room, jaw clenched. Lady Alice stared at him and his impression remained the same as when he had seen her earlier.

Young. Naive. Pretty. Tawny hair. Gentle, innocent blue eyes…

But as he watched, her expression shifted. Not angry. Not yet. But bewildered …

He stepped forward and bowed, a gracious gesture, he hoped.

Silence. Though he could see countless questions in her eyes.

She glanced back at Dame Elizabeth. 'Is this to be announced to the court, then?'

'The betrothal ceremony will be a private affair, though word will become known, of course. However, my involvement must remain secret.'

'And the King's approval?' she asked.

'Has been obtained.'

She did not look as if she believed that, he thought. Not a dull-witted woman, then. So it was as well she did not know the priest who would preside was a secret ally of Henry Tudor, who was gathering an army in exile to take England's throne.

Dame Elizabeth waved her hand, as if she still reigned and the audience was over. 'Sir John, please see that Lady Alice returns safely to the palace.'

One final bow and they left the hall.

The wind from the river whipped around them. Beside him, she shivered. He reached out his arm, sheltering her with his cloak, pulling her close.

He thought of her, suddenly, not as a pawn in this game, but as his *wife*. Married, he would be free to explore the soft warmth of her, to touch her hair and …

Guilt prickled his spine.

They entered the Palace, suddenly engulfed by the scent of Yule greenery, and he let her go, wishing her a night of peace. There was still much she was not to know.

Not yet, at least.

Continue reading
CHRISTMAS AT COURT
Blythe Gifford

Available next month
www.millsandboon.co.uk

WE'RE LOOKING FOR NEW AUTHORS FOR THE MILLS & BOON HISTORICAL SERIES!

Whether you're a published author or an aspiring one, our editors would love to read your story.

You can submit the synopsis and first three chapters of your novel online, and find out more about the series, at **harlequin.submittable.com/submit**

We read all submissions and you do not need to have an agent to submit.

IF YOU'RE INTERESTED, WHY NOT HAVE A GO?

Submit your story at:
harlequin.submittable.com/submit

MILLS & BOON

LET'S TALK

Romance

For exclusive extracts, competitions
and special offers, find us online:

facebook.com/millsandboon

@MillsandBoon

@MillsandBoonUK

Get in touch on 01413 063232

For all the latest titles coming soon, visit
millsandboon.co.uk/nextmonth